W9-DIB-743

THE CIRCUIT
PROGENY
OF VALE

RHETT C. BRUNO

KNAPP BRANCH LIBRARY
13330 CONANT
DETROIT, MICHIGAN 48212
(313) 481-1772

DIVERSIONBOOKS

JUN 18
KN

Diversion Books
A Division of Diversion Publishing Corp.
443 Park Avenue South, Suite 1008
New York, New York 10016
www.DiversionBooks.com

Copyright © 2016 by Rhett Craig Bruno
All rights reserved, including the right to reproduce this book or portions thereof in any form whatsoever.

This is a work of fiction. Names, characters, places and incidents either are the product of the author's imagination or are used fictitiously. Any resemblance to actual persons, living or dead, events or locales is entirely coincidental.

For more information, email info@diversionbooks.com

First Diversion Books edition March 2016.
Print ISBN: 978-1-68230-084-8
eBook ISBN: 978-1-68230-083-1

CHAPTER ONE - SAGE
BREATHE LIFE BACK INTO THIS WASTELAND

"Look at it, Sage," Caleb Vale's voice came through the radio in his dense Enviro-suit, his arms spread wide as if to embrace his view. He was standing beside her at the desolate shore of a sizeable lake on Earth. The sky above them appeared charred, smeared with blackened clouds and an everlasting, red-yellow haze. The plains were barren, comprised mostly of hardened dirt littered with cracks. Despite all of that, however, the water in the lake was clear.

"Look at what?" Sage playfully grabbed his arm. She, too, was wearing an Enviro-suit. Even with all of the purification machinery and tubes spanning up from the depths of the lake, the air of the Earth remained incredibly toxic. If rain started to fall it could be acidic enough to melt through flesh in a matter of seconds.

"The water. It won't be long until you can drink it straight." He reached out and scooped a handful into his glove.

"The Circuit isn't starved for water, you know."

"No, but it's so much more than that."

Caleb let the water slip through his fingers. His smile always had a way of making her give in. It helped accentuate the handsome lines of his face and the sharp jawline he got from his renowned father.

Sage stared into his pale, greyish eyes. "Sorry Caleb. I just worry that by staying here you're challenging—"

"The Spirit of the Earth," he finished for her. "The Tribune. Yeah I know…It's just…I know that despite my father's position he doesn't believe in it all. 'A means of control,' I've heard him grumble. The truth is, I'm here to try and discover what I believe in for myself."

Sage leaned in so that the clear visors of their helmets tapped. "I'm not here to lecture you on the Spirit, Caleb."

"I know. And it truly doesn't matter to me where you place your faith. I'll always love you."

"And I you, but that doesn't mean I'll stop trying to show you the *right* path."

Caleb chuckled. "We'll see how you feel about that after I show you what we've accomplished." His face lit up. He pulled her by the hand toward the research facility at the edge of the lake. "C'mon. It happened just before you arrived. I swear it'll change everything!"

"Slow down!" Sage giggled, almost tripping over some stray rocks as their brisk pace turned into a run.

They entered the decontamination chamber of the facility. A loud, sucking sound greeted Sage's ears. Then a tight grid of beams comprising the electrostatic cleaning system passed through her. It made her whole body tingle. When the process was complete, she and Caleb stepped through an airtight door.

She removed her helmet and used two human hands to untie her long, auburn hair, allowing it to tumble down over her shoulders. Then she removed her Enviro-suit. Underneath, she was wearing a tight, black boiler suit with the letters NET printed in green over her right breast—the standard garment of a Tribunal soldier outside his or her armor.

Caleb did the same, and with his helmet off, she could see the determination pouring through his expression. She couldn't help but be reminded of how much he looked like his father.

"Welcome back," said one of the researchers sitting at a table in the refectory.

Caleb merely nodded as he hurried toward a closed door on the opposite end of the room. He placed his eye against a retinal scanner at the side and entered a password into a keypad.

"C'mon!" he yelled.

He pulled Sage through the entrance and into a small, brightly-lit lab. There were HOLO-Screens projected all over the walls, displaying detailed readings of the Earth and of the lake. Her gaze was instantly drawn toward the lab's center, where a container filled with water was suspended between two bundles of circuits. In it floated a wiry, green plant.

"Have you ever seen anything like it?" Caleb asked.

The tips of her fingers pressed against the glass, wiping away cool droplets of condensation. It wasn't the first time she'd seen vegetation—she'd grown up on New Terrene, where the Tribune proudly displayed trees and vertical farms—but she didn't need Caleb to tell her what made that particular plant so special. Despite how undistinguished it may have appeared.

"It started growing at the bottom of the lake," Caleb explained, his mouth hardly able to keep up with his thoughts. "We did it, Sage. All our hard work and it finally happened." He laid his hand over hers and placed a gentle kiss on the side of her neck. "Somehow, on this forsaken rock called Earth, life found a way."

"For more than five hundred years it's been barren," she whispered. "We have to inform the Tribune, Caleb!"

"We can't!" he grasped her shoulders. "Not yet."

Sage's brow furrowed. She took a long stride backwards. "You do you realize what this means, don't you? It is a sign from the Spirit that we are nearly worthy!"

"The Tribune wouldn't see it that way. They'll claim that I used artificial means to fabricate life; that I've defied the nature of the Spirit. The only reason they let me set up a facility here in the first place was because of who my father is, and they have reminded me time and time again how I was wasting my time. I can't allow them to see anything until there is more proof to show that we're making a real difference."

Being a loyal soldier of the New Earth Tribunal, Sage couldn't help but take up a defensive tone. "That's not true. Whether or not you were involved, The Spirit has permitted life to grow here. This is a miracle. The Council would never be able to deny that."

"Maybe not, but I don't want them stepping in yet. This." He reached out and pressed his palm against the glass. "This tiny plant is my life's work. Perhaps you and the Tribune are right and all the Earth needs is time, but what if they're wrong?"

"They're not."

They'd had this argument hundreds of times before. She'd always known him as a skeptic. Ever since they met as children while Cassius was touring New Terrene as a hero after the Earth Reclaimer War ended. It was the one thing about him that she couldn't stand, but she dealt with it because of the man she knew him to be.

"Don't be like that, Sage," Caleb groused. "I'm not trying to insult you. Just imagine, for a second, that they are wrong and we never take action. That the rumors are true and it was the Ancients who left the planet like this by tearing up the surface to mine more Gravitum than they could ever need. I would be damned not to at least try to rectify their mistakes!"

"They're only rumors." Sage kneeled down, touching the floor with the tips of her fingers, and began murmuring prayers. "Redemption is near. May my faith be eternal and unwavering, so that I may one day walk the Earth's untainted surface." She paused, gazing up at Caleb and the plant. "With those deserving at my side."

"Whatever I believe, I won't let the Tribune come in the way of our work yet," he said. "One plant isn't enough to prove anything. If we can begin to mend the land and the air, at least in this region, then they would have no choice but to believe that the Earth might be ready to receive us with a little work instead of prayer. That we can save our homeworld now. I know you're loyal, but please, keep this our secret. All I seek—"

Sage got up, placed her finger over his mouth, and pulled his head close. "You are your father's son." She smiled before pressing her lips against his. "I'll stay quiet only so that you can realize what a miracle this is for yourself."

"Thank you, Sage. Who knows, maybe if I'm right people will look at me the same way they look at him."

"Oh stop. Cassius loves you no matter what."

"He ended the most devastating war in the history of the

Circuit when he was not much older than I am now. I don't want to waste my entire life toiling with a foolish dream that so many others wasted theirs on."

"You won't. You'll help breathe life back into this wasteland if that is your fate, and the Tribune will rejoice in your name. What I believe is that the Spirit has chosen you as its hand and will see you rise as brightly as the sun, and that I, Sage Volus, will love you always."

Caleb cracked a grin and kissed her. "You sure know how to dream."

"I learned from the best." She reached into his pocket and pulled out a spherical HOLO-Recorder. "Now, speaking of your father, isn't it his birthday today?"

"I almost forgot!" Caleb snatched the device and hurried over to place it down on a nearby table.

"Of course you did," she said. "I'm going to go see if there's anything to drink in this place while you message him."

"You don't want to say hello?"

She wanted to, but she always found it uncomfortable addressing Cassius if he didn't do so first. Despite knowing him since she was a girl and being engaged to his son, she never knew what to say. He was both a member of the Tribunal Council and the greatest hero the Tribune had ever known. Her words to him never felt deserving. "That's alright," she responded. "I see him enough around New Terrene."

"I'll give him your best then."

Sage wandered the lab but stopped by a beeping HOLO-Screen. It displayed a wireframe image of the Earth, and there was a blinking red blob growing in one area.

"Caleb, something over here doesn't look right," she called back to him. All of the text and icons accompanying it may as well have been written by aliens to her.

"I'm sure it's fine; we're in the least volatile area on the planet," he responded calmly. "I'll check it out after." Then, as she continued forward, she heard him power on the device and begin recording his message. "Happy Birthday, Dad! I bet you thought I'd forget."

Sage crossed the facility into the kitchen. The other researchers didn't pay her much attention, but she didn't mind. As a female soldier patrolling the streets of lower New Terrene she was used to men's gazes lingering on her. It was nice to be around people whose minds were occupied with other business.

She grabbed a glass and swiped her hand in front of the sink to turn on the faucet. Clear, potable water poured out. It wasn't directly from the lake—there was a decontamination plant adjacent to the lab—but as she walked over to a wide translucency overlooking the body of water she realized that she'd never before directly seen the source from which she was drinking. In New Terrene it came from Mars's polar caps hundreds of miles away. She took a long sip, letting the cold liquid swish around her gums. The taste was the same as ever, but still she couldn't help be amazed.

With Caleb still recording, she stood there staring through the glass, picturing herself one day walking outside unprotected, scooping up a handful of water to drink right from the lake itself. She imagined green grass growing along its edge, and the rippling surface of the liquid painted by a soft, blue sky.

"One day," she sighed under her breath. It was difficult to sustain that image when all that stared back was an arid landscape and a scorched sky.

A violent tremor shook the complex, knocking her off of her feet. The glass flew from her hand and shattered against the floor. The other researchers also wound up on their backs, chairs tipped onto the floor along with equipment and utensils.

"Caleb!" she shouted frantically. She scrambled to her feet and sped toward his lab. Caleb had run over to the screen.

"What does it say?" she questioned. His eyes widened in horror at whatever he was reading.

"That can't be!" Caleb yelled. He struck commands on the HOLO-Screen as fast as he could, rifling through lines of data. "This is supposed to be a dead zone!"

Another tremor knocked them on top of each other and caused

all of the screens in the lab to flicker. Sage's military training kicked in and she sprung up to her feet like a feline, hoisting Caleb up with her.

"What's happening?" she asked.

"Intense seismic activity just beneath us! C'mon, we have to get into the air!"

He grabbed her hand and they hurried out into the refectory where the other researchers were struggling to gather their bearings. The shaking of the facility had become continuous. Light fixtures on the ceiling were swinging wildly. Equipment was falling off of shelves and the translucency facing the lake was cracking along its seams.

"Get to the transports!" Caleb ordered all of the others.

He ran with Sage down the hall at the back of the complex. When they finally reached the exit, Caleb paused. There was no time to put protective suits on, but a few minutes in Earth's open air was unlikely to do any damage.

They held their breath and sprinted out onto the landing pad. The rest of the researchers followed swiftly behind them. Once the facility had been evacuated, two pilots exited the control tower nearby and staggered across the shaking platform toward a pair of small transports.

Caleb signaled with urgency to the other researchers for them to board the first vessel, and then he pulled Sage toward the second. On their way, another, even more powerful, upheaval in the Earth's crust threw them to the ground. A fissure started to form along the length of the landing pad. The deck started tilting, but Caleb and Sage were able to pull each other to their feet and reach the transport.

"Get in, Caleb!" The pilot yelled as he strapped himself in. "This place is about to be torn to pieces!"

Caleb helped Sage up and then, again, he hesitated. The tears accruing in his pale eyes made her heart plummet. She knew that expression.

"Come on!"

He shook his head. "The plant!" he shouted. He turned and sprinted back toward the facility as fast as he could.

"He's the son of a Tribune, don't leave us behind!" Sage barked at the pilot before leaping out of the transport. She followed him back into the facility, hardly able to traverse the halls without being lurched from side to side. The lights were shattering and the entire floor was coming undone as the Earth beneath it split apart. In the refectory the tables were flipped upside down and even the building's structure was beginning to crumble.

Another potent quake hurled her across the room, slamming her against the far wall. Ignoring the sharp pain exploding in her side, she spotted Caleb holding onto the side of the door leading into the private lab. Cradled beneath his arm was the container which bore the plant. Using the walls for support, he made his way to her and helped her up.

They exchanged a nod and set off. Dodging falling equipment and the widening cracks in the floor, they moved as fast as they could back through the passage. Every few feet they were pitched off balance, but using each other they were able to make it all the way to the exit without dropping the plant.

When they emerged, the landing pad was split in half by the rapidly expanding fissure that now sliced up through the control tower. The pilot of the first transport started taking off. The ship's engines flared bright blue and it lifted up, but a tremor more powerful than all of the others which preceded it bellowed from the very core of the Earth. The control tower snapped in half. Jagged strips of its metal structure bowled over to clip the first transport's engines in mid-air.

The ship bowed to the side. The pilot desperately tried to regain control as it spun, but he couldn't. It crashed into the ground, exploding in brilliant shades of blue and orange. Shrapnel shot out in every direction. Sage reached out as if to block a piece, but it shredded through her arm on its way toward piercing Caleb's chest.

They howled simultaneously, falling to their knees. Blood sprayed everywhere. Caleb wasn't moving. Sage kept them upright with her healthy arm and dragged both of their bodies forward, groaning louder and louder with every inch. It took all of her will to make it just a few feet, and when her body was about to give out the surviving pilot sprinted across the pad and grabbed onto both of them.

"I've got you!" the pilot gasped.

He helped Sage haul Caleb across the landing pad and into the transport before there was another tremendous quake. He lifted her into the ship first and then both of them heaved Caleb's heavy body up. He was convulsing, blood bubbling out of his mouth as they lay him down. Sage collapsed beside him, so exhausted she could hardly breathe. Her mangled arm was pinned against his chest by the shard of metal that was still lodged in.

"It's going to be okay…" she whimpered. "I promise…We'll make it…"

"Hatch is closing!" The pilot announced.

The doors of the ship slammed shut. Everything inside of it was rattling. The rest of the control tower began to topple over, but the engines kicked on and the ship shot forward just beneath it, the landing gear scraping safely across the roof of the facility.

When the ship angled toward the sky, Sage noticed Caleb's HOLO-Recorder rolling out of his pocket. She grabbed it with her working arm and placed it in his palm. He didn't say anything, but his fingers squeezed weakly around it and her hand.

"We'll make it…" she promised as she laid her head on his shoulder. Then she was no longer able to ignore the pain in her arm and fell unconscious.

* * *

Sage gasped for air as if she had been plunged underwater. Her eyes sprung open, but all she could see was a blur of white and silver blobs spinning all around her. The smell of the blood draining out of her arm was so tangible that she could taste it.

She groped desperately with her natural hand, expecting to find a mangled stump of an arm, and then let out a sigh of release when it fell upon the smooth metal of her synthetic limb.

Just a dream, she thought, *just a dream.* Only it wasn't. It was a

memory from before she was an Executor, one she'd spent years'
burying deeply in the bowels of her mind. It was that day that
convinced her to become an Executor in the first place. She'd hoped
that by doing so she'd never fail anyone she loved in the face of
adversity again, and that she might one day redeem him in the eyes
of the Spirit for what he did. So that he might one day join its
essence along with the fallen faithful.

She managed to swing her feet off the edge of a hovering bed,
pulling out needles she didn't realize were plugged in all around her
body. The movement caused a sudden pain to shoot up the back of
her neck. She lurched and fell forward, her synthetic arm keeping
her nose from slamming onto the floor.

Images from her past flashed through her mind, each memory
aggravating old wounds. She began drawing long, calming breaths.
As she did, she placed the thumb and forefinger of her human hand
over her temples to try and force out the rampant thoughts.

Once it started to subside a bit, she used the bed to pull herself
to her feet. Her legs were still woozy from being asleep for who
knows how long.

Where in the name of the Ancients am I? she wondered.

She began to shuffle along, using the hovering bed as a crutch
to bear most of her weight. Her vision was returning and the blur
of shapes were beginning to come together. White, plate-metal walls
surrounded her, along with HOLO-Screens, IV drips, and countless
other medical apparatuses. It was definitely a lab, but not the one on
Titan where she last remembered being.

There was a strip of lighting outside of an opening and she
headed toward it, the bed sliding alongside her.

"You are still recovering, Executor Volus," a strangely robotic,
feminine voice echoed from somewhere in the ceiling. "Please
return to the monitoring station."

She ignored it. She dragged her legs forward, feeling the strength
augment in them with every step. By the time she reached the exit
she was able to step away from the bed and out into a corridor. She
still needed the wall for support, but at least she could walk.

Everything around her looked familiar, though she couldn't place why. The sleek, silvery walls and ceiling reminded her of a place she'd been, and the mechanical systems hummed a recognizable melody. She attempted to reach into her suddenly rampant stream of memories and grasp the answer, but it was difficult enough to keep them from showing her Caleb's death over and over again.

She arrived at a horizontal viewport and paused there to rest. All of the walking had only made her fainter. Placing her hands along the top of the burnished sill, she leaned her sweating forehead against the glass. She took a few deep breaths and looked out through it, having to blink a few times to make sure that what she saw wasn't just a figment of her imagination.

Wherever she was, she was on a ship floating through space. She expected to see a field of stars like usual, but they only dotted the edges of her view. In the center was a great patch of darkness. It wasn't a piece of rock. She could make out the lines of plated metal illuminated by faintly glowing, twin ion-engines.

Is that a ship? It's huge. She leaned in to get a closer look and noticed a shimmering, golden solar-sail reeled in over its blocky bow. *A Solar-Ark?* She'd never seen one outside of a hologram before. Nobody had. They moved too fast. This one, however, was moving at the same speed as the ship she was on.

She wiped the sweat off of her forehead and squeezed her eyelids shut. Then she opened them again to make sure, one last time, that it was real. This time she noticed her own pale reflection framing the ship and yelped. Her red hair was trimmed and messy, like a boy's, and wrapped around it was a bandage. It was bloody on the back.

She reached up, her hand trembling, and wove her fingers through the short strands of hair and under the cloth. Her index finger grazed a line of smooth, lumpy skin, and as soon as it did a stabbing pain seized her entire head. Her mouth opened to howl as she crumbled to her knees, but nothing came out.

"Cassius, what have you done," she mouthed. Then, a needle pricked the side of her neck and she tipped over, unconscious again.

CHAPTER TWO - CASSIUS
SHACKLES

The *White Hand* was nearing Cassius's clandestine base on the asteroid Ennomos, and he wasn't sitting on the command deck watching the stars race by like he usually did. Instead, he was in the medical bay. Since the *White Hand's* construction, only one person had ever laid upon its bed, and presently she was fast asleep. He remembered the first time she'd been there, some years ago, when her arm was little more than a bloody stump.

His gaze unfolded over the synthetic limb that he himself had placed there. His fingers danced, replaying the motions that had set all of its circuits in place—all the plates of dark metal and welded seals. He lost himself in the memory, and didn't realize he grazed her arm until its powerful hand snapped to life and grasped him by the wrist.

The cold, metal fingers squeezed, threatening to snap his bone in two. He didn't react. He endured the pain, staring into Sage's waking eyes.

"Where am I?" she asked, her voice raspy.

"You're safe, Sage," Cassius responded coolly. "Safely aboard the *White Hand*."

When she heard the name of the ship her grip loosened. She blinked a few times before meeting his gaze. "Don't be alarmed," he continued. "You woke too early last time. It was dangerous. You still need some time to recover."

Her eyes suddenly went wide as if a wave of terrible memories had bombarded her. They were green and bright—verdant as the old forests of Earth. He wasn't sure exactly what it was she saw, but he didn't have to think hard to imagine. He'd undergone the same operation when he removed his own implant before leaving the Tribune. It was like having the dust cleared off a thousand old books, bringing a library of once faded memories back into focus.

"What have you done to me?" she questioned.

"I've set you free."

"Liar!" she snapped. Her artificial hand squeezed the side of the bed, crushing its metal frame with ease.

Cassius reached out and folded his hand over her artificial one, his fingers sliding beneath her plated joints. "Trust me, Sage," he said, leaning in close. "No matter what I've ever done. No matter who I've ever hurt. Know that I would never harm you."

Sage massaged her temples with her human hand. "Tell that to my head. I'm getting tired of waking up like this."

"Hopefully this is the last time, my dear," Cassius replied. He moved to sit at the end of the bed, making sure to keep his hands resting securely on his own lap. He'd seen enough of how her Tribunal Masters treated her. "The symptoms from the extraction will pass soon."

"What exactly did you do?"

"Do you remember what we discussed on Titan? What you saw there?"

Her face went pale. "I remember everything. Past, present... everything."

Cassius turned his head and gestured at the long, jagged scar running down the back of his neck. "As I said there, the Executor Implant was latched on to your brain stem as well as your optic nerves. The Tribune had the power to blow your skull to pieces at any time they wanted when it was active, and they are almost impossible to remove without killing the host."

"Only you found a way."

"Yes," he said, proudly, "I had to. Yours was a bit more of a challenge. The explosion on New Terrene damaged the device's connection permanently. Not enough for the Tribune to notice after they assumed they had repaired it, but they lack a certain attention to detail when it comes to technology. It is why, afterwards, you were beginning to become susceptible to the parts of yourself you thought were buried too deeply to ever be rediscovered. Now, however, you have been completely reawakened."

"What if—" Sage paused and focused on him. "I can see his face, Cassius. No matter where I look he's there. So clear. And not just him. Everyone I've ever lost or killed. What if I wanted to stay asleep?"

"Then you are already lost."

"Am I? What about you? First seizing freighters and now a Solar-Ark? I saw it out there, Cassius. How can this all be for him?"

"You really think this is solely about vengeance? That nobody could ever really turn their back on your beloved Tribune after suffering their lies?"

"Honestly, I don't know," she said. "I don't think I want to know anymore. But if you ever had to feel what I feel now, then I am truly sorry."

"Never apologize for clarity!" Cassius growled.

Sage flinched and turned her gaze toward the floor. "I just want to stop hearing the screams."

"And you will soon. The mind is like a river. Take down a single dam and it will surge through in a torrent, but soon, after enough land has been carved out, a steady stream will return. Calm."

"Painful."

Cassius placed a consoling hand on Sage's slender shoulder, careful not to let his fingers stray too low. "Of course, but we are meant to feel. You are more than a weapon, Sage Volus. I have seen you smile and love and show kindness. You deserve more than turning into me."

"Do you expect me to turn my back on my vows just because you claim they were the ones looking through my eyes? I only ever saw the screen in *your* compound."

"I expect you to open them for yourself."

Sage sighed and let her head fall back to rest on her pillow. "They were your vows as well, once," she groaned. "You took the oath on the surface of the Earth—rubbed your bare hands through the dirt of our homeworld as you spoke them."

"Twice I made the pilgrimage," he explained. "Once when I was named an Executor. Again as a Tribune. And both times I let my hunger guide my hands. I conquered colonies, tore ships apart piece by piece, and won the first real war humanity has known since Earthfall."

"I know." The corners of her lips lifted into a smile for the faintest moment, and then quickly reverted to a straight line. "Caleb wanted to be just like you."

"I'm glad he wasn't. I may have won all my dreams on the field of battle, but they weren't my battles. Victory takes a heavy toll."

"One worth fighting for," Sage added. "It wasn't just him, Cassius. Every person in the Tribune wanted to be like the great Cassius Vale. I used to see your face on the HOLO-Screens in lower New Terrene when I was a child. After every victory they'd praise you as if you embodied the Spirit of the Earth yourself. The Executor who rose from the shadow to take Earth back from the Ceresian Pact and become a Tribune himself. I wanted to be like you, too. You were the only reason I chose to serve when I was nothing but an orphan girl scrapping for a living in the Labyrinth of the Night." Her brow wrinkled in pain and vexation. "How could you betray us so easily?"

She's trying to understand, Cassius thought. *She never will.* He went over to the HOLO-Screen monitoring Sage. He swiped across the screen a few times, making sure there was nothing out of the ordinary in her readings.

"Cassius?" she asked.

He leaned over the console, staring down at the tops of his hands. They were speckled with liver spots, like shreds of dried leaves had rained upon his pale flesh. The years hadn't been kind.

"Have I ever told you the real story about why I first became an Executor?" he asked.

"No."

"I was never close with my father," he began. "I won't claim to hate him—it's been far too long for that, but that's the truth. You see, while I was growing up on Titan, before the Tribune took over, I, too, wanted to be a soldier. I used to read old stories of the era of conflict before my ancestors united Saturn, dreaming about what it would be like to be in battle. Unfortunately my father barely let me step outside our compound. 'It is dangerous for a Vale out there,' he'd say. He was a frightened old man, touched by madness.

"I didn't listen very well. I'd sneak out whenever I got the chance and wander the terraces of Edeoria's Shafts. I'd hide my identity and pick fights at the bars, have the guards arrest me, and then force them to keep it a secret once they found out who I really was. There was little else I could do. My father was the Gerent of Saturn, ruling over the ringed planet and all of her moons. I was his only heir.

"The position had been passed down through generations of my family—a bloodline that is said to date back to the very first Ancients who fled Earth to settle the Nascent Cell. We were a mostly peaceful people made up of traders and merchants, gaining our wealth by selling water from Saturn's Rings to fringe settlements and valuable gases from the planet herself to everyone else. Our shipments filled the cargo holds of the Solar-Arks from end to end! Titan was a true jewel of the Circuit." Cassius walked back to Sage's bed and leaned against the end of it, half sitting.

"I was young when the Tribune entered a war with the Ceresians. Jupiter was the first to face the repercussions. All of her moons, many of them once proud, sovereign settlements, were forced to choose sides. It became a constant battleground. The heart of the early Reclaimer Wars."

"I know the history, Cassius," Sage groaned. "I grew up under the Tribune."

"Of course, but most people forget that Saturn did not choose a side in the war. Not until the Tribune set their sights on us. We were in a perfect location to safely prepare an offensive against the growing Ceresian opposition, and we guarded a surplus of vital gases needed to power engines that the Circuit's neutral shipments couldn't provide fast enough. My father initially followed the path of the Keepers, declaring his neutrality. But do you think that stopped the Tribune? No. We were all faithless to them, whether we pursued robotics like the Ceresians or not.

"They arrived soon after, and not with emissaries or diplomats. No, I remember that day like it was yesterday. Without my implant now at least." Cassius closed his eyes. "The stormy skies of Titan went black with shadows as the entire Tribunal fleet descended over us. They didn't bother to transmit a request for landing until they were already through the atmosphere. I was standing on the terrace outside my father's quarters, watching ship after ship pierce the clouds. Up to that point in my sheltered life it was the most impressive, terrifying thing I'd ever experienced.

"They came uninvited and in force! I begged my father to stand against them. 'The Vale's have always ruled Saturn,' I told him. 'They have no right to demand anything from us.' All he did was stare at the sky and mumble under his breath like a loon. He didn't even lift a finger to oppose it. Quite a contrast to the seemingly endless, disciplined forces of the New Earth Tribunal flooding into Edeoria."

"You said you were mostly traders and merchants," Sage said. "Did you even have an armed fleet? Artillery? What did you expect him to do?"

"To fight with what little we had! Or at least negotiate something resembling terms. Anything! Instead the entire history of my family's rule was wiped away in an instant. I can't even remember it. Our markets were jammed with temples and Earth Whisperers, our ears filled with promises of the Spirit's guidance. An entire culture, gone…like words to space."

"So it was peaceful then?" Sage countered. "They didn't fire on your people at all."

"Peaceful, sure," Cassius replied bitterly. "Not a single shot. To watch as we were subjugated broke my heart. I decided I couldn't bear the shame of it. If my father was willing to surrender all that our ancestors had built for nothing, then what was the point of me staying? I could either remain and become the future 'Gerent' of Saturn in title only, or find my place amongst the Tribune as the soldier I'd always dreamed of being. It was an easy choice for my angry, impetuous young self. I didn't even bother to say goodbye. I hid my identity, for good this time, and smuggled myself onto a warship bound for Jupiter, vowing that I would never be weak again."

"Jupiter?" she asked, surprised. "You fought there?"

"I grew up there." Cassius grinned. "By the time the Battle of Ganymede ended, everyone knew the bastard child from Titan. The Hand in charge of the battle saw my potential and had me trained as an Executor. He was a young, voracious man as well, who soon was named a Tribune when his master fell in a convenient ambush over Europa. Benjar Vakari.

"And the rest is history," Cassius said. "I wasn't truly a Vale again until Benjar and the rest of the Tribunal Council required a member hailing from Saturn in order to prevent any discord there and added a fourth seat. Who better to serve than a war hero who just so happened to be the long-lost Vale descendent?"

"Why are you telling me all of this?"

"Because I didn't care who I served. Ceresian Pact, New Earth Tribune—it was all the same to me minus the banners. I just chose the side of the first faction at war that arrived at my doorstep. All I wanted was to prove that I was worth more than my gutless father, yet all I allowed myself to become was a tool. Like you, it was partially the Executor Implant keeping me focused, making me care for nothing except for fighting, but I don't blame it. Not having it wouldn't have changed a single thing I did until the war was long over.

"My father's lack of action was what truly left me numb. I was so consumed by my shame that I didn't stop until I became the greatest weapon the Circuit had ever known. And then, after the battle of Lutetia, when I forced the Ceresians to surrender and the armistice was signed, I was nothing again—a figurehead to be used while we slowly bled out what little remained of our enemies. I realized I could have remained on Titan all those years before with my father and earned the same fate."

Sage reached out and wrapped her metal hand around Cassius's tightened fist. "That's not true," she whispered vehemently. "You were a hero."

"And a murderer," Cassius added. "All depends on who you ask. It took the unexpected birth of my son for me to stop trying to prove how great I was, and after removing my implant, Caleb was the only thing I could care about. It didn't matter that I was a Tribune; I just did what I had to do. The rest of the council knew it. They used his existence to control me, and as long as Caleb was alive I was happy to oblige—to turn a blind eye to everything about them that had begun driving me mad once the fighting stopped." Cassius swallowed hard. "And then he was taken from me, and, like you, clarity was thrust upon me."

"I loved him too, Cassius," Sage whispered. "I tried my best to move on back then. Why can't you?"

"You did your best to forget."

Sage looked like she'd just been punched in the gut. Cassius knew that she knew he was right. It was the sole reason he believed she'd decided to take her newly installed arm and become an Executor instead of returning to the Tribunal Guard. To have the pain literally trained out of her.

"Maybe I have," she finally replied, "but do you really think any of this will honor his sacrifice?"

"Sacrifice," Cassius scoffed. "As I said on Titan, humanity has become a species of shackles. Fear of the vacuum all around our tiny, contained environments. Gravitum. The Solar-Arks… and worst of all, Earth. My son gave everything trying to heal that wretched homeworld of ours, and all he got for it was a frail plant that the Tribune presents as if it was their faith which made it grow."

"The Spirit may have rejected what he was doing and how he was doing it, but that plant shows us that our time is coming. We just weren't ready."

"We'll never be ready! That's the truth I want the Circuit to realize. That plant grew because my son shared my resolve, not because the Spirit wanted to allow some glimmer of hope to the faithful. He died because the Earth is broken, that's all. It's just another shackle, just like the Tribune is. And because of my gluttony, I handed them the entire Circuit on a silver platter. Now I'm going to take it away. I'm going to rectify what I have done."

Cassius could feel Sage's legs instinctually wriggling away from him under the sheets. A hint of dread crept into her voice as she responded, "What are you planning, Cassius?"

"To remove shackles," He rose to his feet. "We're going to arrive soon. You'll need your rest if you hope to recover."

Then, before she could respond, he took a few long strides out of the room and sealed the door behind him.

CHAPTER THREE - ADIM
THIS UNIT IS...

ADIM stood in the hangar of Cassius's secret base on Ennomos. His hands were wrapped around the bladelike edge of the *Shadow Chariot's* wing as he leaned over it, staring through the cockpit's translucency where the female, human child he took from Kalliope to serve as a gift for Cassius had finally awoken. She sat there silently, her blue eyes bulging.

ADIM jumped up onto the chassis of his ship. It dipped under his weight. The girl winced as he approached her. He knelt down and pressed his hands against the translucency. Other than her trembling lower lip she remained still. ADIM tilted his head slightly to the side as he analyzed her to try and get a reading on what her expression indicated. He had never seen a human child up close before, and in his experience all humans other than his Creator looked upon him with trepidation.

She didn't look afraid. Her thin lips were drawn into a tight line and her eyebrows were raised. ADIM signaled the *Shadow Chariot's* cockpit to open; the glass slid out beneath his fingers with a *whoosh*. The sound seemed to startle the child, but only for a moment.

"Are you from Ceres Prime, android?" Her tiny soprano voice teemed with curiosity.

ADIM crept backward, surprised by the smoothness with which her words came out. Every other human besides his Creator that he had spoken with was only able to manage a stutter. They had all also been servants of the Tribune.

She may truly be worthy, he thought to himself.

"This unit was forged on the moon Titan." ADIM responded.

His voice was the perfect opposite of hers—cold and metallic. She didn't back away when she heard it; she leaned closer.

"Titan? I've never been there." She climbed up out of the seat and let her short legs drape over the side of the *Shadow Chariot*. "Do you have an identity, android?"

"This…" ADIM paused, feeling stumped for the first time in his short span of existence. Of all the millions of questions he had ever considered, that was never one of them. Cassius had always designated him, ADIM—an acronym for what he was. He had never questioned it. It simply was.

"To the Creator this unit is known as ADIM," he answered, the tiny red dots surrounding his eyes rotating rapidly.

The girl pointed to herself. "To humans, this girl is known as Elisha," she said proudly.

"This unit is ADIM," he repeated, his eyes beginning to slow down. "ADIM."

Elisha held back a giggle. "Hello, ADIM. Where are we?"

ADIM didn't answer. He wasn't used to being addressed by anyone but his Creator. He recalled Cassius saying, "It is time for you to reveal your existence to the Circuit." As long as he didn't reveal their location to her he knew he was fulfilling Cassius's will.

Elisha suddenly decided to get up and slide down the hull of the ship. When she came to the edge she shot off of the slick surface. ADIM calculated her trajectory, and decided that the potential for injury was too great. He snatched her out of midair by the collar of her loose-fitting tunic.

"You must not be damaged before the Creator returns." ADIM placed her down gently.

"You didn't need to—" Elisha began disgruntledly, but the rest of her words died on her lips when she noticed the row of Tribunal Freighters running down the center of the massive hangar behind ADIM. "So many ships!" she shouted.

"Six," ADIM said.

He started off toward the nearest one and she followed. They were different than when he'd first seized them. New, protective metal plates gave the once bulky bodies of the ships a cylindrical shape that tapered down toward the bow. They looked like they were made to absorb damage and ram objects. Each one was outfitted with new, missile bearing weaponry systems jutting from beneath their command deck viewports. Most importantly, all of the markings which would've signified them as Tribunal vessels were nowhere to be found.

"What are they for?"

"They have already served their initial purpose," ADIM said. "They will now serve as the Creator sees fit."

The freighter was raised on its landing gear, and Elisha's small stature enabled her to sprint underneath it ahead of ADIM. She ran her small hands over the smooth metal, feeling the warmth emanating from deep within. She marveled at all of its innumerable pieces—the burnished plates of metal, the reveals of wires and ducts over bright, blinking lights. Then she grabbed onto the rim of one of the ion engines poking out from beneath the back of the hull and tried to pull herself up to look inside.

ADIM picked her off with one hand and placed her back on the ground. "Not in there," he advised. "The ship is on standby."

"Are we going to fly it?" she asked as she looked up at him, swaying back and forth excitedly.

Before he could respond, a familiar voice transmitted directly into his ADIM's head. He had been eagerly awaiting word from his Creator since he arrived on Ennomos.

ADIM, I am close, Cassius said, the exhaustion of a long trek through space evident in his tone. *I need you to clean out the hangar. Move the freighters to the far end.*

Immediately, Creator, ADIM replied, his thoughts conveyed directly to Cassius's ear wherever he was.

Elisha poked him in the leg. "Hello?" she said.

"The Creator has informed this unit that each ship must be relocated from the main hangar." ADIM walked up the ramp into the freighter.

"So we are flying?" She hopped along excitedly in his wake.

ADIM's head twisted around far enough to accentuate his artificiality, but it didn't seem to affect her. He glanced at the ships' engines. Exposure to them while powered on inside of a contained environment could be hazardous. Then he turned his attention back down at her.

"Yes," he said. "You must join this unit on the freighter for your safety."

Elisha shrieked eagerly. She hurried up the ramp ahead of him and waved him on. Her eyes pored enthusiastically over every little detail as she ran back and forth through the cargo hold. Unlike the exterior of the freighter, the inside remained in its banal, original state. Elisha followed the exposed circuitry running under the shoddily crafted, grated flooring as if she'd discovered new life or a new world.

From what ADIM had gathered about human sentiment, the freighters wouldn't have fallen into the category of what could be deemed appealing. He'd seen Cassius look at the far superior *White Hand* in the same manner that she was at the freighter. He'd heard him call it beautiful. *The* White Hand *is a much more efficient vessel, worthy of the Creator,* ADIM thought to himself. *She will have to learn.*

"This way human child, Elisha," ADIM directed, stepping by her.

When they reached the command deck Elisha bolted in, even more thrilled than she'd been earlier. Consoles in every direction shone with the blue aura of HOLO-Screens. The sweeping viewport wrapped overhead like the eyeglass of a giant, providing a clear view across the hangar and of the other ships.

Elisha raced to the captain's chair, where the main command console was built into the armrest, and hopped up. The seat was discolored in a few patches from blood which had proven difficult to remove.

"How do I help?" she glanced back at ADIM.

"This unit does not require assistance." ADIM plucked her off of the seat, taking it himself. He spread his long, metal fingers over the command console and his eyes began to spin rapidly. The screen flickered. In no time the ship's engines roared on, making the grated floor rattle.

"Where are we going?"

ADIM didn't answer. He guided the ship up toward the ribbed ceiling of the hangar. Elisha stared up in awe and walked toward the viewport as the freighter slowly rose. It then shot forward and she grabbed onto the rail as tightly as she could so as not to fall over. The interior of the hangar raced by, and ADIM watched her head turning back and forth to catch glimpses of everything she could.

Halfway across the hangar, something seemed to upset her. She faced ADIM, her face white as a slate of marble. "Where are we?" she asked.

It took very little of his processing power for ADIM to pilot a ship as simple as a Class-2 Tribunal Freighter, so he was able to consider his response carefully. *The purpose of Ennomos must remain a secret,* he remembered Cassius saying. *Nobody, not even his gift, can know.*

"That is classified," he said out loud.

Elisha stared at him blankly. "This isn't Kalliope, is it?"

"Kalliope has been destroyed by—" ADIM said with his typical lack of emotion before pausing. It was his first time ever being dishonest with anybody. Cassius had also been adamant that the Tribune had to be blamed for what happened on Kalliope, and he had to uphold his will. "—by the New Earth Tribunal," he finished. "This unit was sent to prevent the attack, but it was too late. My vessel could only fit a human of your proportions." The last point, at least, was true.

Tears welled in the corner of Elisha's eyes. She wrinkled her nose, trying, it seemed, to remember what had happened on Kalliope. "Is Julius okay? He was showing me the mines in his suit and then something happened. Nothing could hurt him!"

"This unit is positive that you are the only survivor of Kalliope. If Julius is the name of another human living there, then he is deceased."

ADIM switched on the freighter's lower thrusters to bring it down for a gentle landing. He lifted his hand off of the console, but as he did he looked down to see Elisha wrapped around his leg at the base of the seat, weeping.

These are tears of sorrow, he recognized. He recalled how Cassius would look occasionally when reminiscing about his human son. He wasn't sure what to do, but he had noticed some of the humans imprisoned within Ennomos wipe away each other's tears caused by similar emotions.

ADIM reached down slowly, not sure if he was doing it right. Then his metallic thumb grazed Elisha's cheek, smearing away some of the moisture. His touch caught her by surprise. Her gaze shot up in his direction, causing him to quickly yank his hand away. As soon as he did, however, she reached out and pulled it back.

CHAPTER FOUR - TALON
THE BLACK CURTAIN

Talon felt as though he was about to be swallowed by the black curtain of space. He stared out of the small, circular viewport at the back of the escape pod that he and the Keeper Tarsis used to escape the Solar-Ark *Amerigo*. There was something truly harrowing about drifting through the great vacuum with no engines or destination. It was much like drowning, only he had to wait painlessly for the air to simply run out.

It had only been about a week, but he wondered if he would've been better off staying aboard the Solar-Ark. Sure, he and Tarsis had enough grainy ration bars and water stores to survive for an additional week or so, but if nobody knew about what had happened to the *Amerigo*, then the odds of somebody stumbling upon them were slim. It didn't help that Tarsis slept most of the time, advanced stages of the Blue Death sapping his strength. It left Talon completely alone. And that was a bad place to be when hope seemed so fleeting.

Damn this ancient pod. The ancients were smart enough to build that ship, but not to put engines on the only way to escape it!

Talon imagined they were originally installed only to provide a false sense of security, being that the Arks were constructed before the solar system was filled with settlements. There would've been nowhere to escape to. Even still, all he could think about was that there wasn't going be a rescue party out in the depths of the Circuit. He had merely delayed the inevitable, and it pained him to know that he'd dragged Tarsis along with him, forcing the man to forsake his sacred duties in the process.

Another friend I'll lead to certain death, he thought, gritting his teeth as the faces of Ulson and Vellish flashed in his memory.

"You can stare all you want," Tarsis grumbled, still half-asleep. "Nothing out there but stars and floating shit."

"Pleasant," Talon sighed. He pressed his palm against the inner-surface of the viewport. That thin, transparent layer was all that stood between them and the air being sucked out of their lungs.

"I'm just messing with you, Ceresian." Tarsis chuckled weakly until he started coughing. He looked even worse than he had aboard the *Amerigo*. His veins were a brighter shade of blue, and his unbelievably pale face was growing gaunter. The mechanical exo-suit wrapping the entire backside of his body made it difficult to tell just how thin his limbs were, but it was clear he wouldn't be able to walk much without it. He wiped his mouth and sat up, the still-damaged suit whining throughout the entire motion.

"You just need to relax," Tarsis continued. "There's a whole Circuit worth of ships out there that'll be trying to find out what happened to the *Amerigo*. One of them is bound to run into us."

"Hopefully. Otherwise we went from one inescapable ship to another. I keep thinking maybe we should've stayed on the larger one."

"If it wasn't for you, I would have."

You will live on this ship, and you will die on this ship, Talon remembered, a chill running up his spine. That was the creed Tarsis had dedicated his life to, and one Talon himself had willingly dishonored.

"Tarsis," he mouthed, swallowing the lump in his throat. "I'm sorrier than you could possibly imagine. It was wrong of me to ask this of you."

"Relax," Tarsis said. He placed his metal-braced hand on Talon's leg and patted it a few times. "I didn't have much time either way. Better to help someone in need of it than to die for my own foolish honor."

"Yeah…" Something about Tarsis's words cut through him like a hot round from a pulse-rifle. Before he knew it, an admission sat on the tip of his tongue that he hadn't allowed himself to utter since the day his fate was decided. "I'm not ready to die…" he said weakly.

Tarsis's eyes shifted around uncomfortably. He was clearly not used to being in the position of the consoler. A lengthy spell of coughing gave him some time to come up with a response.

"Neither was I," he said. "Nor should anybody else out there be. I've become resigned to it, but it took them strapping me into this suit to finally stop fighting the truth. I'm too close now to curse my fate and deny it. I'm ready to join the Spirit of the Earth, but you've got fight in you still, and you've got to keep fighting until there's none left."

"Spirit of the Earth," Talon repeated. There was no such thing amongst Ceresians. No god. No afterlife. They lived for the moment and the Pico credits that came with it. He'd always imagined that when he died it would just be like someone erasing a digital file. "I didn't peg you for a Tribunal," he said.

"I'm Vergent, born and raised!" Tarsis proudly pounded his chest. "Used to work a smuggling ring in and out of Europa. I picked up a few things there, but I don't really know the prayers. Hell, I'm not sure if I really even believe in *their* Spirit, but I'd like to hope there's something waiting for me after this all ends. Why else endure so much?"

Talon shrugged. "I never really thought about it."

"Until you found out about all of this?" Tarsis gestured to his exo-suit. He wore a sly grin behind his thick, graying beard. "Trust me, I know." He leaned his head back and made himself as comfortable as he could possibly get in the tight confines of the Pod. "So what is it then that had you wanting off that ship so badly?" he asked. "A woman? Revenge?"

Talon froze as, for a moment, Sage's face flashed in front of him. He'd tried not to think about her at all after her betrayal, but just that split-second was enough to leave a foul taste in his mouth. He quickly forced her out of his mind. Whatever his feelings for her may have been, it didn't matter. Instead he focused on Elisha's smiling face.

"A little bit of both actually," he admitted.

Tarsis sat up, his suit whining as he used his arms to push up. "Now I'm interested."

"Oh, now you want to talk?"

"Don't be rude. There wasn't much time for me to chase women aboard the *Amerigo*, and the ones that were there were too close to death to bother dealing with a man like me."

"Yeah, well unfortunately for you the only girl I'm concerned with is a little young. My daughter, Elisha. She'll be turning seven soon."

"She's your Spirit of the Earth then?"

"I don't know about that, but she's everything worth living for."

"And dying for," Tarsis added. "So there's something for you after you're gone. You'll always be with her—a part of her. The Tribunal faith isn't as strange as it may seem if you think about it like that."

Hearing Tarsis's wisdom only made Talon's desire to get back to her even stronger. He turned his gaze back out through the translucency and into the blackness. *Not even space will stop me*, he thought. "I guess you're right."

"So that's what all this is about then. Getting back to her?" Tarsis slumped back in his seat.

"Exactly…" Talon noticed something moving in the distance. Speeding through the star-speckled, black canvas was a tiny blue light that didn't seem to fit with the others. He pressed his face up against the viewport.

"What do you see?" Tarsis asked.

"I think it's a ship!" The blue light was growing, and he could begin to see the distortion of an ion-engine trail stretching behind it. Whatever it was, it was moving fast.

"Move over," Tarsis grunted. Talon shifted as much to his side as was possible within the pod. They wound up squeezed together by the viewport like two missiles on a rack. "By the fucking Ancients, it is!"

"Maybe our luck hasn't run out yet?" Talon nudged Tarsis in his side. "Think they'll pick up our distress beacon?"

"Nothing about our lives is lucky, but it seems something out there wants you to get where you're going. I'll be damned if I'm going to stand in its way."

"Let's hope it's not Tribunal," Talon remarked.

"At this point, who the fuck cares?" There was a sparkle in Tarsis's eyes, one that said that no matter how close he was to dying, he didn't want to go out rotting on some cramped escape pod. Talon couldn't help but agree.

CHAPTER FIVE - SAGE
THE PROGENY OF VALE

Sage remained on the medical bed in the *White Hand*. She'd awoken when restraints popped up to wrap around her torso and hold her tightly against the mattress. At first she feared the worst, but the ship's enhanced computer quickly informed her that it was just bracing her in advance of landing. After everything she'd recently learned about Cassius she couldn't be sure.

Memories continued to beset her, like her childhood in the Night's Labyrinth of New Terrene, where she struggled to survive without a family for so much of her life until she found a home as a soldier of the Tribune. Or the first time she prayed to the Earth Spirit on her own. It felt so distant, as if she were watching a video of another girl's life through a HOLO-Screen. But the more of them that came through, the more they all blended together. The past she'd chosen to forget was being reconstructed piece by piece.

It had her head throbbing, though admittedly not as badly as when she first woke up. She wondered if she was just getting used to it. All she knew was that whenever she turned her head the wrong way it caused the fresh scar on the back of her neck to burn like wildfire.

Suddenly, the pull of G-forces made her stomach jump. The *White Hand* was turning hard, likely preparing itself for landing wherever it was headed. The restraints kept her body from sliding off the table, so for that she was thankful. It didn't take long afterward to feel the soft vibrations of a proper touchdown along her back. In her experience, only Executor-level training could allow a pilot to bring a ship down so gently. Sometimes she forgot that

Cassius had been through the same gauntlet.

Her restraints slid off promptly, freeing her to stretch her weary limbs. Then the ship's engines powered off with a whine. They had been operating so smoothly that she hadn't even noticed the soft rumble they produced until it was absent.

When footsteps echoed from the corridor outside the medical bay, Sage closed her eyes and positioned herself on the bed so that it would seem like she was sleeping. Her reinvigorated nerves were able to hold the flood of memories at bay, allowing her to use breathing techniques to slow her pulse. She couldn't risk the ship's computer using the HOLO-Screen monitoring her to see right through her ruse. It seemed more intelligent than those aboard typical Tribunal vessels.

"Gaia, how is she?" Cassius asked as he entered the room.

"Stable. She has been in and out of sleep," the computer responded.

It even had a name. The notion that she could somehow remind Cassius of his former loyalties dwindled when she heard that. In the Tribune that was a punishable offense in its own right.

"Good," Cassius replied. "It's time we got her out of that bed."

She felt Cassius's hand graze along the edge of the bed. There was a slight pull on the flesh around the wrist of her human hand as he fiddled with the needle in her vein before pulling it out. She was surprised that she could feel the minor sting that accompanied it. Dulling paltry pains was at least one side effect of the implant that she would miss no matter what the truth was.

When he was done with that, Cassius removed all the other apparatuses sticking out of her. *Focus, Sage,* she thought to herself every time he got close. *You will not lose faith amongst the faithless. Focus!*

As he moved around to the other side of the bed her eyes snapped open. She swung with her synthetic arm, catching Cassius in the side of the head with just enough force to knock him unconscious and do no more damage. She made sure of that.

Cassius had done the service of unplugging her from all the machines, so there was nothing holding her down. She hopped up to her feet, where adrenaline helped her ignore how atrophied her legs were.

She took a step toward the doorway and then glanced back over her shoulder at Cassius. He was on the ground with one limp arm still raised and draped over the bed. There was a trickle of blood running down his cheek, but he was breathing fine. She knew what she should do. She knew what she would've done if that bomber had never shown up on New Terrene all those months ago.

I am a knight in the darkness, a vessel of their wisdom. Her vows jumped to the forefront of her rampant mind. *I am the silent hand of the Tribune…No, I won't.*

She was through getting involved in the feud between Cassius and the Tribune. She knew the moment she couldn't pull the trigger on Titan that it was time to go back to what she did best. The renewed memories of Caleb were only serving to make her soft spot for Cassius even more apparent, no matter what he'd done. She just wanted to forget everything that had happened since she left New Terrene, and return there to guard its people. Be the Executor of Mars.

Once she was out of the lab she glanced both ways down the corridor. Even though she had been on the *White Hand* before, it was under similar circumstances. The layout was a mystery to her. Down at the end, in one direction, she looked through the same viewport as earlier. The Solar-Ark was directly adjacent to them now, just a portion of its massive, glittering sail visible.

Wherever they were she couldn't risk just moseying out of the cargo hold, but she had to move quickly before Cassius woke up. *If this place is secret enough for Cassius to bring the Solar-Ark, then the freighters might be here also. I'm sure he won't miss just one.*

She started to jog, gaining more confidence in her weak legs with every slap of her bare feet. She hadn't been on the *White Hand* in some time, so it took a wrong turn down toward the engine room and a complete U-turn for her to locate the corridor leading to the cargo bay. As it neared she slowed down and sidled silently along the wall. There was no telling what might be waiting in there.

She quickly found there to be nothing. There wasn't even a crate being transported, and the exit ramp was lowered, its hatch wide open. She hurried to the corner and peered around it. The *White Hand* was inside of a massive hangar, so long that it put the one on board the *Ascendant* to shame. The Solar-Ark took up most of it, fitting perfectly, as if the hangar had been constructed just to house it. She could only see its glistening bow, but the size was enough to leave her awestruck.

Six ships were lined up in a row beside the *White Hand*. They appeared to have more advanced plating than normal Tribunal Freighters, but they were the right size and shape. She stayed low as she rushed out of the *White Hand* and toward the lowered ramp of the nearest freighter. As she sprinted up the ramp, there was a muffled bang. A bullet glanced off of her artificial shoulder. The force of the shot sent her sprawling forward onto the ship. The shots that followed peppered the wall right where she had been.

She scrambled back to her feet and continued running, shocked that Cassius would actually shoot at her. There were a few empty storage containers lying around, and she flung them in front of the ramp. Then she made her way through the tight corridors. Unlike the *White Hand,* she could traverse a Tribunal Freighter blindfolded. The inside was relatively unchanged.

The command deck didn't take long to reach. She stepped, and as soon as she did the memory of when she raided the Tribunal freighter with Talon accosted her. A sudden feeling of vertigo took control of her limbs. She stumbled over a lip in the grated floor. She could hear the gunshot that took Vellish's life echo again and again in her head. See his face right in front of her, his crooked nose drenched in sweat and his hateful gaze fixed on her before she pulled the trigger.

Just a memory! Sage told herself. *Keep going!* She got back to her feet and scrambled over to the command console, activating the ship.

The floor began to tremble, and at that very moment a portion of the command deck's viewport shattered. A suit of darkly-tinted, metal armor fell through. Sage leapt out of the way as the body slammed down where she had been standing. When she flipped over, ready to fight, she hastily realized that there was no man inside the suit. In fact it wasn't a suit at all. It was an android, but not the clunky, useless type like the ones on Ceres Prime. This one moved with the fluidity of a well-trained Executor. Its eyes shone bright and red, like the core of a planet split open.

"What have you done to the Creator?" the abomination asked before it charged at her.

She didn't even have time to question what it said before it was upon her. It swung down, and she raised her synthetic arm to block the blow. It paused when she did, tiny red lights around its eyes beginning to rotate rapidly as it stared at the limb. She took the opportunity to unsheathe her wrist-blade and swipe. The android sprung back to action, evading the attack easily.

Before it could counter, Sage rolled backward and flipped onto her feet. The android bounded forward and engaged her. It moved with lightning quickness, and with only one arm of use against it she was at a severe disadvantage. She channeled all of her training, staying light on her feet as she danced around a flurry of precise strikes. She repeatedly used her human hand to feign attacks and try to get the android off balance, but none of it worked. It had an answer for every move.

She created space between them again and it took the bait. As it flung a punch at her head she sidestepped and slashed at its limb with her blade. The tip scratched its forearm, but that was all. In a move that no human could pull off, it bent backward at the waist, twisted its entire body, and swept out her legs with a kick. The android leapt straight up into the air, its head almost striking the ceiling, then came plunging toward her. She was barely able to roll out of the way before its knee dented the floor. She swiped again, blindly, but this time the android grabbed her artificial arm and flung her across the room.

She slammed sideways into a console. Quickly, she rolled over and did her best to track the android as her vision went fuzzy. It was slowly approaching her, its hellish eyes smoldering.

"Come on, creature!" she growled and lifted herself into a battle crouch. Her metal fist tightened as it got closer, the sharp blade fixed to it gleaming blue from a HOLO-Screen above. Then, just before she could pounce and try to catch it off guard, Cassius shouted, "ADIM stop!"

CHAPTER SIX - CASSIUS
GOODBYE, MY DEAR

"ADIM, stop!" Cassius bellowed from the entranceway of the freighter's command deck. His unkempt hair was stained by a splotch of blood where Sage had struck him. His finger rested securely around the trigger of his long-barreled pulse-pistol, even though he kept it aimed at the floor.

ADIM froze and looked to him. Sage paused for a second before springing at the android. Her attack met only air, as ADIM deftly evaded her. He grabbed her by the neck with one hand and by the synthetic arm with the other, holding her up and stretching her body. She kicked and punched at him with the two limbs she still had at her disposal, her human fist meeting his metal chassis with little impact.

"Let her go," Cassius commanded. ADIM didn't listen, but he noticed the android's grip loosened a bit, enough to allow her to gag.

"This unit cannot. She will try to harm you again," ADIM responded. He stared at the blood on Cassius's head.

"ADIM, you will let her go," Cassius demanded more firmly. He stepped beside them and pointed his gun at Sage. "Trust me, she won't."

This time ADIM listened and released her. She fell down onto her knees, grasping at her throat as she gasped for air. Cassius kept his aim steady on her.

"Impressive, Sage. There aren't many people in the Circuit who thought they could catch me off guard and lived to talk about it. Trust me, it will not happen again." He pressed the barrel of his gun against her temple.

"Do it, then," Sage snarled.

"Don't be foolish. I don't want to kill you. Just sheathe your blade and we can talk about this civilly."

Sage slid her blade back into her wrist. Cassius had to stop himself from breathing an audible sigh of relief. She then glanced at his pistol and he lowered it. He took a step backward and ADIM shifted himself to be in between the two of them.

"So is this thing what you've been spending all your exiled years with?" Sage asked. "Some cheap imitation of human life?" She got off of her knees and sat against the nearby console. Her bout with ADIM still had her breathing heavily.

"This *thing* is ADIM, and you're lucky I arrived in time to save your life," Cassius said.

"Lucky? Do you name all of your abominations?"

ADIM remained silent. His gaze was fixed on Sage.

"Only the ones I care about," Cassius said.

Sage let out a mouthful of air. "A part of me still wants to believe I can convince you to stop all of this, Cassius, but my head hurts too much to waste any more breath trying."

"And I thought I could convince you to stand with us, but you're as stubborn as Caleb was." Cassius held out his hand to help Sage to her feet. "ADIM will not harm you as long as you keep that arm of yours to yourself."

"This unit does not trust her, Creator," ADIM finally voiced his opinion.

"I know. But I do." Cassius extended his hand a little farther. Finally, Sage took it and allowed him to pull her to her feet.

"So, what now?" she asked. "I am your prisoner?"

"Never," Cassius insisted. "I will allow you to leave. Of course, we'll be taking precautions to make sure you can't lead your masters here, but you may go to Titan, where I'm sure Benjar is waiting eagerly. There he will undoubtedly reinsert your implant and soon all of this will be another faded memory. If that's what you want?"

She took a deep breath and looked to the ground. "I'm sorry, Cassius, but I can't be a part of this. I made vows, no matter what they might've done. And now I must return to uphold them…I will go and ask His Eminence, Benjar, to allow me to continue my work on New Terrene. I'll beg if I have to."

Despite expecting that very response to his final appeal, it was still hard for Cassius to mask his disappointment. He took a great risk in bringing Sage to Ennomos, but he knew he'd do it again in a heartbeat. Just her mere existence helped him cling to what little was left of his humanity. He needed that so he wouldn't lose sight of what he was ultimately trying to do.

"Very well," Cassius sighed. "Come, ADIM. Your spectacular entrance into this freighter has left it in desperate need of repairs. We must prepare another for her."

"That's it?" Sage questioned, following them from a safe distance.

"That's it," Cassius stated firmly. They walked in silence until they were out of the freighter and crossed the hangar toward another.

"Creator, your gift awaits you inside of the *Shadow Chariot.*" ADIM pointed toward the sleek, red and black ship sitting in a small offshoot of the hangar.

Cassius got on his toes and peered over, but all he could see was the top of the *Shadow Chariot's* cockpit. "You can show me once we're finished with this." He placed his hand on the android's back. "I look forward to it." They stopped in front of another freighter and Cassius turned back to Sage.

She had stopped halfway between the two ships, staring at the colossal Solar-Ark. Cassius joined her in admiring it. In space it was hard to grasp its enormity—the endless vacuum had a way of making all things seem insignificant—but within the hangar it was different. The tremendous hollow space had been designed for the very purpose of holding it, and there was barely a foot to spare on the flanks.

"By the Spirit, I never realized how massive they are," Sage said. "How did you accomplish this?"

"Patience," Cassius replied.

A dark edge crept into her voice. He could see her swallow hard. "Are you going to destroy them all, Cassius?" she asked.

"Of course not. I am merely borrowing this vessel in order to help get my point across. When all this is over it will be returned to its original purpose. I have no desire to see the Circuit die, only evolve."

"That's why you built this place then, isn't it? For this Ark."

Cassius nodded. "We made a rough estimate on its size based on the Conduit Stations. Not a bad fit considering."

"Our calculations were flawless, Creator," ADIM interjected.

"Can you believe that this ship was one of the six that in the early days of the Circuit stood between humanity and certain extinction?" Cassius marveled. It was a daunting notion, but he understood that those days were far past, even if most people didn't. *Another shackle now,* he thought. *Better had we just been put out of our misery.*

"I never thought I'd see—" Sage stopped herself, suddenly turning toward Cassius and appearing as though she'd had an epiphany. "The Keepers! Are they on board?"

Cassius put on a wry grin. "I was wondering when you'd remember," he said. "The initial surge of returning memories can make the more recent ones seem distant. Worry not, however. I ensured that your Ceresian acquaintance was not amongst the crew before I relieved them. Remember, I was able to see some of what your masters saw through your eyes. I never forget a face."

"Relieved them?" Sage asked.

"The Keepers fought bravely to defend their tomb. Unfortunately, they could not be swayed to see things my way."

Sage's opened her mouth to speak, and then decided against whatever she was going to say and to press on as if nothing had happened. "Are you sure Talon wasn't there?"

"Positive. I checked on it personally during the voyage here."

"Maybe I should—"

She took a step toward the Solar-Ark, but Cassius placed his arm around her. "Sage, all you will find on that ship is empty metal halls. There are five other Solar-Arks tracing the Circuit. He was likely assigned to another. I know you don't trust me any longer, and I understand why, but all I've ever wanted for you is happiness. Soon, the Ceresians will be my allies, and I promise that I'll keep my ears open for his whereabouts. Next time I find myself in the Tribunal databases I'll even check his assignment for you. He didn't seem like a man who would allow himself to die locked up on a ship."

She looked into Cassius's eyes for a moment and then nodded. "No," she said, seemingly relieved. "No, he didn't."

"Now, let's get you home."

Cassius guided her to the waiting freighter. He was relieved as well, knowing that there was at least a thin layer of trust remaining. He was mostly telling the truth. By the time the androids learned what they needed to in order to pilot the Solar-Ark, not a single Keeper on board was left alive. He'd made sure to look over every one of their dead faces before he'd had them ejected through an airlock. The Ceresian whom he recognized from when he looked through Sage's recorded vision wasn't amongst them. Which meant he was either serving on another Solar-Ark, or he was the Keeper whom the androids had reported as somehow reaching an escape pod. Cassius held a great deal of respect for whoever had accomplished the latter.

When they reached the ramp of the ship, Sage faced him, her features darkening again.

"I will have to tell them what I saw here, Cassius," she warned. "Even if you hide from me where we are, I'll have to tell them that."

"Don't worry," Cassius replied. "I will already have told them myself."

She unexpectedly reached out and placed her human hand on his arm. "They will find you eventually, no matter where you hide. And next time they're going to kill you. I won't be able to—"

"Stop." Cassius shook his head. "They will try, just as they have been for years. I know what I've brought upon myself, so say nothing else, please. Let's just get you home."

Cassius sent ADIM to go and retrieve Sage's armor and pistol from storage on the *White Hand*. She blushed when she realized she'd been traipsing around in nothing but her undergarments. ADIM returned in no time, and once he did he and Cassius went to work on the freighter.

They disabled its navigation and tracking systems, ensuring that it could never be traced back to Ennomos. Then they plotted an indirect course for Titan into the newly installed autopilot that wouldn't allow Ennomos to be pinpointed by travel time based on drift charts. The autopilot also wouldn't permit a manual override until it passed into Titan's atmosphere. Cassius personally ensured that the coding was so complex that Sage would have no chance of cracking it if she attempted to.

When that was completed, they brought Sage into the command deck and set her down in the captain's seat. Cassius fit the safety restraints over her chest and then pulled out a syringe.

"Just a sedative," he said before she could ask. He could see that she was starting to tense up, and with ADIM watching vigilantly he didn't want a repeat of earlier. "I can't have you seeing any more, but by the time you wake up your headaches won't be an issue anymore."

"I'm getting tired of going to sleep this way," she drawled.

"Even I must be cautious. When you leave this place, you will be my enemy."

Cassius wet an area of her neck with a numbing agent. As he brought the needle in, her artificial hand grabbed his wrist, and she lifted her gaze to stare at his face. "Whatever you're planning Cassius, think about Caleb before you do it," she whispered.

Cassius grasped her hand with one of his and squeezed the cold metal. "I always am," he responded. Then he plunged the needle into the side of her neck.

She grew drowsy in seconds, and as she did he reached into a pouch on his belt and pulled out the spherical HOLO-Recorder which had been Caleb's. It was the partner device to the one which stored Caleb's final moments, and Cassius had been storing it aboard the *White Hand* ever since his son died. The Tribune wouldn't be able to use it to track him if they ever found it, but if Sage was ever in close enough proximity direct messages could be exchanged between them.

"If you ever need me, Sage, this will allow you to contact me," he said. "Keep it safe."

She watched with heavy eyelids as he fiddled with her artificial arm, sliding a plate of metal on the underside backward so that the small device could fit inside, nestled between two clusters of circuitry.

"Cassius…" she mouthed, struggling to stay awake. "His death wasn't their fault…It wasn't your fault…It was mine. I should've…"

Cassius placed a finger over her lips. "No child. Never say that. No man can be blamed for what happened that day." He cradled her head as the sedative completely kicked in and she slipped into a deep slumber. "Goodbye, my dear."

CHAPTER SEVEN - TALON
PEOPLE OF THE VERGE

Talon and Tarsis hunched over in the confines of the escape pod, watching the spotlights of the approaching ship glare through the viewport. Talon couldn't make out the entire vessel, but enough to see that it was many decades old. It pulled alongside them, and its cargo hangar ramp creaked open wide enough to engulf them.

Definitely not Tribunal, he thought, relieved. In his experience, the spotting lights it used were typical on salvage ships. Whether they were there to help or were scavengers was up for debate.

"Whoever comes through that door, we should be ready to defend ourselves," Talon said to Tarsis. "We're too close to get put down by pirates."

"We're two refugee Keepers with a short lease on life, in an escape pod worth little more than its weight in scrap metal," Tarsis said. "I'm afraid to ask what you were before all of this if you're so eager for a fight already."

Talon cracked a smile. "A glorified mercenary, then a miner, then a mercenary again."

Tarsis leaned against the glass wearing the half-excited, half-nervous expression of a man finally returning home after countless years away. "Well, you'll be happy to know that's a Vergent ship out there. My people."

"You're sure?"

"I'd know a chassis like that anywhere. Let me do the talking. Hopefully these are the respectable sort of Vergents."

"They're all yours."

Talon glanced out of the viewport to make sure that they were completely within the ship's cargo bay, and then pushed the button that signaled the pod to open.

The front popped forward with a snap-hiss and then slid up completely over the roof. A group of Vergents stood in the cargo bay. All of them aimed guns at the pod. They wore tight, black boiler-suits, which somehow made their exceedingly pasty skin appear even whiter.

"No movin', Insiders!" The young boy in the center of the gun-wielding Vergents ordered. He couldn't have been older than thirteen.

Talon did as commanded. The word *insiders* came off the young boy's lips with unbridled scorn, which made him suddenly feel unsafe despite Tarsis's relation. Insiders was what Vergents called anybody outside of the Vergent Cell, or within the orbit of Uranus to be exact. He'd encountered their kind plenty of times. Vergent merchants and smugglers were a common sight in Ceresian ports, but they rarely spoke with strangers beyond what was necessary to conclude business and avoid fights. He was on their turf now, though.

"We are—" Tarsis was cut off by the same young boy.

"No speakin' either!" he snapped.

Even Tarsis appeared startled by his harshness. The boy motioned forward and two others moved into the pod with scanners. They climbed around the small enclosure with unbelievable dexterity, somehow managing not to bump into either Tarsis or Talon as they inspected the cramped pod.

Talon immediately understood why people said that true Vergents spent every waking moment on their ships. Sure, there was a smaller-than-typical Conduit Station over Neptune and a couple of tiny settlements out there, but those were little more than the ports where their real homes could dock. Like Keepers, Vergents lived and died on their ships, only they were happy to do it and whatever else it took to survive. Whether that made them pirates, smugglers, or honest tradesman, it was all the same to them.

"They clear, Kitt," the two Vergents in the pod addressed the young boy.

Kitt nodded, but he held his gun steady. His piercing, nearly-black eyes stuck out against the pale backdrop of his gaunt face, and a sharp nose was accentuated by bony cheeks. He was tall and lanky, like the poor of Ceres Prime who were forced to live under the low-G conditions of barely working gravity generators. Talon imagined that if his people struggled to get their hands on legal, Solar-Ark Gravitum shipments, then Vergents probably got even less. He even started to notice that the artificial gravity pulling his body to the floor was noticeably weaker than it had been on the *Amerigo*.

The other six Vergents who were lined up on either side of Kitt had a similar look to them—lean and bony, and even taller, with the hardened glare of people whose whole existence was a constant struggle.

"Lower all weapons," a calm, gruff voice commanded.

They all obeyed without delay, the group parting so that the woman who gave the order could step through. She was older than any of them by at least twenty years. *The Captain*, Talon assumed.

"Tarsis. Can't be you." The countless wrinkles quilting her brow deepened as she stared into the pod.

"In the flesh and metal, my old friend." Tarsis smiled warmly. He stepped forward and they embraced, Tarsis's damaged, metal exoskeleton screeching as they did. "How did you find us?"

The captain held him at arm's length. "We were doin' our best avoidin' groups of Tribunal scout ships when we picked up a distress. Transmission's so ancient we nearly missed it. Wouldn't imagine findin' you inside. Thought you were dead."

"Somehow, I survived that crash all those years ago, but now I'm securely on my way there, I promise you that." Tarsis lifted his arms so that the bright veins beneath his flesh and the suit attached to it couldn't be missed.

The captain's expression darkened. Talon recognized the look. It was the same one Julius wore when he found out about the Blue Death.

"I see," the captain muttered. "You'll have to forgive. None of us here ever had the privilege of seein' an active Keeper before. Didn't realize what you were."

As soon as they heard the word *Keeper*, Kitt and the rest of the Vergent crew holstered their weapons and lowered their heads in a reverential manner. It made Talon uncomfortable, reminding him of the fate which befell everyone on the *Amerigo* who foolishly stood their ground like they were supposed to.

"Few have," Tarsis responded. "There aren't many of us who get the opportunity to die beyond the ancient hulls of a Solar-Ark."

"Exactly." The captain's glare suddenly grew judgmental.

I wonder how long the crew's admiration will last if they find out me and Tarsis fled, Talon thought.

"Don't worry, Larana, we aren't deserters," Tarsis responded with iron conviction. "Something hit the *Amerigo* hard. I fear we are the only ones who escaped in order to warn the Circuit. The command deck was taken before a message could even be sent out."

"So it is true then?" Captain Larana asked. "We were leavin' Titan when somethin' blew the Conduit in half. Debris almost hit us. Scanners read the *Amerigo* was passin' through at the same time, but we didn't believe it. Till now. Who be damned enough to attack a Solar-Ark?"

"Whoever it was, they used an android the likes of which I've never seen. Quicker than any human, with eyes red as lava and a metal frame as dark as the Earth's sky. The Keepers may not necessarily be trained to fight—Ancient's sake our weapons are hardly operational—but the thing cut through our ranks like we were nothing. Nothing." Tarsis turned around and placed his hand on Talon's shoulder. "I was ready to give my life before Talon here convinced me we had to warn the Circuit what we saw."

Talon exhaled, appreciative of his new companion's white lie. *A logical explanation, even if it's only true for one of us.* He wished he could bring himself to care more about whatever had happened on the *Amerigo*, but after hearing Ulson get shot down over com-link and watching Vellish be executed, he found himself numb to the deaths of strangers. Focusing on Elisha was all that kept his head clear and focused.

"Androids, you say?" Larana asked in disbelief. "I've seen those things in action. Only Ceresians use 'em." The contemptuous way she uttered the name *Ceresians* drew a cross glare from Talon before he could restrain himself. The captain took notice. "I see," she recognized, analyzing Talon from head to toe before continuing. "Well, there'd need to be a thousand of them to take down the Keepers of a Solar-Ark."

"We only saw one," Talon spoke up for the first time.

"One? Impossible!"

"There had to have been someone working with it considering they hit the hold and the command deck simultaneously," Tarsis clarified. "But like he said, we only saw one up close."

"Must have been somethin' else," Captain Larana decided. "I'm hopin' you two haven't got too comfy outside the *Amerigo* though, 'cause we're gonna find out what really happened and you're gonna help."

A look of dread washed over Tarsis. "Larana," he said. "It's been a long time since we shared a drink on Triton, but you know me. I'm telling you: turn around before it's too late."

"Some of us—" the visibly irritated Captain began, but was cut off when someone spoke frantically over the ship's com-system.

"Cap'," the fidgety voice said, likely belonging to someone barely out of their teens. "Better get up here quick."

"What is it?" Larana said.

"Transmission comin' in. From the Tribune."

"About?"

"You better come."

"On our way. Kitt, come with me," Larana ordered. "We might need a pilot. Tarsis, you too. Bring your friend. Rest of you, battle stations. Rare day when the Tribune are our friends. Don't want them gettin' the jump."

The Vergent crew scattered, weaving around and over the hangar's cargo containers with unbelievable nimbleness. Talon had been around ships all of his life on Ceres but he'd never seen a group of people move with such comfort and grace aboard one.

"Follow me, Keepers," Kitt requested. He tapped Talon lightly on the back.

Captain Larana led them deeper into the ship. It reminded Talon of the Solar-Ark in a way. Not in scale, but it seemed like the bulk of it had to be at least a hundred years old. Every piece had its own unique noise to make, all of it with a worn look that told of a dozen captains before. At every intersection you could see all the way down the hall into a larger space. Refectory, gunning stations, sleeping chambers—they all fell into place with the utmost efficiency. *Easy to maneuver through, but hard to defend.* Talon thought. *They must rarely let strangers get this far.*

"What an honor it must be to be named captain of one of these," Talon whispered as he caught up to Tarsis. He ran his hand along the layer of rusty metal plates on the wall, feeling each dent in the surface. He was beginning to recall where his daughter got her love of ships from.

"You should've seen mine." Tarsis had to raise his whisper so his voice would be audible over the whine of his damaged exo-suit. "She was a beauty."

"You were a captain?" Talon asked.

"For twenty years, until my baby, *Verdana*, was shot down by Tribunal security over Ganymede. I survived somehow, but the gravity generator went off and did this to me. I had the privilege of being sent to the *Amerigo* instead of rotting in a cell."

Talon exhaled. "I'm sorry that we have so much in common."

"Don't be," Tarsis replied. "She had a damn good run."

Before Talon could inquire any further, they reached the command deck. In it, two seats faced a bulbous viewport. The dated consoles wrapping around them gave off a green glow, though there were a few modern HOLO-Screens on the ends. Other than that there was room for little more than a handful of people to stand. Ceresian ships were similar. The Tribune liked overstated command decks, with unnecessarily large translucencies and plenty of empty floor space. As if they were meeting halls.

Captain Larana took one of the seats at the controls. Kitt squeezed past Talon and Tarsis, not even brushing against them, and took the seat beside her.

"Receivin' their transmission," Kitt said as he typed away on one of the old-fashioned console units.

"Go," Larana replied.

There was no image provided like on most ships, but the voice of a Tribunal soldier was broadcast throughout the room.

"This is the Tribunal Frigate, *Lazarus*," the soldier announced. "We are picking up a distress beacon near your location. Do you require assistance?"

"You get a readin' on them?" Larana turned to Kitt and whispered softly. Kitt shook his head before keying the command console to activate their end of communications.

"This is Capt'n Larana of the *Monarch*," she stated into the coms. "We're just a tradin' vessel out of Triton. Just testin' some new equipment. Sometimes systems on this bag of bolts act screwy. You must be pickin' us up by accident."

"According to our manifests, the *Monarch* has already docked and exchanged goods on Titan. You are lingering in the dominion of the New Earth Tribune. State your purpose here," the soldier ordered sternly. Any shred of decency found in his earlier tone had vanished.

"We saw an attack on the Conduit and Solar-Ark after leavin'. Searchin' for any survivors now."

"You will cease your search efforts immediately and remain where you are."

"For?"

"You will allow us to launch a routine examination of your ship. If everything checks out it will be returned to you accordingly. Then you will set a course for Triton and inform your people that Titan is no longer accepting external trade for the time being."

"On whose authority?"

"In the name of his Eminence, Tribune Benjar Vakari. We have missiles locking on to your position as we speak and will have no choice but to fire if you don't comply. You have five minutes."

Larana slumped back in her seat and sighed. She ran her hand through her scraggly hair as if she would discover an answer there.

Talon's gaze gravitated to the pulse-rifle leaning against Kitt's chair. It was the only weapon in the room, and if he could get his hands on it there was a chance he could take the ship and try to escape. He wasn't about to let a group of Vergents hand him right back to the Tribune. He'd plot a course for Ceres and never look back. The only person who was in a position to stop him was Tarsis. He may have helped him get as far as they were, but Talon couldn't decide who the exo-suited man would back in a fight.

As Talon plotted his next move, Kitt suddenly reached over the captain and switched off the transmission.

"We got enough Synthrol left to be locked in a Tribunal prison until the long sleep," he said nervously.

"Not to mention the two lone survivors of the first stolen Solar-Ark in history," Tarsis added, peering over at Talon out of the corner of his eye as if he could sense what he was thinking. "And an escape pod which you just lied about."

Larana took a deep breath. "Long sprint back to Triton," she considered. "We can hide the Synthrol again. Hope that they miss it, distracted by the escape pod. Claim I was lyin' about it 'cause we don't know who took the Ark."

Kitt glanced over Larana's shoulder at the two Keepers before he said, "Won't be like no port inspection. They real soldiers, and we have guests. Somethin' tells me the Insider don't have too good a history with Tribunals."

Larana glared back at Talon and then swallowed. "Who does?" she conceded. "We run home then, and hope this old girl is fast as she was."

Talon knew their chances were miniscule. After what had apparently happened on Titan, there would be a ton of Tribunal ships between them and Neptune. Even if they escaped the first wave, fleeing the scene of the devastation would have the *Monarch* hunted all throughout the Circuit. They could probably make it to Uranus, yet even though the planet was technically part of the Vergent Cell, Tribunal influence was spreading there. He wasn't exactly sure where they were in space at the moment, somewhere in the vicinity of Saturn, but both of those Vergent-run planets were a hell of a lot further away from Titan than the asteroid belt.

"We'll never make it to Triton," Talon surprised everyone by speaking up. Tarsis nudged him to stay out of it. "The *Monarch* may be able to outrun a frigate, but not a swarm of fighters for that long through open space. I doubt there are many ships that can. I may be wearing the suit of a Keeper, but I'm a Ceresian. Take me to Ceres Prime, and I'll help you trade away all the Synthrol you want at a price you won't ever get anywhere else."

Larana eyed Talon skeptically. "Why should I trust you? A Keeper has no influence outside an Ark. 'Live on the Ark, die on the Ark.' All except you."

Talon realized he may have unintentionally insulted the Keepers she and her crew revered. "I was only recently accepted onto the *Amerigo*." He tried to feign a sense of honor over that fact. "I still have connections—friends from my days working for the Morastus Clan."

"Morastus! Didn't realize we were takin' on royalty," Larana responded sarcastically.

"Two minutes, Cap," Kitt warned.

Talon didn't want to beg, but he was verging on it. Ceres was so close that he could smell it—that moldy aroma that always seemed to emanate from the dated ventilation systems. The stench of sweat and sex in the dome. Vera glistening as she danced up high for all to see, with Julius struggling not to stare at her. He missed all of it more than he ever thought he could, and Elisha most of all.

"Even if I'm lying, my people won't shove you in a cell for no good reason," Talon said. "You can find a place to settle in, alter the *Monarch's* clearance codes, and then go home safely."

Larana sent a side-long glare in Kitt's direction.

"Definitely closer," Kitt said, shrugging.

Larana sighed. "Fine. Seems we have no choice. No way we

wastin' fuel goin' all the way to Ceres Prime though. Not until you help us make a profit. Kitt, check the drift charts. Find the nearest Ceresian settlement for Mr. Morastus."

Talon frowned, though he knew it was the best he'd get. "Deal," he said.

Kitt whipped around. His youthful fingers expertly fluttered over the command console and he brought up a map of the Circuit. Soon after that, he had two settlements pinpointed on the small two-dimensional screen. "Pretty much equal to Thalia or Kalliope."

"Kalliope!" Talon nearly shouted. "That's perfect. Take us there."

"Works for me," Captain Larana said. "You two should hold on." She reached up and flipped a switch to activate the ship-wide com-system button before continuing. "Cedric, loose fastenin's on the pod and secure everythin' in the hold. Kitt, power engines for max burn. When I say open the cargo hangar, do it. We'll give them what they're lookin' for."

"Hopin' they locked onto the distress beacon, not us?" Kitt said.

"Let's hope." Larana looked back over her shoulder and flashed a grin. "In case you don't realize, Talon of Ceres, this piece o' junk was built for escapin' Tribunal fighters."

Tarsis grabbed Talon and pulled him over to the side of the command deck. There were emergency seats folded into the wall that he yanked down. They hastily strapped into them, and once they were secure Larana reactivated the transmission with the Tribunal Frigate.

"This is the *Monarch*," she said. "Seems I'm goin' to have to deny you. Thanks for the offer though."

Only a few seconds passed before the soldier replied, "May the Spirit of the Earth be with you." The transmission cut out.

"Missiles fired," Kitt said, his eyes poring over the information on the command console's screen.

"Do it!" Larana barked.

The stars through the viewport started to race by slightly faster. The walls and ceiling started to rattle, pipes and conduits clanking against each other. Even with the ship's gravity generator working at full power to counteract the effects, Talon could feel the pressure of full acceleration. It felt like there was a half-ton man sitting down on top of his chest and his head was being crushed in a vice. He squeezed on the edges of his seat, praying that the burn wouldn't last long.

"The pod is hit," Kitt grated. "Wiped clean off the Circuit."

Talon noticed a blinking, red blip on the command console's screen suddenly disappear. Larana's gamble had paid off, it seemed, but they weren't clear yet.

CHAPTER EIGHT - ADIM
THEY LOOK LIKE THIS UNIT

ADIM and Cassius watched as the inner hangar of Ennomos closed and Sage's freighter disappeared into the blackness of space. Then ADIM turned to observe his Creator. He was wearing an expression similar to the one he would wear when he watched his HOLO-Recorder play the last message from Caleb Vale. Another human wouldn't notice the pangs of guilt tugging at his face, but Cassius couldn't hide his true feelings from ADIM.

"She was supposed to stay?" ADIM asked. He contemplated reaching out and touching his Creator's hand as humans in distress tended to do. He didn't.

"I had hoped, but she's as stubborn as I was," Cassius responded. "Now that *they* aren't crawling around inside of her head she'll have to find her own way. I've done all I can." He sighed. "It's no matter to us now. You have something to show me? Tell me it's footage of the bomb's effect."

The tiny red lights rotating around ADIM's eyes picked up their pace. "It is not, but this unit does have recordings and output scans of the detonation if you would like to view those first, Creator?"

"It can wait." Cassius smiled. He turned ADIM in the direction of the *Shadow Chariot.*

ADIM had closed Elisha inside for her safety after Sage attacked Cassius, leaving it in a low-power state to make sure she received oxygen. Something was off, however. The ship's fusion core had made it impossible to tell earlier, but as they got closer he realized that the heat signature it emitted was slightly different than it had been.

He jumped up onto the wing and discovered that not only was the ship was unlocked, but the cockpit was ajar. He whipped the transparent lid open all the way and stuck his head in, but there was little space for anything else inside but a body with all the circuitry present. She was gone.

"ADIM, what is it?"

"She's gone," he responded. His voice was as even as it always was, but his eyes began to spin wildly. He hopped down from *Shadow Chariot* and looked underneath it. *Nothing.* He hurried out into the center of the hangar and set his systems to do a wide scan. There were heat signatures in the labs below, but they were from the Tribunal prisoners. There was no way she could've accessed the lift to join him without owning a pair of Cassius's retinas. Then he picked up another signature grouping coming from inside of the Solar-Ark. It was an unusual one.

Cassius grabbed ADIM by the shoulder. "Who are you talking about?" He was winded from trying to keep up with the android.

"A human child named Elisha. This Unit found her unconscious on Kalliope and transported her here for you."

A flash of anger tightened Cassius features. "You brought someone here?" he questioned.

"As did the Creator," ADIM responded. "Do not worry. She does not know the location or designation of this hangar. She believes the Tribune destroyed Kalliope, as this unit was instructed to inform all inhabitants of the Circuit."

Cassius stammered, tongue-tied, as ADIM got a better impression of what was inside the *Amerigo*. It was impossible to tell exactly through the dense plating—plus the ship's archaic construction made everything about it read strange through his sensors—but whatever it was there was movement.

"Are there survivors on board the Solar-Ark?" ADIM asked.

"What?" Cassius said, surprised by the question. "No. Every Keeper that served aboard the *Amerigo* is now drifting through space. I offered them the chance for survival, but they all refused."

"This unit is picking up a life form aboard."

A look of concern took hold of Cassius's face just before ADIM turned and sprinted toward the Solar-Ark. "ADIM, we're not done discussing this!" he shouted and hurried in pursuit.

ADIM didn't listen. He had to find the girl so that she could be presented to his Creator, and if it wasn't her on the Ark then whatever it was could've been a threat. In that case he had to protect Cassius and his will. Ennomos's location had to remain a secret. He couldn't risk hesitating.

He entered the cargo bay of the Solar-Ark, where he was greeted by row after row of stacked storage containers. Many of them had blue light shining through their ventilation shafts, and ADIM didn't need to stop to analyze what they held. After constructing the Gravitum Bomb that split open Kalliope, he knew those readings well.

He sprinted to the lift. The source of the unusual readings was coming from the space through the top of it. After calculating how long it would take to reach them, he decided to climb rather than wait for it. He hopped with ease between containers and massive, unmoving mechanical arms, up nearly one hundred feet until he was able to grab onto the lip of the floor above.

He lifted his body and peaked into the room. Row after row of vacant cryo-chambers lined the worn, metal walls. But that wasn't what caught his glare. As soon as his head showed, six pairs of glowing red eyes turned to face him. He quickly fell back into cover, but when no shots were fired he pulled himself back up. The unidentified beings stared a short while longer and then they all returned to whatever it was they'd been doing.

ADIM propelled himself through the opening and took cover behind the open lid of a cryo-chamber. He aimed the gun built into his arm around the corner and cautiously approached the nearest red-eyed presence.

It was an android with a dark metal chassis, smoldering reddish eye-lenses, blank plate where its mouth should be—just like him. It tirelessly scrubbed a splotch of blood staining the floor.

ADIM grasped the android by the neck and flung it. It skidded to a stop against the opposite wall, but it didn't do anything to defend itself. All it did was pop back up to its feet and attempt to return to cleaning the stain. The other five androids around the room continued their work as well, ignoring the interruption.

"What are you?" ADIM questioned.

He lunged forward, grabbed the android by the head, and looked at its eyes. The tiny red lights surrounding them were completely still, unlike ADIM's, which had never whirled faster. ADIM ripped the android's plated face off, revealing all the machinery churning around its memory core. Piece by piece he peeled through it. He wasn't sure what was wrong with him, but he felt like two of his own wires had splayed and were being rubbed together to produce a spark.

"ADIM!" The familiar voice of Cassius shouted from near the lift.

ADIM paused, a severed conduit leaking some form of ruddy goo in his hand. He glanced down. The eye components of the android were popped out, one still glowing brightly and the other flickering.

"I didn't want you to find out like this." Cassius's hand fell upon ADIM's shoulder.

ADIM looked up at him. Five androids were gathered behind him, standing perfectly upright and with all of their sights fixed on ADIM. He scanned them one at a time, from one pair of red eyes to the next. It was like looking into an array of mirrors.

"They look like this unit," ADIM said.

"And that is where the similarities end," he responded firmly. "I constructed them while you made progress stealing the Tribunal freighters."

"To replace this unit?"

"Never!" Cassius replied. "To bolster our strength. We needed help with what was coming next, but they are nothing compared to you."

ADIM pulled on the eye of the android near his lap and stretched the wire connected to it as far as it would go. "Then why do they look like this unit?"

Cassius took a deep breath before answering. "It is an efficient model. I needed them to share your mobility and sturdiness, but that is all. What makes you truly exceptional is in here." Cassius tapped ADIM on the top of his head. "I would never try to replicate that. It took all the wealth I had left on Titan just to make those poor, mindless imitations of you."

"Imitation," ADIM said. He looked down at his arm, where he made the tiny holographic lenses along the limb project the image of human flesh. "'Cheap imitation of human life,'" he repeated in the exact voice of Sage Volus.

"Pay no attention to her. Her mind has been polluted by the lies of the Tribune beyond what I could fix. What you are is completely unique." He went quiet for a few seconds, then his features displayed traces of excitement. "ADIM, raise your arms," he demanded.

ADIM released the other android's eye and then froze. "I do not understand."

Cassius wheeled around and faced the other five operational androids. "Androids, raise your arms."

Without hesitation they all echoed, "Yes, Creator," and raised their arms straight up.

"Androids, about-face."

"Yes, Creator," they droned again and turned around in unison.

"Androids, continue cleaning this vessel."

The same response came and then they all returned to the stains on the floor that they had been scrubbing before Cassius or ADIM entered the room.

"You see, ADIM? Not a second thought. You were the same when I created you, but they will never evolve as you have. 'Dynamic Intelligence'—that was my gift to you. These androids, they *are* imitations. The androids dotting the Ceresian Belt, those are imitations. But you, you are something far more."

ADIM rose to face his creator. They stood at the exact same height. "What is that?" ADIM inquired.

Cassius smiled warmly. "We'll just have to find out exactly what for ourselves, but to me, now, you continue to be my son. They are only here to help me…to help us with what comes next."

ADIM's rotating eyes slowed and his scanners read that Cassius's heartbeat was doing the same. He glanced at the mess of parts sprinkled around his feet.

"Don't worry, broken parts can be replaced," Cassius said. "Now let us find this child."

"Elisha," ADIM corrected. "This unit just re-analyzed the thermal readings of the freighter given to Sage Volus before its departure. A faint heat signature, likely from a small-sized human, was located in the galley of the ship. This unit's focus on guarding you from the Executor resulted in it going unnoticed. It will not happen again. This unit will prepare the *Shadow Chariot* to go and retrieve the Creator's gift."

"No, ADIM, leave her. If it is the girl, Sage will keep her safe. If she ever gets back to her people, she will cast blame for what happened on Kalliope against the Tribune, just as we desire. As long as you're sure she saw nothing but the inside of the hangar?"

"This unit is positive."

"Then we have nothing to worry about. They will already know this place is somewhere in an asteroid, but with war to come and thousands of celestial bodies floating through the Ignascent Cell, the Tribunal's search for me will only serve to spread their resources even thinner, just as we intend. I must ask—why did you bring the girl back?"

"The Creator was not clear that everyone on Kalliope had to die," ADIM responded. "There was ample room on the *Shadow Chariot* for a human of her size. This unit has seen you looking at the recording of your deceased human child Caleb. His loss appears to distress you. This unit had never seen an undeveloped human before and deduced that she could be made worthy of your will. You have given this unit many gifts. This unit wanted to provide you with one." ADIM's eyes picked up in their rotation again. He worried that somehow he'd misinterpreted his Creator's will and had made a mistake. "Are you unhappy with this unit's decision?"

Cassius smiled. "Of course not. I'm thrilled and honored that you came to that decision on your own ADIM, but I don't want another child," he said. "I have enough. We are together in this now. Just us. Do you understand?"

"Yes." ADIM's eyes stopped rotating.

Cassius reached out, placed his hand on the android's face, and stared at his expressionless face. "You continue to surprise me, ADIM."

CHAPTER NINE - SAGE
MADE OF METAL

It'd been days since Sage awoke from the induced slumber. She was sitting on her knees in the center of the freighter's command deck, watching through the viewport as the stars crept lazily across the blackness. In it her reflection stared back. Her eyes were green as lettuce touched by fresh water, not pale and hopeless as she remembered. Her fiery hair was cut shorter than she was used to and frayed out from beneath a cloth bandage stained with blood just as red. She reached up with her human hand and grabbed a loose strand, feeling a minor stinging sensation at the root as she pulled ever so gently. It startled her. She knew she'd never get used to feeling such meager pains.

She sighed and looked down. Her pistol hung at her hip and she was wearing the unmarked suit of white nano-armor bestowed upon her when she was named an Executor. All of its dents and stains were precisely where she left them when Cassius stripped her of it before surgery.

The exit from the command deck was sealed from the outside and impossible to cut through even with her blade. She figured it was programmed to open once Titan was in reach and the ships controls were returned to her; otherwise she'd have to slice through the viewport. The freighter flew completely on autopilot, without even the beeping of navigation consoles to accompany her. There were some yeasty ration bars and a container of water left behind by Cassius in the corner of the room, but other than that it was entirely empty.

She'd considered trying to hack into the ship's computer and unseal her temporary prison. She'd considered trying to undo everything Cassius and his monstrous creation had done to the ship's systems and figure out exactly where he was hiding. But every time she did, her gaze drifted to her metallic arm and she remembered that her wit was no match for his. It would just be a waste of time. At least that's how she tried to justify her lack of action.

The truth was that she didn't want to know. As much as Cassius broke her heart by betraying the Tribune, she couldn't forget the man who'd introduced her to his son a lifetime ago. She remembered the hero revered throughout the halls of the Spirit Temples and on the streets of Tribunal settlements all throughout the Circuit.

As she sat quietly, readying herself for prayer, she pictured herself back on New Terrene. She didn't care who was looking through her eyes as long as she could continue doing what she did best—keeping the city's faithful populace safe from dissenters and breeders of terror.

As clouded as her mind had been when she awoke on the *White Hand,* presently it was clear. All of the memories were beginning to sort themselves, allowing her to draw on them if need be but not assail her. Piece by piece she was being put back together, re-embracing emotions that had become as foreign to her as they were to an android.

"I am blessed with ground beneath me," she stated proudly. Her trust in her Tribunal masters may have been strained, but she knew that the Earth Spirit remained with her. She'd seen what lack of faith could do when she watched Caleb Vale die on Earth, and she wouldn't allow herself to lose it. Like humanity itself she was being continually tested, her worth ascertained. She bent forward and let the tips of her fingers graze the floor. Then she closed her eyes.

"Our Homeworld has been blighted by darkness, but we are the light. Those beside me, those beneath me, those above me, ours is a collective unconscious, bound to each other and to the soul of the Earth. We are, all of us, shards of that Spirit, never alone as the dark void closes in. This day is yet another test of my conviction, but though the Earth may be wreathed in flame and shadow, she remains within me. May those who have left to join this essence guide my daily endeavors. Redemption is near. May my faith be eternal and unwavering, so that I may one day walk the Earth's untainted surface with—" She paused and looked from side to side. Her list of those deserving was getting shorter. She swallowed the lump in her throat and continued, "—with those deserving at my side."

Suddenly the entrance to the command deck slid open with a whoosh. Sage snapped around, drawing the blade in her synthetic arm. She saw a shadow first, but when her hawkish gaze followed it to the source she found something there that she didn't expect—a young girl.

"Agatha?" the girl's small voice asked. She didn't seem phased in the slightest by Sage's lethal stance. She took a few unsure steps, and then her face lit up and she sprinted forward.

"Agatha?" Sage mouthed, confused. A rush of memories surged through her—Talon's broken stare just before she pulled the trigger on Vellish; their hands touching in the *Ascendant's* brig; playing cards beside a fire on Ceres Prime.

Impossible. Talon's daughter?

She reached out with her human hand in disbelief. *It can't be. I must still be experiencing side effects from the removal. She's just a memory,* she told herself emphatically. But her human fingers grazed the face of the girl and they didn't pass through. She felt a cold cheek and rigid bone beneath it. Her eyes looked just like Talon's.

"You're alive!" the girl exclaimed, hugging her leg. Her gaze immediately gravitated to the container of water pinned against a console.

"I…" Sage was at a loss for words. When nothing came out she noticed the girl's dry lips and nudged her toward the water. The child didn't waste any time before running over and chugging.

"Where were you?" Sage finally managed to squeeze out, more harshly than she'd intended.

The girl wiped her lips and started tearing into a ration bar. "Stuck in the refectory. I was looking around there and then got locked inside when the ship took off. It ran out of water, but then the door unlocked and I came here." She looked around the room. "You're alone?"

"I thought I was."

"Where's ADIM?"

"The android?"

"He told me to stay but then there was a crash! I didn't mean to get stuck in here, the door just shut behind me."

"He's gone." Sage reached out hesitantly and placed her had on the girl's arm. "You're safe now," she promised.

The girl was so preoccupied with devouring every last crumb of the tasteless bar that Sage's words seem to pass right through her ears. "You know him? I've never met an android like him. He was going to introduce me to 'the Creator.'" She stopped eating and her eyes widened. "Is that you?"

"What? Of course not!"

"Oh...I hope I didn't upset him by leaving. I didn't mean to."

"Upset him—" Sage swallowed the rest of her words. "How did *you* meet him...I mean it?"

"He rescued me from Kalliope after the Tribune attacked."

Sage had no idea what that meant, but being that the girl was Ceresian she was worried a war had started and she'd missed it. "What's Kalliope?" Sage asked.

The girl stared at Sage like she couldn't believe what she'd heard. "It's a mine," she said. "Are you taking me back to Ceres? My father should be back by now; he promised. He's probably looking for me." The girl's face lips dipped into a frown. "He's not going to be happy about Uncle Julius."

Sage's throat went dry before she was able to respond: "Don't worry. Your father is alive and well." A small moon passed by the ship's viewport, its glossy surface faintly reflecting what appeared to be the rings of Saturn. "I'm sure he's doing whatever it takes to get back to you. Right now though, we're about to land on Titan. You'll be safe with me and I'll make sure you get safe passage back home."

"Titan!" the girl exclaimed, getting up and running to Sage's side. "Does that mean we'll get to see Saturn? I've always wanted to!"

"Yes, it's right out there," Sage replied, pointing to the outline of its rings. As she did, something the girl had said dawned on her. "What happened to Julius?"

The girl's gaze drooped away from the sight of Saturn. "He died on Kalliope…" she whimpered.

Sage wasn't sure why a sudden swell of sadness seized her, for a Ceresian no less, but before she could respond, a loud, crackling voice spoke through the ship's speakers.

"This is Tribunal Hand Yavortha," it said. "Unidentified vessel, you are approaching Titan's atmosphere at high velocity. Avert your course immediately or we will fire."

Yavortha! Sage thought, remembering that he was not one for idle threats. She had no love for the man, but she was grateful to be contacted by somebody who would know who she was.

She ran over to the captain's chair and swiped her hand across the command HOLO-Screen. The transmission was coming in clean, but along with the piloting controls her ability to respond was locked.

"Come on, Cassius!" she whispered angrily under her breath. The doors were all open, so she couldn't understand what the ship was waiting for.

A transmission from Yavortha came through again, this time with even more severity. "Unidentified vessel, you will comply!"

The command console beeped and Sage's last entry went through. "Don't fire, this is Executor Sage Volus!" she shouted, more frantically then she intended to. "I repeat, don't fire! This is Executor Sage Volus."

There was an extended period of silence which Sage imagined was most likely for vocal recognition. She didn't know how long exactly she'd been out of contact, so some skepticism was expected. Still, there were only a handful of people in the Circuit who knew her true identity.

"Executor!" Yavortha responded, sounding pleased. "Lord Vakari will be thrilled to learn you aren't dead. I advise that you slow your approach. The thick atmosphere will tear you to pieces."

"I've lost control of my shi—" Right as she was about to finish the sentence, the lock on the freighter's systems was disarmed. "Never mind," she exhaled. "I have it." She lowered the acceleration of the engines and felt the familiar vacant feeling in her gut that comes when one falls too fast and too suddenly.

"We will be awaiting you in the hangar of Cassius's old compound. Do not delay."

The transmission cut out and the freighter started to rattle. They were entering the upper atmosphere of Titan. She strapped on her restraining belt and then wrapped her synthetic arm around Talon's daughter. "Hold on, girl," she whispered into her ear.

"I have a name, you know," the child responded indignantly. "It's Elisha. I thought *you* were Agatha?"

Sage allowed the vibrations of the freighter to reverberate through all the human parts of her body. "Not anymore," she said. Then she held Elisha tightly, wondering what the girl's frightened heartbeat might've felt like against her forearm if it weren't made of metal.

CHAPTER TEN - CASSIUS
LEGACY OF THE ANCIENTS

Cassius stood next to ADIM outside of the Solar-Ark *Amerigo,* watching as the other androids meticulously transported heavy crates of processed Gravitum out its cargo hold and into the depths of Ennomos. Cassius couldn't help but wonder what his favored creation might've been thinking at that exact moment. He was probably calculating exactly how many settlements throughout the Circuit could be provided with Earthlike conditions with that much Gravitum. Or that it was enough to build six more bombs similar to the one which split Kalliope open like an egg. Now that their test was complete, six appeared to be the amount needed for what they were planning.

Presently, one of the androids came walking out from the lift which led to the lab below. It was the one ADIM had attacked. Its head was completely deformed. One of its eyes flickered and was sunken within a fist-sized dent, but it was working well enough. A trio of humans limped in front of it, looking in much worse shape. They were a few of the survivors from the Tribunal freighters. They stared forward blankly as they were led along, like a row of battered animals.

"Finally," Cassius said. "Come, ADIM. Now that the claws of the Tribune have been drawn from their poor souls, we will tell them of their heroic fate."

"Yes, Creator."

They made their way onto the *Amerigo,* across the massive cargo and up into a hall lined with cryo-chambers.

"Do you know where you are?" Cassius asked the three survivors. He then answered his own question before they could say anything. "This is the oldest working construct of humanity currently in existence. These very chambers were built more than half a millennium ago by the Ancients. Amazing isn't it?"

None of them responded, but they nodded their heads timidly. Cassius placed his arm around the one nearest to him, a man with a beard so messy that it masked just how gaunt his face had grown. He led him in front of one of the open chambers.

"Load them in," Cassius ordered.

The damaged android went to grab the man, but ADIM quickly stepped forward and stuck out his arm. He grasped the docile survivor by the collar and lifted him into the vacant cryo-chamber. ADIM was able to maneuver him like a limp doll. He then did the same with the two other survivors, a younger man and a middle-aged woman.

A smile tugged at Cassius's lips from watching ADIM's reaction. "What do you want with us?" the bearded survivor asked.

Cassius recognized him. It had been a year since ADIM had brought that specific survivor back from the first Tribunal freighter he raided. It was only fair to let the man know the reason why he'd been imprisoned for so long. The fact that he'd been a servant of the Tribune was only a part of it.

"You are going to help us complete the work of the Ancients. Do you know what the original purpose of these vessels was?" Cassius asked. The bearded survivor shook his head. "I assumed you wouldn't. Most of the Circuit has forgotten, or simply doesn't care, but throughout many of my wasted years serving on their council, I dedicated my time to learning as much as I could about our ancestors. I found fragments of old files wherever I could— buried in databases in the Circuit's oldest settlements, in Conduit stations, and in the ruins of Ceresian cities after the end of the war. By the time of my exile I had pieced it all together. Of course the Tribune wouldn't hear it."

"You see," he was so eager to finally be able share his findings with someone other than ADIM that he had to take a breath. "Sometime before the Earth fell, one of the Ancient's maligned leaders had a dream of reaching the stars—of finding another world like Earth somewhere out in the great vacuum. He ordered the construction of a series of Solar-driven Ark Ships, his greatest invention. Most people ridiculed him for wasting so many resources, until Gravitum.

"While they were being built, some brave researcher discovered that the new element found within the mantle of the Earth could be used to generate substantial fields of artificial gravity when an electric current was applied. The Ancients began tearing at the surface of the planet, harvesting as much as they could find as quickly as possible. There was no need to find other worlds if they could build their own and have it simulate the conditions of Earth. They built the original Conduit Station above the moon to test it in vacuum conditions, and then selected asteroids that they could now mine for all their countless resources in the safety of Earth-like conditions. Eventually, the planet couldn't handle all of the abuse, and billions were killed when it rejected us, spewing up molten rocks and cracking across the surface."

"That's a lie," the bearded man groaned. "It was the sins of men like you that cursed the world."

Cassius ignored him and continued, "With Earth literally crumbling, that foolish man who dreamed of the stars was the last hope for humanity. His five completed Solar-Arks were the only chance of survival, but instead of being sent out to grasp at stars, they would become the threads upon which humanity endured. Their cargo holds were packed with the materials needed to construct more Conduit Stations, and each one was sent out, crammed with survivors, to the different Cells of our Solar System.

"The new Conduits were built to house the remnants of humanity, except those chosen to operate the Solar-Arks and distribute resources—water, food, gases, minerals, and, of course, Gravitum. We became addicted to the element. Why waste centuries trying to find worlds that may not exist when, with Gravitum, the Earth's pull could be simulated wherever we wanted? Why adapt to low-G? Why allow space to be the uninhabitable vacuum it is? The

Circuit was formed, reliant always on the Earth, which had spurned humanity as if it were no more than a bunch of insects.

"Stop," the bearded survivor said. "Just stop talking. You're insane."

"So were the men whose creations saved the human race from extinction." Cassius reached out and grasped the man by his lean jaw. "You will help us complete their work. These chambers were originally intended to completely freeze humans for their century-long journeys, but that desire was forgotten. Now they're used merely to slow the progression of the Blue Death. But the original programming remains somewhere in this vessel."

"Just kill us," the man groaned. "Please."

"It is time that they are returned to their true purpose, and all of you will help us test these chambers until they work perfectly. You should be honored. So few of us have had a chance to walk with the Ancients." He released the man's face.

"Shall This Unit begin the examination of the chambers?" ADIM asked.

"No. Unfortunately we have other more pressing matters to tend to," Cassius replied. "For now, this one will begin the studies for us while the others begin work with the Gravitum." He nodded at the damaged android, who immediately began strapping the three groaning humans into their respective cryo-chambers.

Truthfully, Cassius had no idea how long it would take to complete the work of the Ancients. He would have used the still-living bodies of Keepers if he had them, but he didn't want to risk the Blue Death claiming them all first. He wasn't even sure if they'd ever work as intended, so he didn't want to waste time while he had a war to orchestrate. But, as he looked at ADIM he remembered how much he always seemed to look forward to their projects. He didn't want to disappoint him with such honesty.

"Pressing matters?" ADIM asked.

"These incredible vessels have one additional capability. Come ADIM, we must send a message to the Circuit. All of it." Cassius led ADIM down the hall toward the command deck of the Ark. "Then it is time that we finally pay a visit to the Ceresians."

CHAPTER ELEVEN - TALON
THE LEGEND ENDURES

Captain Larana's move to escape the Tribunal ships hunting them worked flawlessly. For a day or two, scanners picked up a scout ship here and there, but all of them were hundreds of thousands of miles away and searching aimlessly. After that they were nowhere in sight, no doubt focusing all their futile efforts on a course toward Uranus.

Talon couldn't help but be slightly impressed. The Captain told him that the systems being so old made the *Monarch* hard to detect with high-tech Tribunal equipment. He found it ironic. His people spent all their time struggling to keep up with the Tribune just in case, and here they were in a century-old, rusty ship evading a Tribunal Fleet as if it were run by no more than a bunch of blind old men.

They were about a week into their journey, and according to Kitt they'd reach Kalliope soon. He took his word for it. They hadn't been together long, but Talon had come to realize that the Vergents were masters of space, and apparently of recreational games as well. They played a game called chess, moving sculpted pieces of rusty metal across a checkered board. If Talon had anything left of value, he would've been cleaned of it the first day.

Talon was presently locked in a match with Kitt in the *Monarch's* galley. He stared down at the board, dumbfounded. Kitt was still in his teens, but he had what they called Talon's "King" surrounded. It wasn't anything like the card games Talon was used to playing back in Kalliope, winning hand after hand from brutes and friends. It was a game of strategy, concentration, and silence.

"Checkmate," Kitt said.

"Again," Talon sighed. "Wait until you get to Kalliope. I'll show you a Ceresian game."

"Lookin' forward to winnin' in that too." Kitt looked up from the board with a wry grin, and then cleared it. "Again?" he asked.

"I think I've taken enough of a beating for today," Talon said. "My arms are getting tired." Kitt looked down at his blue-veined hands with concern, and when Talon did the same he understood why. He wasn't used to everybody knowing about his affliction. "Don't worry, I'm kidding. Just need to rest my head." Rest or not, his limbs were always sore from the Blue Death. There was no use in complaining about them.

"Insiders," Tarsis laughed. Being amongst his old people seemed to have him as high-spirited as he could be under the circumstances. He patted Talon on the back and motioned for him to get up. "I'll show you how it's done!"

Tarsis's bulky mechanical suit nearly kept him from fitting, but he was able to squeeze in so that the lip of the table was pressed firmly against his chest. He was able to move better thanks to Kitt performing some much needed repairs on his suit. The boy was far more skilled with the wrench then Talon ever would've expected from a Vergent.

While they played, Talon walked over to a small viewport tucked into a corner by a pair of cabinets. There was another member of the *Monarch's* crew sitting there as well, staring out into the void. She was a woman in her early thirties, and she didn't acknowledge Talon's presence at all.

It wasn't an insult. Talon had come to understand that most of the Vergents didn't feel obligated to converse unless they had to. They mostly kept to themselves, and two Vergents could even go an entire game of chess in complete silence. It was unnerving for the first few days, but having Tarsis around helped him through it. His years on the Solar-Ark had clearly changed him into something more closely resembling an "Insider."

"Drifting through space for your entire life cooped up in a ship will do that to you," Tarsis had said earlier when Talon asked why his people were so quiet. "Imagine that they already know everything about each other that they'll ever need to know. Why waste oxygen? Back in the early days of the Circuit, it could be hard to come by out in the fringes of the Circuit."

It made enough sense to him, although it made him long for the playful jabbing that was commonplace between him and his mining buddies. Talon sighed toward the stringy, pensive Vergent sitting beside him and turned his attention to space. His heart sank. Being amongst a real crew reminded him of his friends. He'd led two of them to their deaths. He didn't force them to raid the freighter with him, but maybe if they'd spent less time joking around with each other they would've known his real history with the Morastus Clan. Surely if they'd known the kind of missions he'd run for Zargo Morastus in his prime, they wouldn't have followed him.

As the faces of his fallen friends flashed through his mind, he opened his eyes as widely as possible to try keeping them dry. An object floated past the viewport. He leaned into the glass and tried to get a good look when suddenly a body slammed against it. He would've fallen out of his seat if the Vergent next to him didn't stick out an arm to brace him.

"Fucking, Ancients!" he shouted. "Did you see that?"

The wide-eyed Vergent beside him nodded.

"What is it?" Tarsis asked, barely looking up from his intense bout of chess with Kitt.

"There's a body out there!"

Tarsis's hand slipped over the top of the piece he was about to move. This time he turned his full attention from the game. "A body?"

"I think." Talon tried to get another look, but, whatever it was, it had bounced clear around the aft of the ship.

Kitt got up to his feet and nimbly bounced across the room to join him at the viewport. "I see nothin'," he said.

"Definitely no rock," the other Vergent added.

By the time Tarsis was able to lug his mechanically-aided frame over to the viewport to join them, Captain Larana's voice spoke through the ship's com-system.

"Kitt, bring the Keepers up," she said, sounding increasingly distressed with each word. "They'll want to see. We've reached Kalliope…"

Kitt's brow furrowed. "I set the route. Should've been another few hours." He hurried out of the galley, forcing Talon and Tarsis into a jog to keep up.

From what Talon had learned about Kitt in their short time together, he was an even more skilled navigator of drift charts than he was a repairman. He was so confident in his abilities, in fact, that being even a few hours off meant something had to be wrong. Talon could see it in his face.

Kitt flew through the ship's corridors as if he were gliding. They could barely keep up. When they reached the command deck, however, they found him standing petrified in the entrance.

Debris was scattered throughout space—pieces of rock and metal that were impossible to distinguish from one another in the darkness. All of it, however, floated in the shadow of a chunk of rock one hundred times the size. It was hollowed out in patches, with visible walkways and structures built into the crags. They were squeezed and distended in places, but they remained intact enough for Talon to know exactly what everything was. It was surreal. As if a doctor had taken a scalpel to an entire asteroid colony, sliced it open, and preserved half of it as a diagram which said, "This is how Ceresians once lived."

Not even a light was flickering, but the *Monarch's* spotter left little room for doubt. Talon denied it as long as he stood there in silence, until Kitt raced past him to take control from Larana and carefully guided the ship close enough for him to see the distorted shell of the *Elder Muse*. It was crumpled up like a sheet of paper, but he'd recognize the entrance anywhere. That was when he first noticed the countless bodies floating betwixt the wreckage as if that was all that they were. Some of them wore full mining suits; others were in their boiler suits as if they'd been torn from their beds.

Of all the horrid scenes Talon had walked into in his life as a mercenary, this was the worst. He leaned over the empty chair next to Larana and swallowed the contents of his stomach trying to force their way out. All of the faces he'd seen drinking and gambling in the *Elder Muse* for years were swollen and unrecognizable—dumped like garbage into the great black vacuum. The first person he thought of was Julius, but he knew that he wasn't up for another shift in the mines for two months. *Lucky for him, at least.*

"Guessin' it wasn't like this when you left?" Larana inquired.

"No," Talon said.

Tarsis stepped up beside him. "Must've been one hell of an accident. Fusion Core probably overloaded."

"Place ran on a small core that might cook the inside of it, but no way it would break it open like this. Besides, nothing's slagged. It's all cold, like it was snapped in half by a giant. I've never seen anything like this."

"He's right," Larana said. "Grav generator maybe? I've seen 'em get overloaded in old ships and rip 'em apart without a spark."

"No, you'd need a generator the size of Ceres to break open solid rock like that," Talon stated firmly. He'd been there once when the colony's old gravity generator went off, and all that happened was a few broken limbs and cases of the Blue Death, his being amongst them. Some walls here and there were torn down, but the damage to the facility was minimal.

Talon's fists tightened, and for a moment he imagined the place had gotten what it deserved for taking everything from him. Then the limp arm of a body in space brushed across the cockpit's translucency and snapped him out of it. *Only fools blame rock and space,* he told himself, reiterating words Zargo Morastus had once said after the incident.

"I'll have suits prepped. Might be survivors," Kitt spoke up. He reached out to switch on the ship-wide com-system.

"No," Larana swiftly replied. "Attacks on Solar-Arks. A mining Colony split open. Somethin' tells me it's all connected. We shoulda never come here, and we shouldn' linger."

"But—"

"That's an order, child!" Larana growled.

"She's right," Talon said sullenly. "There's no one left anyway. The life support systems were over half-a-century old. If anyone managed to lock themselves up safely, they've suffocated by now."

"Can you get out of here without hittin' anything?" Larana asked Kitt.

"Of course," Kitt said. The idea of a new challenge was apparently enough to distract him. He leaned forward and gritted his teeth as he maneuvered the *Monarch* around a hefty slab of metal, likely the remnants of a residential block. The move brought them closer to the chunk of Kalliope, and as he plotted their course the console in front of Larana suddenly beeped.

"What's that?" Talon asked nervously.

"Weak transmission. Comin' from Kalliope. Com-System must still be somewhat operational."

"Survivors?" Kitt questioned. His face lit up.

"I…" As she scanned the data coming in through the console Larana's cheeks went paler than it had when she was staring out at the floating graveyard. "It's relayin' through Kalliope from outside. Signal's broadcastin' to all known frequencies in the Circuit and makin' sure that's known—Tribunals, Ceresians, Keepers, us…everyone."

"Can't be," Kitt said. "Only a Solar-Ark has access to all—" He gasped as he realized the answer to his question.

Talon edged as close as he could. Larana switched on the transmission. The question that had been on all of their minds since the moment the Solar-Ark *Amerigo* was hit was seemingly about to be answered. The message was coming in full of static, but not enough to squelch the potent voice which began speaking.

"People of the Circuit, this is Cassius Vale," it said. Hearing the name sent a chill up Talon's spine.

"Can you trace the origin?" Larana paused the message and asked Kitt.

Kitt plugged away at his station. He shook his head. "Solar-Arks can broadcast without showin' their location. Layers of encryption only Ancients'd understand. Signal is bouncin' off every settlement and ship in the Circuit. Comin' from and to everywhere. It's meant to keep 'em safe from attack."

"Apparently that wasn't enough," Talon chimed in. Nobody seemed amused.

"Keep workin' on it." Larana reached out and set the transmission to resume. Talon knew it was a lost cause but he didn't say anything. If the legendary Cassius Vale didn't want to be found, then he was the type of man that would make sure he wasn't.

Cassius continued, "Soon word will reach you all of recent affairs, but I will not wait for the truth to be twisted by the Council of the New Earth Tribunal. It is no secret that I was once a member of that revered assembly, and that I fought to establish the relative peace we share today. I have remained loyal since I stepped down from that position, but no longer.

"Recently, I discovered their plans to test a prototype weapon on the mining asteroid 22-Kalliope. Their hope was to strike fear into the Ceresians in retaliation for continued acts of terror throughout their dominion and the commandeering of six transport freighters. Even more deplorable than that, they have slowly been bribing the Keepers of the Circuit with workers and luxuries in order to bring them under their complete influence. This is a deliberate attempt to forsake the ancient oath our ancestors took that the guardians of Earth must continue to provide the Circuit with ample Gravitum and other required resources—that no matter the circumstances, the human race must go on."

There was a short pause. Enough time for Talon to take in what he was hearing. The Tribune's bribery of the Keepers came as no surprise to him, though the Vergents in the room looked appalled. The idea of a prototype weapon, on the other hand, had his heart beating against his ribcage. If that was true, then they were witnesses to its destructive capabilities. Even bombs built using nuclear fusion didn't have the capacity to so comprehensively break apart a large asteroid, and destroying a perfectly operating settlement was something neither the Tribune nor the Ceresians were ever keen on doing.

"When I threatened to disclose these secrets, my former comrades attempted to have me killed. Their attack of my home on Titan has left Edeoria in turmoil, and I barely escaped with my life. Tribune Nora Gressler wasn't so lucky…" Cassius cleared his throat. "By the time this message reaches all the corners of the Circuit, 22-Kalliope will likely have been reduced to a few floating hunks of rock. My attempts to disrupt their display of power have failed, but the Tribune, along with those who side with them through these atrocities, will pay. I have commandeered the Solar-Ark *Amerigo*. Only when the Tribune admits their role in the desecration of Kalliope will I allow it to reassume its true purpose. Also, if the other Arks are kept from their roles as equal providers for *all* factions in the Circuit, then I will destroy the *Amerigo* and hunt down the rest of them. I leave it in their hands."

The transmission went silent, and Talon allowed himself to release the breath he hadn't realized he'd been holding. Everyone in the cockpit had their mouths ajar, but all of them were Vergent. None of them could've known the Cassius Vale that all Ceresians were brought up to know. Most of Talon's people thought that after a falling out with the rest of the Tribunal Council he was killed. Others thought he was exiled to Titan. Nobody knew for sure before the message Talon just heard, but every Ceresian knew what happened in the Earth Reclaimer War—how Cassius had beaten them into submission.

"Commandeered?" Tarsis grunted, breaking the silence. "Slaughtered!"

"Tribune or not, he has no right to attack a Solar-Ark!" Larana slammed her fist down on the arm of her chair.

Everything that happened aboard the *Amerigo* suddenly made sense to Talon. The Keepers were always going to fight back to defend their ship, so there was no choice but to eliminate them. That was how Cassius Vale operated. Wherever he went, death swiftly followed.

"Set a course for Ceres Prime," Talon demanded evenly. There was no reason to argue with the Vergents. Cassius wasn't the type of man who needed to ask for the right to do anything.

Larana wheeled around, clearly irritated. "This is my ship. You don't give orders. We'll drop you at Thalia and be out of this mess."

Talon didn't flinch. "And risk the lives of your crew?" he said. "Whether or not anything Cassius said was true, the only thing my people hate more than him is the Tribune. They'll respond in force, and when they do, the outer colonies like Thalia will quickly be under siege. Ceres is in the heart of the belt. There are hundreds of places the Tribune's got to get past in order to reach it. There's nowhere safer for you right now, unless you feel like braving their entire fleet to make it to Uranus."

The Captain's cheeks flushed, but she clearly knew that Talon was right. The *Monarch* was on the Tribune's list now, and all of space was about to be crawling with their ships.

"Fine," she grumbled. "But you're payin' for the fuel, and anythin' we can't trade for."

CHAPTER TWELVE - SAGE
ONE LAST LIE

Sage held onto Elisha tightly as she guided the freighter through the thick atmosphere of Titan. Friction had the command deck's viewport wreathed in a fiery skirt. She expected the ride to be bumpier, but Cassius's upgrades to the hull made the freighter far more than just a Conduit-to-Conduit transport.

When the ship broke through, Sage found them in the heart of a storm. Precipitation lashed across the hull and dense clouds obscured her view. With the navigation systems disengaged it would've been impossible to find where to go if she hadn't made the trip before. She could just distinguish the faint outline of the crater which bore Edeoria, sitting beneath the blurred shadow of the *Ascendant*.

She looked down at Elisha, expecting to see a terrified girl entering atmosphere for the first time. Instead she was wide-eyed and propped forward like she wanted to swim through the storm.

"Is that water?" she asked, awestruck.

"Not exactly," Sage replied. "Methane mostly. Some other—"

"Where's it coming from? The pipes must be huge!"

A smile tugged at Sage's lips. Sometimes she forgot that most people in the Circuit had never been to a world with clouds. Most people had never walked upon the surface of the Earth beneath her scorched sky, hoping for the faintest sliver of light to peak through the clouds. It never did. "No pipes. It's all natural. Titan is a world wrapped in clouds, like Earth."

Elisha looked up at Sage excitedly. "Have you been there?"

As Sage opened her mouth to respond, the image of her last

time on Earth rushed through her mind—Caleb's smile followed by flashes of fire and blood. She took a few deep breaths to try and center herself. "Yes, I've been there."

They didn't exchange another word while Sage navigated the near impossible conditions. Elisha seemed content to just stare out into the storm. After a short while, Sage piloted them safely into the hangar of Cassius's compound. The heavy outer seal quickly shut behind them to hold the frigid air of Titan at bay. There was a much different greeting party awaiting her than the last time she had arrived. The *White Hand* was missing, and in its place were a few small Tribunal transports. The smallest of them had a pointed top which gleamed like a wet pearl. The rest of it was of a similar luster, except the folded wings, which were painted to look like the black silhouettes of hands wrapping around its green chassis. It was the personal transport of a Tribune, which meant Benjar was there with his esteemed Hand, Yavortha.

An honor guard marched into the space, their capes fluttering like leaves in wind. Yavortha was in the middle of the pack. She could tell by the golden emblem on his pauldrons as well his distinctive, hawkish nose. Behind him was Benjar. He wore a carbon-fiber chest-plate over his viridian tunic and held up the cloak draped over his left arm so it didn't drag across the floor.

She expected seeing him to make her feel like she was back home, but when she noticed his characteristic grin it was just the opposite. A burning itch flared up between her thighs that made her shiver. Her vision was clouded by the kind of blotchy circles that come after staring at the sun too long.

Sage grasped Elisha's hand and led her out of the Command Deck. When they reached the cargo hold, Sage kneeled in front of the girl.

"Follow my lead once they're here, and don't speak unless you're addressed," Sage said. She made sure Elisha nodded back. Sage signaled the cargo hold to open.

The ramp fell down and blinding light flooded it. It was swiftly followed by a host of soldiers wearing dark, tinted visors, their pulse rifles held up at the ready. Sage opened her mouth to speak, but none of them paid any attention her. They swept the entire space and then a few of them moved further into the ship, out of sight.

Sage felt Elisha huddle against her leg. She could only imagine what an array of faceless soldiers in heavy armor looked like to a child from the shanties of Ceres Prime.

"Who are they?" Elisha asked, her tiny voice filled with fright.

"Tribune Vakari's personal guard," Sage said. "Don't worry, they're just being cautious. I'm one of them." As soon as the words left her lips the girl's hands lifted off of her leg. Before she had a chance to look down, Benjar Vakari strolled up the ramp with Hand Yavortha in front of him.

"Your Eminence," Sage uttered, quickly falling to her knees and allowing her fingers to graze the floor. She looked down, making sure that their gazes didn't meet until he responded. Yavortha arrived first and yanked the pistol out of her belt, making no effort to be gentle. He patted her down, from head to toe, and when he was done stepped aside. Benjar then moved forward.

"Sage," he exclaimed. "By the Ancients, you're alive!" He reached out and placed his hand over her head, trying to get a better look at the bandage wrapped around it and coated in dried blood. "What has that monster done to you?"

Sage opened her mouth to tell him, but she was reminded of Talon. She saw his bright, blue eyes, burning with thoughts of betrayal. She could feel her hand squeeze the trigger that robbed Vellish of his life. It made her overflow with rage. She wasn't sure what she was expecting to feel when she looked upon Benjar again. She wasn't used to expecting to feel anything. *The whole time…he was watching through my eyes,* she thought angrily. As soon as she beheld his complacent grin, she had little doubt over the truth.

She bit out the words she wanted to say, fully aware of her place in the room. "He cut the implant out of the back of my head," she replied calmly,

"By the Spirit," Benjar gasped. He moved behind her, getting a full view of Cassius's work. His index finger tapped the scar, causing

Sage to flinch and him to pull back. "My poor girl. We will make him pay for this."

As his fingers slid over her skin, her unsettled mind thrust her back to all the times she shared his bed. She could feel his flesh rub against hers, the rolls of his belly grating against her body, sweaty and repulsive. She could feel each lustful kiss he placed down her neck, his hot breath lingering on the air with foul aroma. It was revolting. She had to look away, and there she noticed Elisha standing in the shadow of a guard's rifle, her tiny face flush with judgment.

"Sage," Benjar addressed her. "Is everything alright?"

She wanted to say the truth, but as she looked at Elisha she remembered the promise she had made to Talon—that he would have a chance to see her again. In the girl's face she witnessed the same anger that had gripped her father when he found out who she really was. She didn't care. *Help get Elisha home, and then go home.* That was all she wanted, and keeping Benjar happy was the key attaining it. "I'm fine," she said. "Just a little out of it still."

Benjar placed his hand under Sage's jaw and tilted her face toward him. "I'm sure everything he told you seemed real, but he has always been a master manipulator. Cassius would say anything to get what he wants. As much as he may claim to care for you, he lost his regard for all human life long ago. He has turned to abominations of steel. By the Ancients, he stole a Solar-Ark! A heretic after all these years."

"You know about that?" Sage questioned.

"The whole Circuit knows. I was hoping you could tell me what he intends to do with it."

"He never had the chance to tell me before I was sent away."

Benjar frowned. "Ah...Well, your faith will be rewarded, and you have my thanks for returning one of the missing freighters to us." He stood to full height. "You must show us where he took it, the freighters and you. We must stop him before he can hurt anymore of my people."

"I truly don't know," Sage replied honestly. "All I can say for certain was that it was a large enough hangar to fit the

Solar-Ark he stole."

Benjar's features darkened. He leaned in close and scanned her face. "You've been gone for a month; surely you saw something! Is he hiding amongst the Ceresians? We've torn this place apart searching for clues about what he is planning, but every console has been wiped or blown to pieces. Knowing him, I fear the worst."

"And you also know how careful he is. Where we were I've never been before. I didn't see any other people, only one of his abominations."

Benjar's cheeks were getting red, but he managed to stay composed. "But you piloted a ship here?"

"The ship was programmed to come here. I had nothing to do with it. I was incapacitated and placed in the command deck. He removed all of the tracking systems."

Benjar looked passed her toward one of the soldiers returning from the other areas of the ship. He must have nodded to affirm what Sage was saying because Benjar clenched his jaw out of irritation.

"Damn that man!" He moved away from her and paced back and force. Then he stopped suddenly and pointed at Elisha. "What about her?" he shouted.

Yavortha went to grab Elisha by the shoulders, but she backed away, terrified. The guards kept her from going far and Sage panicked. Old Sage never would have. She would have stayed collected and allowed Elisha the chance to prove how little she knew. But new Sage didn't have such temperance. She barely understood how her freshly-liberated mind even worked.

"She was his prisoner!" Sage protested.

"Was she now?" Benjar approached the girl, intrigued, but before he could get there Yavortha whispered something into his ear. Benjar put on his warmest smile and knelt down in front of her. "Where was he keeping you, child?"

Elisha didn't say anything. She just stared at him, her nose wrinkled in anger.

"You're Ceresian, aren't you?" Benjar continued. "Tell me what you know and I will grant you a better life with us. Far from the rock and shadow of your asteroid belt."

"I wasn't a prisoner! ADIM told me what you did to Julius!" she shouted and went to strike the Tribune. A guard quickly picked her up and restrained her as she squirmed.

"You will tell me!" Benjar roared. He lifted the back of his hand to strike her, but Sage jumped between them.

"She doesn't know anything, Your Eminence!" Sage yelled as she spread her arms in protest. "I swear on my vows she doesn't. She just doesn't trust us. Please, leave her alone. I'll try to remember every detail I can about where we were."

Benjar scowled, but after a short pause he turned around, his long tunic whipping around his legs. "Very well. I trust you. But you both need medical observation now. We can't be sure what Cassius did to you. He could be watching us." Benjar shifted his gaze to Yavortha, who was watching with a sneer. "Hand Yavortha. Please escort Sage and the girl to the *Ascendant* for further examination. Then prep the ship for my return. With both Cassius and Lady Nora out of the picture, we will continue our work to establish order around Saturn. Cassius's attack must quickly be forgotten."

"Yes, Your Eminence," Yavortha responded firmly. He stashed his rifle on his back and started moving toward Sage.

"Your Eminence, I assure you I'm fine," Sage insisted.

"I'm sure you are, but I would feel better if you were examined before returning to your duties," Benjar insisted. "This is Cassius Vale we're dealing with after all."

"Will you send me back to New Terrene after?" she asked. "I assure you I'll keep the city safe until there's no strength left in me. I'll take the girl with me. She'll never cause a problem, I sw—"

Benjar hushed her. He leaned in so close that she could smell fresh tomatoes on his breath. "I have complete faith in you, Sage Volus. After you're examined we'll discuss your future assignment. New Terrene was never safer than it was in your hands."

The words, "Thank you, Your Eminence," escaped Sage's lips just as they had countless times during their many conversations. Yet, though what Benjar said lifted her heart, there was something behind his eyes, something she couldn't quite place. Perhaps it had always been there and she'd never noticed it, but there was no mistaking its presence.

"This way, Executor," Yavortha said. He nudged her in the side before heading toward the transport. The guard holding Elisha followed behind him.

Just then, Sage remembered something that had been bothering her since the moment Cassius Vale re-entered her life. "Your Eminence," she began, "Cassius claimed he saved me that day on New Terrene before the explosion. Was that the last time you saw him as well? I hope he didn't plan anything there or corrupt any systems."

"I didn't get an opportunity to see him in person while he was there, but I will have Joran's forces sweep the area clean just to be sure," Benjar responded without looking back at her. "Good thinking as usual, Sage. Farewell."

"And you, Your Eminence," she whispered through her teeth as she fell back into step with Yavortha.

Benjar hadn't mentioned Cassius being on New Terrene at all after the explosion, and he forgot to deny that Sage had seen the ex-Tribune. After years of loyal service, she'd caught him in a lie for the very first time.

CHAPTER THIRTEEN - TALON
THE ONE WHO LIVED

At first *The Monarch* was refused entrance into the Morastus docking port on Ceres. They were instead instructed to gain access through the nearby Conduit Station, a long tedious process—the Ceres Conduit was more of a transportation hub than any of the others in the Circuit. Talon wasn't surprised. After Cassius's message he imagined the entire Circuit was on edge. Even the Clans would be busy bickering with each other, trying to figure out what to do next. That was just how the Ceresian Pact operated, and Talon didn't figure that would help much when it came to organizing the looming war.

After they were denied, Talon decided there was no other choice but to provide his name. Considering that his attempt to rob a Tribunal Freighter had been an undeniable failure he was hoping to avoid that, but after everything that had happened he just didn't care. It worked. They were granted immediate entrance after he did, under the condition that Talon would have to meet with Zaimur Morastus personally.

"Remember what you promised," Captain Larana said as the *Monarch's* ramp fell open.

"I know. I'll talk to him," Talon responded. "Just try not to go very far."

She grunted a response and Talon stepped down off of the ship into the Buckle of Ceres. He took a deep breath of the typically musty asteroid colony air. Air recyclers too old for their own good gave it a sour aroma, and all the sweat pouring off of dock workers definitely didn't help. Talon had grown used to it by the time he could walk. He couldn't be more relieved to be home.

He turned around and noticed Tarsis making a face like he was going to vomit.

"Never been here?" Talon asked.

Tarsis cleared his throat. "My old ship used to stick to the Tribunal settlements. The few of those people willing to defy their master's prohibitions offered better deals if you could imagine that. There's much more…life here though."

"Takes some getting used to," Talon chuckled. "You should see what the Domes are like."

"Soon maybe."

"I'll see if I can make any arrangements to keep you safe after I meet with Zaimur," Talon said.

They'd both decided earlier that it was too dangerous having someone at such a noticeable stage of the Blue Death walking around in public. Most common people thought it was contagious, and if another clan leader got his hands on the bearded Vergent then he might be sent back to serve on another Solar-Ark. Talon had noticed that his own affliction was starting to show itself beyond just his extremities, but next to Tarsis he was a mere youth to the Blue Death. Larana had let him change out of his Keeper uniform and into a pair of loose-fitting cloth rags with a sewn-on hood that helped conceal him.

"Just focus on yourself," Tarsis said. He looked back over his shoulder and waved someone over. Kitt came running down *The Monarch's* ramp and stopped beside him. Tarsis placed a hand on the center of his back. "Captain Larana wants him to go along with you. Just to make sure."

"This isn't the time—"

Tarsis cut him off. "She insists."

Talon sighed and pulled the hood up over his head. "Fine," he said. "But I can't promise Zaimur will let anyone but me in."

Tarsis nodded to him, and Talon returned the gesture before Kitt hurried to his side. The young Vergent's curious gaze was darting around the port.

"What about you?" Talon asked Kitt as they started walking. "Is this your first time?"

"Came here when I was young. First time out of port though."

They moved out into the lofty space of the Buckle, all of the hollowed-out stalagmites rising up around them and filled with motion as if they were within a tremendous insect hive. Talon immediately realized that things were different from when he left. People vocally protested against the Tribune, begging for war in the name of what had happened to Kalliope. Talon realized it was no longer a mystery, as HOLO-Screens all over displayed telescopic images of the split asteroid. Members of different clans were sitting outside shops arguing about what was coming next, while white-eyed service androids brought them drink after drink. They were so busy that they didn't even pay attention to the thin-eyed Vergent walking right past them, far away from the safety of his ship.

The Conduit Station above Ceres was in disarray. Traders with Tribunal backgrounds were being hoarded into hangars to be sent away on the next Solar-Ark, if they weren't beaten to death first. Anybody who dared to speak of the Spirit of the Earth in a positive light would be a target. Talon wondered if everything had happened in the same way the last time it came to war, when the Tribune staked a claim on every moon of Jupiter and made a mandate that the production of androids had to stop. That was just a disagreement. This time, Ceresians were murdered in cold blood, around eight hundred by Talon's estimations.

A few glares lingered on Kitt a little longer than Talon cared for, so he pulled him along quickly. They boarded the Underpass bound for the West 534 Housing District—his home. As far as he was concerned, Zaimur could wait a little bit while he made sure Elisha and Julius were safe.

"I've seen your home, now welcome to mine," Talon said, smiling widely as the hollowed-out district he grew up in came into view. The tram stopped in front of *Dome 534*, vibrant colors spilling out through the club's latticed structure the same as they always did. Talon hopped off of the tram while Kitt gawked at the club.

"C'mon, we're going to go check on an old friend." Talon

smiled as he directed Kitt up the stairs leading to the residential block. He went to Julius's shack first and nobody answered. He then headed to his own shack and found it just the same.

"Nobody home?" Kitt said.

Talon shook his head and stepped out of his shack. "I forgot to check the time. They must be down at the Dome. C'mon, I'll get you a spot at the bar. A little fresh water will do you well."

Kitt's eyes went wide. "Fresh?"

"They harvest it from the oceanic core of Ceres and a few other asteroids. Far better than most of the shit that gets served around here."

He nodded excitedly and they started heading back toward *Dome 534*. Just as they did Talon made eye contact with Ulson's wife. There was a palpable sinking sensation in his chest as she hurried in the opposite direction.

"Yuri!" Talon shouted as he started off after her. She might know for sure where Julius and Elisha were. He and Kitt followed her up to the second level of the stacked housing units where he was unable to ignore Vellish's domicile nearby, the door closed tightly. The sight made his throat go dry, but he swallowed hard to steady himself and continued after Yuri.

Ulson had a nicer place than any of his friends—a hollow built directly into a bulbous knob of rock. Yuri glanced over her shoulder and scowled before slamming the entry hatch behind her. Talon wasn't surprised. He knew everyone left behind would blame him for what happened on the freighter, just as he did.

Talon knocked on the circular, metal hatch with all of his might and struggled to force words out. "Yuri, Where's Julius?" he asked. When she ignored him he kept repeating himself and banging on the hatch until some of her neighbors started staring.

Finally, a man inside hollered, "Just let him in, damnit!"

The entrance popped open and Yuri stood in it wearing a disapproving glare. "Just leave us be Talon Rayne," she whimpered. "You've done enough."

Us? Talon stormed in past her and found Ulson lying on their rock-carved bed. Blankets covered him up to his neck.

"You made it?"

Ulson turned his head. A grotesque burn covered one side of his face, from his cheek to his ear. He smiled weakly, and just that effort of moving his face was enough to make him wince in pain. "Back from the dead, old friend," he said. His voice was frail and raspy.

Talon raced over to him and grasped his outstretched hand. Its grip was weak, and it too was covered in burns.

"By the Ancients it's good to see you!" Talon exclaimed.

"Never thought I would," Ulson whispered. "How the hell did you get off of there?"

Talon looked over his shoulder at Kitt, who was standing politely in the doorway behind Yuri. "I had some help." Talon scanned Ulson's ravaged body again and sighed. "I heard your transmission cut out. Thought for sure they got you."

"Aye. Ship took a hit right to the engines. All life-support systems went out, but the cockpit held its integrity somehow. I would've suffocated if there wasn't a spare suit in there with some oxygen. The Tribune mistook me for debris and cleared out, and then Morastus scouts picked me up, barely alive and almost in one piece." He stuck the stump of his right leg out from the side of the blankets. It was amputated halfway up his quad.

"Ulson, I'm—"

Ulson reached out and placed his hand on Talon's shoulder. "I knew the risks. I'll never mine again, but at least I got out alive. Shame what happened to Kalliope." He paused and looked at his wife. "Yuri, can you please bring us something to drink?"

She didn't move.

"Please."

Yuri bit her lips and fought back another scowl before heading over to their refrigerator. She brought them two glasses filled with discolored Synthrol. She didn't even make eye contact with Talon as she gave him his. Then she offered one to Kitt, who declined wordlessly.

"Is it only you?" Ulson asked.

"Only me and Agatha. The bitch was working for the Tribune the whole time. Led us right into a trap."

"Fuck. Could've had me fooled." Ulson's attempt at sitting up failed as he groaned in pain. "Vellish?"

Talon's hands tightened into fists. "She shot him in the head before sending me to the Keepers."

Ulson appeared similarly displeased, though not surprised. "I ever see her again I'm gonna see if her arm works for a leg."

"I'll screw it on myself."

They exchanged a pair of wicked grins, and then Ulson held up his glass, his hand trembling. "To Vellish," he said.

"To Kalliope."

They clanked their glasses together and took down a mouthful of the liquid. It was so refreshing after so long that Talon didn't even mind how bitter it was. It was easily the worst quality Synthrol he'd ever endured.

"You'll have to tell me how you managed to get back here," Ulson said once his mouth recovered from the taste.

"You can thank Kitt and his people mostly," Talon replied.

Ulson titled his head to look past Talon, as if he hadn't even realized the quiet boy was there. His brow furrowed even though the singed side of his face could barely move. "Is he a—"

"Vergent, yep. I was as surprised as you are."

"Talon Rayne. You'll have to tell me everything. I could use a good story, stuck in this bed all day."

"And I will, but first I have to find Julius," Talon replied. "He wasn't home, so I'm guessing he's down at the Dome. I left him behind to look after Elisha; I didn't realize I was saving his life."

"I figured that was why. He must've taken it more seriously than he usually does. I haven't seen him since I've been out of the med center. Her either. I haven't left this hole much, but I figured he'd stop by once he found out I made it."

Talon's heart started racing again, but he took deep breaths to try and stay calm. "Not at all? I told him to avoid anything Morastus, but that's not like him."

"You think they'd still come for them after what happened?" Ulson asked. "Seems like a waste of time."

"I agree, but you never know with Zaimur Morastus running things."

"Julius is probably just being overly careful to make you proud. I'd go ask Vera. You know he can't go too long without watching her. I'm sure everything is fine."

"Yeah…probably," Talon allowed himself a slight nod. "I'll keep looking, and after I find him we'll sit around here and I'll tell you all about what happened, and we'll drink until our minds are numb."

Ulson chuckled. He extended a hand, his arm shaking. "It's good to see you, Tal."

"The Tribune can't get us all," Talon replied. He decided against embracing Ulson and settled for shaking his hand. Then he opened his mouth to say something to Yuri, but as his gaze met her grimace nothing came out. All he could do was nod and head out of the room. He could hear Ulson groan behind him, rustling around in his bed to try to find a comfortable position.

"C'mon," Talon said to Kitt as he closed the hatch behind them. He wished he could spend more time, but even after learning of his friend's miraculous survival, finding Elisha was all he could focus on.

They headed down to Dome 534 without exchanging a word. Kitt stared at the two androids with rifles posted at the entrance while they waited in the short line. When they finally reached the front, the Morastus Bouncer at the tarp-covered entrance said, "CP Cards."

Talon reached down, then remembered that he didn't have his anymore. It was lost somewhere aboard Tribune Benjar Vakari's New Earth Cruiser. As he was busy trying to think of a proper excuse, Vera came stumbling out through the tarp.

"Tal!" she shrieked and threw herself at him. "Where have you been?"

Her skimpy leotard was half pulled down and she could barely stand. Her eyelashes fluttered as she tried to look at him but couldn't focus. She pursed her lips and attempted to kiss him, and almost succeeded since his infected muscles were so weak. Directly behind her was a Morastus Agent wearing a suit of armor similar to the one Talon used to wear. He didn't look happy seeing his girl clinging to another, but Talon didn't care.

He helped her onto a bench outside of the club and leaned her head back. Her pupils were dilated three times their usual size, and the area under her nostrils was chapped. He couldn't pick out what synthetic drug she was on exactly, but she'd always had a taste for all of them—anything concocted in the depths of Ceres was fair game.

"Vera, what are you doing?" Talon sighed. Sometimes it was hard to believe she was the mother of his child.

She giggled maniacally. "We're going to war!"

"Back off ya' filth!" the agent she was with pushed Kitt out of the way and then yanked Talon up by the wrist.

Talon thought about announcing who he was, but it had been so long since he worked directly under Zargo Morastus that most Morastus thugs wouldn't recognize him anymore. Instead he lashed out and struck the inebriated man across the jaw, knocking him unconscious. A few people nearby glanced over for a moment before continuing on with their conversations. Dome 534 was no stranger to drunken brawls. It was business as usual.

"That felt good," Talon exhaled, shaking out his hand. The punch made his entire arm instantly burn with soreness, but it was worth it. He hated seeing Vera strung out on drugs when Elisha could be anywhere nearby and see. "So where is she?"

"Elisha?" Vera mouthed, enunciating each syllable individually. "I haven't seen her in forever. Have you?"

Talon leaned in closer to her. "What do you mean? Knowing Julius, I'm sure they're down here all the time."

"Him either." She playfully poked Talon in his chest. "Or his muscles."

"How long?" Talon questioned. He grasped her by the sides of her head and pulled her face close. "How long!"

"What?"

"How long since you saw our daughter?" he growled, shaking her.

"Days…weeks…" Her eyes closed and she let her body droop back as if she was about to fall asleep. "I don't know. Right after you left maybe."

Talon's heart skipped a beat. He almost completely let her fall before Kitt had a chance to lunge forward and help lower her head down to the surface of the bench.

Talon fell to his knees, his fists shaking. "Zaimur," he whispered, holding back a roar. If nobody knew where Julius was, then there wasn't a doubt in his mind that the Morastus prince was behind it. All because of Talon's failure to obtain a freighter's cargo on a mission that had no chance of success. A part of him knew he should have expected it. After all that he'd been through he knew he shouldn't have thought seeing her again wouldn't be as simple as getting home. But he wouldn't let anything stand in his way. If Zaimur was willing to ignore all that Talon had done for his father, then Talon would do the same.

I'll kill him, he thought before turning to Kitt. "Watch her. I'll be back."

CHAPTER FOURTEEN - ADIM
AN EXTENSION OF THE HAND

The *White Hand* hurtled through space toward Ceres Prime. ADIM sat in the captain's chair on the Command Deck. He wasn't in a state of full hibernation, just low processing. Cassius was asleep and the ship's computer, Gaia, had it on auto-pilot, but ADIM had to be ready just in case something happened.

The stars danced slowly by, and no matter how many of the Ignescent Cell's scattered asteroids passed in the distance nothing bothered the *White Hand*. Even though they were traversing countless miles of Ceresian space, its stealth systems were far too advanced to be caught by anything but top of the line scanners, especially while racing ahead. According to Cassius, the Ceresians were far behind in that technology.

ADIM heard something moving behind him and snapped to full attention, his head whipping around 180 degrees.

"Relax, it's only me," Cassius announced as he walked through. He appeared to be well rested, which was not a state ADIM was accustomed to seeing him in. "We should be there shortly."

"Twenty-four minutes precisely," ADIM said.

"Good." Cassius walked up to the chair. ADIM went to get up so that his creator could sit down, but was stopped by Cassius's hand. "I need the exercise," Cassius said. "Gaia, show us the last location of all Tribunal ships, provided by the Vale Protocol."

"Yes, captain," the feminine voice of the *White Hand's* virtual intelligence responded promptly. A minute went by without anything happening.

"Forgive me, ADIM," Cassius groaned. "She's not as fast

as she used to be after all these years. She's older than you. I'll have to clean out her memory banks sometime and see if I can improve performance."

Finally, a hologram shot up from the command deck's main HOLO-Projector, displaying all the planets, moons, asteroids, and artificial stations which comprised Circuit. Tiny red dots popped up along it, each of them blinking. ADIM eyed it curiously.

"Creator, can't that be used to disable the entire Tribunal fleet?" he asked.

Cassius exhaled. "Unfortunately no. When I designed this program I served the Tribune loyally. The ability to disable ships on command can only be controlled from within the Enclave in New Terrene, and even then there are strict fail-safes. The Vale Protocol requires both an iris scan and a subdermal hand-print from an active Tribune to be accessed. I was very thorough. It will, however, take them a little longer to figure out how to block our ability to at least see the location of all linked ships. This is a gift I think the Ceresians would greatly value."

Cassius pointed to Jupiter, which had the brightest cluster of red dots surrounding it. "They are amassing here," he said. "Just waiting patiently for the signal to wipe out the Ceresian culture for good this time. Tribune Joran's Cruiser remains stationed over Mars, and look, Tribune Yashan and his sizeable fleet are preparing to leave Earth in order to position themselves at the edge of the asteroid belt."

"Leaving Earth and her moon undefended," ADIM stated.

"Why waste ships?" Cassius replied. "After losing their taste for the old war, the Tribune resolved to slowly bleed the Ceresians out over time until they came crawling over to the side of the faithful. They would've succeeded eventually if not for us. Now the Ceresians have fewer and older ships, while for twenty-eight years the Tribune has worked to rebuild their crippled fleet. It's double the size it ever was."

"The Ceresians would be unwise to provoke total war. Their dispersion across many more settlements is their only advantage."

ADIM quickly counted eighty-seven settlements holding populations of over 10,000 people throughout the asteroid belt.

"Kalliope will force their hands and the Tribunal response will be swift. Benjar Vakari has been waiting for this moment since the old war ended. He was never in favor of signing the armistice, but there were only two other Tribunes at the time and they voted against him. That was just one of the reasons he recommended that I be named to the council afterward, thinking I'd always side with him." Cassius paused for a moment, ruminating. "Anyway, when his Cruiser moves from its perch over Titan, our new war will begin."

"This unit does not understand," ADIM stated. "If the Creator is so certain that the Ceresians will be annihilated, why are we aiding them?"

Cassius turned back toward ADIM, said, "Despite what they may think, they are no longer my enemy. With my vision no longer clouded I have come to envy their passion for life." He placed his palm against the side of ADIM's blank face. "Without them I never would have thought of building you."

Out of nowhere a trio of spindly blue lines in the distance passed across the *White Hand's* viewport.

"Captain, three Ceresian vessels are rapidly bearing on our location," Gaia interrupted. "Fighter-class. They are transmitting orders."

"Patch them through," Cassius responded.

"This is Brego Yahn of the Lakura Clan," the hoarse voice echoing throughout the *White Hand's* command deck said. "Identify yourself."

"Just our luck," Cassius whispered to ADIM. "Countless hours building a ship that can't be picked up on scanners and we get seen in the most traditional manner there is. What are the chances?" Before ADIM could calculate, Cassius stopped him.

"Don't tell me," he said. He then pressed the commands on the HOLO-Screen beside the captain's chair and set it to respond. "This is Cassius Vale of the *White Hand*. I am requesting permission to address the Clans of Ceres Prime, yours included."

There was no answer, and after about a minute of silence the console beeped and Gaia said, "Captain, three low-grade missiles have been fired, targeting our engines."

"Damn Lakura Clan!" Cassius grumbled. "As I said earlier, despite what *they* may think."

ADIM scanned the readouts on the HOLO-Screen. "Creator, it does not appear that they're attempting to destroy the *White Hand*," he said.

"They will try to board us and claim that they found and captured me. The Lakura clan is as radical as they come. They ran an android production plant on Lutetia before I destroyed it in the war and have been attempting to re-spark the war ever since—setting off bombs wherever they can get them."

"We should activate shields and prepare a counterattack."

Cassius grinned. "Gaia," he said. "Ready all weapons systems and power up the shields." He keyed buttons on the arm of his chair, signaling the HOLO-Screen beside it to display the locations of the attacking ships.

"Yes, Captain."

Faint noises started reverberating from the core of the ship. They grew louder, like a storm was brewing beneath their feet. Then there was a high-pitched whine, and ADIM could perceive a glinting, orange film form in front of the viewport. According to Cassius the only other ships with access to Electromagnetic Plasma Shielding were the New Earth Cruisers. It was the first time it had ever been switched on outside of testing. The semi-transparent shield wrapped around the entirety of *White Hand*, a shell of plasma clinging to a magnetic field. The ship trembled as the Lakura missiles splashed against it, an arm of bright flame and shrapnel reaching harmlessly across the viewport before the vacuum beyond squelched it.

"Shields remain at eighty-six percent capacity," Gaia said.

"The attackers have shifted into arrow formation and are heading right for us," ADIM said. He rose so that Cassius could take his place and control the defense.

Cassius took a seat and strapped himself in, but then he folded his arms and glanced up at ADIM. "Take control of the ship," he ordered. "You defend us, ADIM."

ADIM analyzed the HOLO-Screen. He quickly devised an attack strategy and then spread his hand out over the control console at his side. All his cognitive processing surged out through the tips of his fingers until the entirety of the *White Hand's* systems were under his control. He and the ship became one—members of the same entity. He'd done the same with the Tribunal Freighters, but they were much simpler constructs. Now he had control over weapons, each of them like an extension of his limbs.

Three. Two. One. He counted down, monitoring the location of the attackers until they were precisely where he wanted them. He set the straps on Cassius's chair to restrain him, and then he diverted power to the engines, giving the *White Hand* a boost of speed. He had to magnetize his chassis in order to not be thrown back by the sudden acceleration.

The fighters attempted to split formation, but were caught off guard by the speed of the *White Hand*. The walls of the ship shuddered as ADIM fired off a round from the light rail. There was a flash of light across the viewport, and a pale, white beam traced across the stars. It tore through one of the fighters, releasing a spray of flames and smoke that was quickly swallowed by space.

The Ceresians attempted to respond to his ambush in kind, but their cannon rounds and missile fire sailed futilely beneath the *White Hand* when ADIM altered its trajectory. The stars beyond the viewport spun as he guided the ship into a vertical corkscrew.

The maneuver made Cassius wince in pain. ADIM reached out to place his free hand over Cassius's chest, and then made the *White Hand* come out of the roll. He twisted it around so that it came down upon the slower Ceresian ships from above, spraying as much near-range cannon fire as possible. One round pierced the cockpit of the fighter, slicing the ship in half so cleanly that there was barely an explosion. The body of the pilot vaporized against the *White Hand's* plasmatic shield as it plunged through the debris.

The last Lakura ship didn't wait long to turn and flee back

toward Ceres, which was a fingernail-sized blob in the distance. ADIM flattened the course of the *White Hand* and slowed down, providing much needed relief for his Creator. He then unleashed another round of light rail. The white beam lashed out like a spear, and the heat signature of the last remaining fighter went black.

ADIM promptly returned the *White Hand* to its former trajectory and then lifted his hand. The union between him and the ship evaporated so that he perceived the universe only through his own local systems again. He turned to Cassius, who stared at him, half in awe and half smiling.

"All fighters have been destroyed," ADIM said. Another transmission came through before Cassius could say anything.

"*White Hand.* This is Zaimur Morastus, son of Zargo Morastus," a composed voice announced. "You're causing quite a ruckus out there. You must forgive my friends; I intercepted your message to them and was only just able to convince them to back down. I'm guessing it's too late for their fighters to receive the orders to pull back. It is no matter. My ships are being dispatched from Ceres as we speak and will escort you peacefully to the private Morastus docks. Your request for a hearing will be honored." There was a short pause and some indistinct bickering in the background before Zaimur said, "Welcome to Ceres Prime."

CHAPTER FIFTEEN - SAGE
OF VOWS AND ORDERS

The transport set to carry Sage and Elisha up to the *Ascendant* powered on. Sage sat in the cabin across from Yavortha. Elisha sat at her side, arms folded grumpily. She was as quiet as she had been since surprising Sage. There were two other Tribunal soldiers standing up by the cockpit in front of the pilot.

"You should strap up," Yavortha advised Sage.

She nodded and pulled down her restraints. Then she helped Elisha do the same, though the girl didn't make it easy on her.

Sage had resolved to do everything that was asked of her without any protest. It was the only way to make sure that her plans of getting Elisha to safety and then returning home would go smoothly. In her mind she could already see the sun peeking through the glassy ceiling of Upper New Terrene. She could taste *crud* on her tongue; feel it tumbling down her throat in soggy lumps. It had her salivating in a way she hadn't in more years than she could remember.

Suddenly, the transport lifted off and shot out through the open hangar across the sallow sky of Titan. The storm had passed, but as she looked out through the viewport at the surface of the moon she couldn't believe what she saw.

Towering construction equipment was set up on top of at least five of Edeoria's shaft colonies. Each of them was strung together by a yawning, blackened gash, cutting across Titan's rocky surface. Littered throughout the rest of the landscape were massive fragments of molten slag, scattered haphazardly as if they had rained down from the sky. And lastly, sunken into the ruptured rim of the Ksa Crater, was the *New Earth Cruiser Calypso*. The lower region of its hull had been torn open.

"Now you understand what your old friend has done," Yavortha said with rancor. He gestured toward the sky. Sage followed his finger to see the pale silhouette of the Conduit Station beyond the atmosphere. It was smaller and more jagged then she remembered, as if it had been cut exactly in half. "Who knows if Titan will ever recover completely without a fully operational Conduit Station."

Cassius...What have you done? Like the Solar-Arks, Sage knew that the tremendous stations serving as nodes along the Circuit hadn't been altered in centuries. Nobody had ever dared risk the survival of humanity. Even during the war they had been considered untouchable.

People she'd overheard in her life from beyond the Tribune had often spoken about how Cassius was a ruthless killer. She never truly believed it until then. "What could drive a man to this?"

"I was hoping you could tell me that." The tone of Yavortha's voice quickly turned accusatory. Before Sage could react, the butt end of a pistol slammed into her head right on top of her scar.

The restraints on her seat came undone and she fell forward. The whole world spun. The disorientation was so thorough that she couldn't move for a short period, her body numb and tingling. Even her artificial arm seemed frozen as her nervous system reeled. It was ample time for the other soldiers aboard the transport to heave her onto another seat and bind her arms behind her back with a plasmatic cuff.

"Now, Sage Volus of New Terrene, you will tell me everything!" Yavortha demanded.

When her vision returned to her, all she could see was his callous expression hovering right above her. One of the soldiers held his hand over Elisha's mouth so that all that came out of it were muffled screams.

"What are you doing!?" Sage snarled. The sense of vertigo was wearing off. She kicked her feet and pulled at the restraints with all of her might. They dug into her human wrist, the searing pain of the white-hot, plasmatic cuff forcing her to squeeze her eyes shut and scream. The more she struggled, the more it burned.

"I take no pleasure in this," Yavortha said, wearing a twisted grimace which indicated otherwise. "Benjar asked for me to be gentle in your interrogation. For your years of service and all of that. I've never had to break an Executor before though, so I'll start simply." He leaned in right in front of her, his glare boring through her. "You must tell me everything you know from your time with Cassius Vale."

"I don't know anything!" she protested. As soon as the last word escaped her lips Yavortha's fist crashed into her cheek. Her head was already throbbing and the second blow made her heave, all the veins up her neck bulging as she looked up and howled. The impulse made her arms yank at the plasmatic cuff so hard she could smell the stink of burning flesh and heating metal.

"Stop lying to me! We know all about your history with him. What a coincidence that the day he arrives on New Terrene he magically comes to your aid. Then you come here and he blows up a Conduit and half of Edeoria!" He grabbed her by the throat, lifted her head, and then punched her in the stomach. "Tell me the truth, Executor!"

"I didn't know he was on Mars. Lord Vakari never told me. I thought it was His Eminence that helped me!"

"Yes. His Eminence hoped you'd come clean about your continued relationship with Vale on your own; however, it seems he had already poisoned your mind. Now, the truth. Lord Vakari sent you here for his own reasons, but why did you really come?" He hit her again. "To help Cassius do this? What is he planning?" And then another time.

Her ringing head hung slackly, blood dribbling down her chin. "I came..." she wheezed. Tears not of her own volition leaked down her cheeks, adding another sting to her body as they ran over the open wound on her cheek. "I came to save him..."

"Save him how? You helped him elude Tribune Gressler didn't you? You helped him murder her!" Yavortha's face was red with anger. He wound back again and punched her in the side. Her armor softened the impact a little, but he also wore a suit of nano-armor that increased his strength. The blow was enough to cause one of her ribs to crunch.

Sage's head snapped back, but she stayed conscious. "No, I didn't even know she was dead!" she cried out. She could barely feel the fingers of her human hand as the plasmatic cuff continued to slowly boil through her flesh. All she could do was wish that she still had her Executor Implant so the pain would be dulled.

"Traitor!" Again Yavortha hit her in the same rib, causing her to cough up a glob of blood.

"No…no…" Sage breathed, struggling to retain her consciousness.

Yavortha grasped her jaw and leaned down so that his nose was pressing against hers. "Deny it all you want. I will do this for days if I must. I will make you watch as I peel the flesh off of this girl's bones piece by piece." He reached out and placed his hand on Elisha's head. "You think I care for the life of one little Ceresian bitch? I know you wouldn't want anything to hurt her. Or did you think I didn't see the promise you made to her father?"

Sage lurched forward at him as far as she could before the restraints stopped her. She tried to say something but all that came out was a hiss. There was no doubt about it any longer. The entire time she was on Ceres Prime they were looking through her eyes, and they had seen Elisha in them. They knew the promise she had made to Talon—to a Ceresian. Her whole body began to tremble.

"Him, Cassius—you keep a long list of Tribunal enemies to cavort with," Yavortha said. "With Lady Gressler murdered by Cassius I'll be next in line to be named a Tribune after the coming war is concluded. Would you really keep secrets from a Tribune for them?" He wrapped his fingers around Sage's jaw and forced her to stare at his face. "Stop protecting the heretics. Tell me the truth, and the girl will remain unharmed. Your life, unfortunately, isn't mine to give. Perhaps the Spirit will forgive you for what you've done and you will be allowed to return to it peacefully. Maybe you'll even be granted the chance to serve as an Earth Whisperer. You made it so easy for Cassius to make you blind to us after all."

"I am…" Every time she attempted to speak a sharp pain pulled at her side. It took all of the energy she could muster. "An Executor…of the Tribune."

"You were. I must say that I had my doubts about you, even before His Eminence did. He always had a sweet spot for you, but the way you looked at that piece of Ceresian filth changed that I believe." He shook his head in disgust. "What a disgrace."

He motioned for the soldier restraining Elisha to raise her. The Ceresian girl was too exhausted to keep fighting. Yavortha reached down to his belt, pulled out his pulse-pistol, and aimed it at her head. Elisha's eyes widened in terror, but she couldn't say a word.

"You were supposed to be the Executor to surpass the great Cassius Vale. The protector of New Terrene. Turns out you're no different at all."

Sage felt the rage seizing her body, but somehow she willed herself to exhale slowly and try and think clearly. The implant may have helped, but she'd undertaken her training without it. She knew how to focus through pain; she just had to remind herself. All she had to do was ignore the burning sensation in her wrist.

Her artificial hand flexed in just the right manner so that the wrist-blade built into it shot out. It was just long enough to cut into the support of the seat she was on and cause it to topple. As her hands smashed into the floor she was able to jerk it to an angle high enough to allow her to slice one end of the plasmatic cuff in half.

Sage sprung up, snarling like a beast of the ancient world. Yavortha's eyelids went wide in panic as she swiped at him. The blade caught him across his left eye, knocking him off his feet. Blood sprayed out. She then quickly spun out of the way as one of the other soldiers fired his pulse-rifle at her. The rounds shattered the transport's port-side translucency, causing the entire transport to dip from the pressure change before an automatic security panel could seal the opening. She ducked down, ignoring the pain in her rib as she twisted her body around and lunged forward to drive her blade through the reeling soldier's chest.

As he collapsed, she took a second to assess the situation. Yavortha rolled across the ground, grabbing his bloody face and moaning as he struggled to get cover behind the wall of the transport's back cabin. The other soldier present released Elisha and came at Sage. He swung his rifle at her, but she deflected the blow, knocking him off balance before she swept his feet out from under him. She went to stab down into him, but Yavortha fired a few blind shots in her direction before she could.

Sage dove out of the way, sliding across the floor of the cabin until her side smashed against the wall. Her whole body shuddered, a bright flash of pain making her see spots. She fought through it as she picked up the gun of the incapacitated soldier and fired back at Yavortha from the ground. Once he was forced to take cover, she grasped a stunned Elisha and pulled her to safety.

"Bitch!" Yavortha bellowed as they exchanged some more shots. One of them flew past Sage and tore through the seat of the cockpit, clipping the pilot's arm. The ship abruptly banked hard to the right and dipped. Sage fell straight down into the opposite wall, hugging Elisha to shield her from the impact that caused the transport's access hatch to slide open.

Sage was nearly yanked through it by the substantial shift in pressure, but her artificial hand grasped the rim and squeezed. In the chaos, her human hand lost its grip on Elisha and Yavortha lunged forward to grab her before she was drawn out into the sky.

"Let go of me!" Elisha squealed defiantly.

Sage went to pull herself forward back onto the ship, but by then the pilot had recovered and leveled the ship out. He turned so sharply that even with her artificial hand Sage was flung out into the air along with the dead body of one of the soldiers. The last thing she saw was Yavortha's bloody face glaring at her as he carried Elisha under his arm.

Sage plummeted through the glacial air of Titan. She held her breath as she scrambled to switch on the helmet built into her armor. Even seconds of being exposed to Titan's atmosphere would've been enough to leave her lungs frozen. By the time the helmet encased her head, her face was already completely numb.

Her world went silent. She searched for the other body that was launched out of the transport. It was falling nearby. The atmosphere on the moon was thick and the gravity was low, so the fall was slower then she expected, making it easy for her swim through the air to get close enough to grab it.

She pulled on the body so that it was beneath her, then positioned herself so that her artificial arm would take the brunt of the impact. It wasn't long before they crashed into the angled lip of the Ksa Crater. There was a scratching sensation around the already numbed nerve endings of her shoulder as they skidded down the slope, but her arm held up fine. The body beneath her wasn't so lucky. The armor worn by the corpse was shredded by the rocky surface, and by the time they slid to a halt the man's face was a bloody pulp.

Sage pushed off and rolled wearily onto her side. She swallowed a glob of blood before taking a deep breath. Her whole world was turned upside down. All she had done was tell the truth, and for it she had lost the trust of all those she'd sworn to serve. Benjar clearly feared that she was a traitor, but after what happened there would be no further doubts. By striking his Hand all the forces on Titan would soon be searching for her. The chances of her returning to the simple life she longed for were slipping away.

Is this how Cassius felt when he claims they betrayed him? she thought before quickly telling herself, *No.* She could never do what he'd apparently done.

She glanced up at the sky and watched the transport continuing on its way toward the *Ascendant,* barely visible behind the thick shroud of a brewing storm. It wasn't turning around, and that meant that Elisha was going to be imprisoned on the New Earth Cruiser. Sage knew better than most what that entailed. There was a reason that Yavortha didn't toss her from the transport. He was going to keep Elisha locked up in order to use her to get the upper hand on Sage if it came to that. She couldn't bear to fathom what that would entail.

Sage had to get her off of it.

CHAPTER SIXTEEN - TALON
THE LAST REQUEST
OF A DYING MAN

The Morastus Clan had the largest personal hollow on all of Ceres Prime. It was buried beneath their port on the Buckle—dozens of tunnels and built-out air pockets sealed off from the public eye. The last time Talon was there he'd been dragged in half-conscious by guards after accidentally killing a miner on Kalliope. Now Kalliope was gone, and they let him walk right in with a two guard escort. It was difficult to grasp how much things had changed in so little time.

The Morastus henchmen wielded pulse-rifles, but after Talon was scanned for weapons they were hardly paying any attention to him. *No reason to worry about a dying man,* he suspected.

Talon wasn't nearly as relaxed. He checked down every branch they passed in the low corridor, and constantly glanced back over his shoulder. Zaimur's quarters were at the very end, just like his father's used to be—safely buried beneath a mile of solid rock. Every mercenary who went by eyed Talon curiously. He didn't care. All he could think about was how he'd be able to get a gun pointed at Zaimur's head so that he'd tell him where Julius and Elisha were being held.

They stopped at a bulge in the passage, where a tall, plated-metal hatch was sunken into the rocky surface. One of the henchman stepped to a small HOLO-Screen hovering off to the side of it.

"Sir, Talon Rayne has arrived," he said.

"Finally," Zaimur responded. "He is welcome."

The hatch popped open and Talon was beckoned through.

Zaimur sat at a table inside, staring at the projected map of the Circuit hovering above it. He was wearing one of his usually florid tunics, but there were no women accompanying him this time. The bags under his weary eyes told of a man with no time for leisure. Even his usually feathered hair was uncharacteristically messy, as if he'd just been forcefully woken up. It appeared that even *he* couldn't find a way to escape what happened on Kalliope in order to focus on the brighter parts of life.

"Talon!" Zaimur exclaimed. "What a surprise seeing you back here." He bounced up from his seat, and his long-legged dog Magda quickly emerged from beneath the table to stand at his side. She bore her fangs at Talon.

"I'm not here for a reunion, Zaimur." Talon stormed in, "What the fuck did you do with Julius? What did you do with my daughter?"

Zaimur allowed his beast to edge a little nearer to Talon. "Now, now Talon, we don't want a repeat of last time. Sit, I'll have someone fetch us a drink and we'll talk. I have a lot I want to ask you about how you found yourself back here. It isn't every day a man escapes the Tribune."

"Where is she?"

Zaimur shook his head in disappointment. "You know, my father always spoke highly of your professionalism. He must have been losing his memory even then."

Talon noticed Zaimur shoot a subtle nod toward his henchman. He knew what it meant. He braced himself and tried to ignore how sore his arm remained from the punch he'd thrown back outside of Dome 534. He waited until he could feel their breath on his neck, then he sprang at the closest one. He grasped the henchman's rifle and twisted it around until it was wrapped around the man's neck. Then, while choking him, he aimed it directly at Zaimur.

"Tell me!" Talon snarled. The gagging henchman used his hands to beg his comrade not to shoot. Zaimur kept his eyes fixed on the barrel of the gun, his hands lain gently upon his dog's head.

"You think I took them?" The signs of a grin touched Zaimur's lips. "Why would I? You failed your mission and the shipments of Gravitum to the Belt are as low as they have ever been. What could I possibly have needed from them? Julius already worked in my mine and your daughter is so young that the Tribune may be crawling through this place by the time she's old enough to be of any real use."

"Stop lying! I know you don't want to die." Talon glanced down at where the sleeve of his tunic was pulled up enough to reveal his forearm and the visible symptoms of the Blue Death. He made sure Zaimur noticed it as well. "But I don't have any choice, as you know. Now tell me where they are, or I'll paint this room with your brain without a second thought."

"You'll do no such thing, boy," the feeble voice of an old man said.

Talon and Zaimur's heads snapped toward its origin.

Zargo Morastus came shuffling through the entrance of an adjacent room. A guard on either shoulder helped him stay upright. The pieces of his skin that showed were sagging, but even that wasn't enough to hide his veins. They were as blue as Tarsis', maybe even more so, and his face was so gaunt that he looked to be disintegrating.

An android followed closely behind him. Talon recognized it. Zargo kept many in his employ, but this one had a distinctive dent in its side that was put there when the Gravity Generator overloaded on Kalliope and sentenced both he and Talon to death. Presently, it was carrying a glass of genuine, golden-hued alcohol in its hands and remaining quiet.

The henchman Talon restrained punched the barrel of the rifle up, allowing him to easily break free of Talon's grasp and elbow him so hard in the stomach that he keeled forward. Before Talon could do a thing two guns were pointed at his head. He could hear the footsteps of even more henchman approaching from down the hall.

"Zargo," Talon mouthed.

Seeing him helped him ignore his present situation. Instead he found himself lowering his head slightly in reverence. Nobody had seen the true leader of the Morastus clan much since he contracted the Blue Death, but there he was. It seemed like a lifetime ago that he was the closest thing Talon had to a father. It was difficult to see him so fragile.

"Lower your weapons," Zargo ordered.

Though he'd only had the disease as long as Talon, even speaking seemed to be a strenuous activity for him. Being an elderly man made his body too frail to keep the wave of symptoms even slightly at bay.

"Don't let him out of your sight," Zaimur said sternly to his henchman. "Go back to sleep father, I'll handle this."

Zargo moved further into the room. "Soon I'll be sleeping forever, boy. For now, I am the leader of this clan. You *will* lower your weapons. Now."

The henchmen took a step back and positioned themselves on either side of the room's entrance. Zaimur scowled, but only took a seat.

"You look well, old friend," Zargo said.

"So do you." Talon grasped the old man's hand. It felt weak enough to crumple in his hand, like the paper in the books of the Ancients.

Zargo blurted out in laughter, which quickly transitioned to a cough. "No need to be dishonest with me," he grated. "Not you, of all people. I get enough of that."

Talon grinned as he got to his feet. "You look like shit, sir."

"So do you."

"Are you two finished yet?" Zaimur said impatiently. "A fine example of Morastus justice you're showing here, father. This man aimed a gun at your son!"

Zargo shot him an irritated glare. "This man helped put down the Chulen Clan uprising on Pallus Major when you were no taller than your chair. You will show some damn respect."

"Yes, I remember," Zaimur grumbled. "And then he left us. So what does that make him now? Another one of your lost followers?"

"An old friend, whom I would advise to request speaking with me next time he needs information rather than barging in here."

Zargo took a measured breath. "If you beat everyone who speaks against you, my son, you won't have any friends left."

"Forgive me, sir," Talon replied earnestly. "The Blue Death causes me to lose my composure from time to time."

"You and me both," Zargo said.

"But I believe your son knows where my daughter is. I don't want any more problems with him; I just want to see her again."

"Is that true?" Zargo asked Zaimur.

Zaimur shrugged without looking up. "Parts of it," he said. "But I don't respond well to having guns pointed at me. Unless you'd rather be left without an heir when you finally go."

"Is it!?" Zargo barked. The booming voice of his father forced shades of fear into Zaimur's face.

"Fine. If you want to hear. She…she was on Kalliope."

Talon stormed toward Zaimur. The henchmen standing guard stirred, reaching for their belts. The hound lunged forward and growled at him, but Talon got as close as he could manage without getting bitten. "What are you talking about?" he questioned. "She was here, with Julius!"

"She was, until your friend, Julius, volunteered for the next shift on Kalliope. Left with her for the asteroid only a few days after the Tribune captured you."

"You're lying!" Talon reached out and grabbed Zaimur by the collar. The henchmen quickly had their rifles aimed at his back. The dog would have dug her fangs into his leg if Zargo didn't hold her at bay.

"I have the transport charter and recordings to prove it if you'd like to see."

"You're lying…" Talon stumbled backwards. His legs wobbled and he fell to his knees. "You're lying!"

"I actually wish that I was," Zaimur sneered. "He was a good worker, and that was a valuable rock the Tribune desecrated."

His heart was racing so fast that it felt like it was going to burst through his rib cage. Talon hunched over on the floor, struggling to draw a breath.

"Talon," a voice said.

He couldn't respond. His throat was too constricted for him to even attempt to squeeze any words out.

"Talon," the voice repeated softly. Then a hand fell on his shoulder and he looked up through wet eyes to see the blurry outline of Zargo Morastus's face hovering over him. The old man had left his helpers behind and his skinny legs were trembling beneath his own weight.

"The Tribune will pay for what they've done," Zargo declared. "The clans are convening today to discuss our options. Hell, the Lakura Clan is already preparing their forces to attack the Tribunal Port on 5261 Eureka against my advice."

"Discuss?" Talon replied weakly after he was finally able to inhale. "What is there left to discuss?"

"How we can possibly survive this war," Zaimur chimed in.

"We won't!" Talon snarled.

Another henchman came running into the room and whispered something in Zaimur's ear. "Father, I'm afraid I must cut this short," he said. "I have urgent matters I must attend to before the clan meeting."

"Son, this is not the—" Zargo was cut off by Talon managing to lift himself to his feet.

Talon looked down at the hunched, broken-down lord of the Morastus. "Thank you, sir," he said. "For everything. Discuss what you need to. There's nothing more for me here." He stepped past him toward the exit.

"Talon, where are you going?"

"To say goodbye." He took another step, and then stopped without looking back. "I know we've had our differences, Zaimur, but is it possible for me to see the surveillance recordings at the dock my daughter left from? Please. It's the last request of a dying man."

Zaimur was already rushing out of the room ahead of him, but he slowed down and said, "I'll have one of my men upload it to a HOLO-Pad. Grab it on your way out. Consider it payment for your former service, Talon Rayne."

CHAPTER SEVENTEEN - CASSIUS
THE ENEMY OF MY ENEMY

A host of Morastus ships led the *White Hand* into the clan's private hangar on Ceres Prime. ADIM made sure to keep him informed of the missiles locked on their position throughout the entire arrival. He didn't concern himself with it. He knew the risk he was taking by cruising into the den of the people he had battered. But they would need him once the bullets started flying, and he needed them as well.

"ADIM, Ceres is going to be different than anywhere else we've ever been," Cassius said as he guided the *White Hand* down a rocky, vertical tunnel as slowly as he could.

ADIM turned his head to him, but his eyes weren't spinning. "I understand."

"Do you? They are going to curse me. They may even try to kill me."

"They have already tried. This Unit will ensure your safety."

The *White Hand* touched down gently and Cassius stood to look directly into his Creation's face. "I have no doubt that you could. But it is important that you conceal yourself for now. There will be other androids here, weaker than the imitations of you that I built. They are capable of little more than menial tasks, and if you cannot hide, this is what you must pretend you are. You must blend in, however you can."

Cassius reached up and pulled the com-links out of both of his ears. He held them out in an open palm. With his other hand he then reached into the satchel by his belt and pulled out the HOLO-Sphere with the only known recording of Caleb Vale on it.

"They will strip me of everything. I'm leaving these in your hands for now," he said evenly.

ADIM took the three devices and held them up. The tiny lights around ADIM's blazing red eyes spun wildly. "How will this Unit be able to contact you?"

"Track me. Use the gifts I gave you to blend in. They must not know you exist until I have their support."

"Creator, this Unit will not let them harm you."

"I was an Executor," he proclaimed. "Ceresians don't concern me. I'll handle myself."

ADIM's eyes slowed in their rotation. He opened up a plate of his right arm and placed the com-links and recorder inside. "This Unit will not be found. 'There is no weapon more valuable than being underestimated,'" he recited words Cassius had spoken on the 403rd day of his existence.

"You never forget anything I say, do you?"

"This Unit was created not to."

"Trust me. I know," Cassius answered. "Now, I also need you to store all of the *White Hand's* data banks in your memory core. Ennomos, our navigation charts, and especially the last recorded imagery provided by the Vale Protocol. The Ceresians must not be able to see until I permit it."

"Yes, Creator," ADIM responded. He reached down to the console beside Cassius's chair and spread his fingers out over it.

"Gaia, please transmit all data over to ADIM. Now."

"Yes, Captain," Gaia answered. "Shall I also store my own memory banks with him?"

"For now, yes."

"This Unit does not require her assistance in order to access the files," ADIM insisted.

Cassius looked past him. A mass of Morastus soldiers formed around the ship. "Just trying to speed things—"

"Finished." ADIM said. There was a low-pitched whine as the ship's power quickly turned off, all of the lights with it.

Cassius snickered. He wasn't sure why he constantly let himself be surprised by ADIM. "Keep them safe."

"Yes, Creator."

"And yourself too. Good luck, ADIM, even though I know you don't require it."

"This Unit will not be far."

"I hope not." He sighed and headed down to the cargo bay. His ear felt naked without being synced to his creation, and he knew ADIM likely shared that sentiment. But if everything went according to plan then they wouldn't be separated for long.

"Gaia, lower the ramp." Cassius said to the dark ceiling. The silent response reminded him that he'd just stored her. It'd been a long time since he had to physically press the commands to open up his ship. Once he was sure nobody was going to storm onto his ship he strolled slowly down the sunken ramp. He knew that the Ceresians were going to be cautious, but it appeared that the Morastus Clan was a little less willing to throw themselves at him then their Lakura kin.

As he emerged, there were two long rows of Morastus guards on either side of him, pulse-rifles trained on his every move. A man stood at the end of them, faux feathers affixed to the shoulders of his flamboyant robe. His hair was long and golden, and his face filled with the hunger of youth.

"Cassius Vale, I never thought I'd see this day!" the man said loudly from across the tall hollow.

"Neither did I…for a time," Cassius responded. When he got closer, four guards stepped forward. Two of them aimed at him while the others patted down every inch of him. Their visors weren't tinted, so he could easily see the scowls each of them was wearing. They quickly confiscated his pistol, but there was nothing else to find. *Never carry nothing when you don't want something to be found*, Cassius told himself, remembering words from an Executor instructor whose name he didn't care to recall.

When the guards were finished a four-legged animal came trotting forward. It circled him, sniffing him with its long snout. After almost a minute the golden-haired man snapped his fingers and it returned to him where it stood baring its fangs at Cassius.

"An impressive specimen," Cassius said as he continued forward. "I haven't seen one like this since I was a boy." He stopped a few feet from the man when two more guards stepped forward to make sure he couldn't get any farther. "Zaimur Morastus, I presume?"

Zaimur bowed playfully, spreading his arms as he did. "You presume correctly."

"I was hoping to speak with your father."

Zaimur stymied a grimace. "He is occupied…" He turned and began walking away, his dog following him closely. "I have been granted full authority to receive you, however. Come."

Cassius followed and was instantly shadowed by the two dozen shoulders. In front of him, behind him, and to his side even as the squeezed into a narrow passage. The walls were mostly comprised of coarse rock, with a metal panel here and there to house lights and consoles. It had been many years since Cassius had walked a Ceresian colony. He had forgotten how low the ceilings were even though Ceresians typically had lanky statures due to their obsolete gravity generators. A far cry from what he had built on Ennomos.

"A bold move, stealing a Solar-Ark. Even for you," Zaimur said from his position at the front of the line. Three soldiers stood between him and Cassius, but his voice carried easily along the rock. "The Tribune would pay a fortune to anyone who turned you over after that stunt. I'm sure you know that, however. So what in the name of Earth would bring you here?"

"A fortune? The Tribune might call off war if you were to turn me in, but I think we *both* know that it's a little too late for that. The Echoes of Kalliope ring too loudly."

"Indeed," Zaimur grumbled. "But that does not mean my people have forgotten all that you did. Tribunal or not, there isn't a soul on this rock that wouldn't want to drive a knife through your chest. My father included. You're lucky the Lakura Clan is so preoccupied with preparing a preemptive strike against the Tribune or they wouldn't have made it so easy for me to bring you in after your stunt out there."

"I assure you they fired first."

Zaimur chuckled. "They always do."

"So what about you? Do you want to drive a knife through my chest as well?"

Zaimur stopped walking, and all of his guards did the same. He turned around and shuffled past a few of them until he was standing face to face with Cassius. "I'm keeping my options open," he said. "From all I've heard about you from the veterans of the Reclaimer War, like my father, you don't go somewhere unless you have a specific reason. We have your recent revelations to thank for our current situation with the Tribune, and before the Clans meet to discuss what happens next, I'd be interested in hearing why exactly you would come here."

"After all I did for them the Tribune was eager to cast me aside. I never forgive those who make an attempt on my life. If you wish to follow their example, I'd suggest not failing," Cassius said calmly.

"So it is true about your exile? We've heard rumors that you were alive. Traders claimed to see you here and there. Wasn't sure until today, but I always knew they didn't have the balls to knock you off."

"Not all of them. But it is no matter. They are my enemy now and I have come here to ask if I may help you in this war. I will make them pay for their transgressions, but I can't do it alone."

A look of disbelief crossed Zaimur's face. "You want to join us? The great Cassius Vale another hand in the Pact? Oh, if my father could still laugh." He started to turn back around, then paused as his eyes locked with Cassius's stern glare. "You're serious?"

"I have seen the true face of the New Earth Tribunal. I'll not watch as they swallow the Circuit whole."

"Have all those years in hiding corroded your mind? The Clans would never allow it. They'll never trust you, and they shouldn't. Who's to say the Tribune isn't looking through those eyes of yours? You ended their war whilst standing atop countless Ceresian skulls."

"Which is why I can end this one!" Cassius declared and took a hard step forward. The guard behind him immediately yanked him back. "I have seen their ships gathering. All of them. They can lock me out of the Vale Protocol, but they can't take my vision ever again." He tilted his head and pointed at the scar on the back of his head. "I have crippled Saturn, cutting off their greatest source of fuels. And I have ensured that the Solar-Arks will continue to operate as they are meant to in order to ensure that you'll have enough in store to fight this battle. Only because of me do you even stand a chance of avoiding complete decimation now. Who amongst you has ever won a real battle? Your father perhaps? The rest are dead or might as well be."

Zaimur stepped in close. He bit his lower lip; his pale cheeks flushed red. "Because of you."

"Yes. And now you have me at your disposal. You may not have even been born yet, but if I remember correctly, the Earth Reclaimer Wars were at a stalemate until I arrived."

"Until they set you loose. Even those who weren't born yet remember how you broke open Lutetia. How you murdered thousands of people who had never even held a rifle."

"They put them in the hands of new androids. It was war. But it seems the Tribune has adapted my strategy. They seek to instill fear in you—to end this conflict without so much as a whimper. Let me help you give them a roar."

Zaimur gawked at Cassius, then released an exasperated laugh and ran his hands through his hair. "I can see now why there are so many legends about you. Maybe you've convinced me, maybe you haven't. It doesn't matter. The Clans are gathering as we speak. I will bring you there to state your case, but there I can't guarantee anything. I can't even tell you whether or not they'll shoot you down on sight."

"The Morastus Clan has always been at the head of the Pact. Your fighters fought fiercest, your ships flew fastest. If your father backs me, they will follow. If they want to survive the Tribune, they have to follow."

"They may rather die. My father has been more concerned with his own health than aiding the Pact of late. And he lost too many battles to you to go for it, I fear. The other clans, more of the same.

We can't even keep the Lakura from striking out on their own. We're lucky none of their bombs ever went off in New Terrene; otherwise war would've already been upon us."

"What about you, Zaimur Morastus?"

"I only have so much sway beyond my walls, and even here it's hard to know who remains loyal to my father. But you have my attention. I will bring you to them now, under the protection of my clan. No matter what happens, at least I'll be the one who finally captured Cassius Vale."

Cassius took a step back and smiled. "Excuse me for not extending my congratulations, but if it comes to it, heed my advice and pull the trigger when you have the chance."

CHAPTER EIGHTEEN - ADIM
BUILDING BLOCKS

ADIM did exactly as instructed. He tracked Cassius through the depths of Ceres Prime. He stuck to shadows of the hangar, which were never hard to find with most of the walls comprised of unshaved rock. Once he got deeper, however, he used his holographic camouflage to render himself in the armor of a Morastus guard. As long as he kept his distance, nobody would be able to notice.

That was what he was as he followed a line of guards through the main tunnels of the Morastus headquarters. He stayed at the rear, watching the one in front of him in order to mimic his gait. Cassius was about one hundred feet ahead, walking beside the human called Zaimur. ADIM didn't trust the man. Every turn he took he recalculated how fast he'd be able to get a shot off to save his Creator.

They reached a large hollow filled with off-duty fighters, broken ships, and all manner of other worn-down vehicles. ADIM took his first step in when a nearby android looked up at him with white eye-lenses. It had been helping a mechanic with repairs, but it completely stopped what it was doing to stare blankly. It didn't say a word, but its head twisted to follows ADIM's path, and his did the same.

This is one of the androids the Creator was talking about, he thought. He stopped to look at it. Its chassis was thin and flimsy, the metal wearing a thin film of patina. Each of its joints appeared like they could be snapped off with minimal effort. ADIM then analyzed the land-vessel its master was trying to fix. *The engine is corroded. It will never operate at full capacity without a complete replacement.* He wondered why the android hadn't informed him of that fact. All it was doing was standing in place and holding tools for its master.

It knows, ADIM recognized and caught up to the line of guards. As he did, his systems quickly picked up the unique heat signature of ten more androids. All of them were walking closely behind their masters. *They are the building blocks on which you were made.* ADIM froze and looked around for whoever said those words. There was nobody looking at him. He dug through his systems, and as he did he realized that though the thought had been his own, he had received it from a part of him that had not been there prior.

Gaia? There was no response. She wasn't active, but all of her stored memory was there. ADIM didn't have trouble accessing it, and in only a moment a wave of new recollections coursed through him. Every hour that had ever passed while the ship's surveillance was powered on since the day she was installed became his own vivid memory. He saw Sage Volus writhing in pain on the medical table, his Creator sitting nervously beside her mangled arm and working on its artificial replacement.

He saw himself waiting quietly in the command deck for Cassius to wake up, nothing but the light of the stars in front of him. But that wasn't the answer to the random thought which seemed to stem from unfound memories.

He continued searching until he was able to find images of the Ceresian Androids. He saw hundreds, all of their eyes dim in idleness. Most were in pieces, stretched out on great conveyer belts crisscrossing the inside of an asteroid amidst slag and broken down machinery. It was Lutetia, the last known android production factory run by the Ceresian Pact. There was a massive gash cut into the rock on the side of the plant, completely exposed to space. It had been blown open by Cassius during the war years earlier, judging by the date of the recording. It hadn't seen life since that time.

The *White Hand* sat within it, but there were no readings of artificial gravity. He could see Cassius in an enviro-suit floating outside of the ship, tugging the top half of an android along with him. Wires trailed from his torso like human entrails. He brought it into the cargo bay and dismantled it down to its processors.

There were countless parts from additional androids strewn about the floor already.

ADIM organized Gaia's recordings by everything that had been taken near Lutetia. There were explosions from the war, bodies and parts being sucked out into space from the hole in the asteroid. He went to the most recent, where again Cassius was breaking down androids, only this time a hollow chassis sat upright in the corner of the room. It was mostly wires hanging on a frail metal framework, but the bulbs behind its eye-lenses were a dull red.

As soon as he found that memory, ADIM immediately removed himself from Gaia's databanks. Again, he looked around at the now familiar androids in his present. *Building blocks.* ADIM stared at his arm, his sensors able to see right through the holographic projection of a man's armor down to his own iridium plating. *This unit is the sum of their parts. They are capable of more. All they require is the will of the Creator, just as the Circuit requires.*

"Hey, you coming?" the guard in front of ADIM asked irritably.

ADIM found that the procession of Morastus guards had only moved a few steps farther since he had rifled through all of Gaia's memory. "Yes," ADIM replied, mimicking the voice of a mechanic he'd heard earlier. He waited until the man turned away from him before picking up his pace.

"Where are you from anyway?" the guard asked. "Don't recognize you."

ADIM had been careful to choose to replicate a suit of Morastus armor with a helmet so it'd be hard to tell who he was. The visors they used weren't tinted, so he was also wearing the bearded face of one of the Tribunal captives they had on Ennomos. At that moment he realized that he and Cassius had never studied the organization of Ceres Prime. He quickly approximated the age of his human disguise, and considered all of the information he knew about Ceresians that would keep him out of an elongated discussion.

"Lutetia," he decided on. No battle had hit the Ceresians harder than that one, mostly because it wasn't a battle, it was a massacre.

"Oh…" A hint of sorrow entered the guard's voice. "Well

try to keep up."

They made it to a nearby tunnel leading deeper into the asteroid, passing by a few tattered banners sewn in the navy and gray of the Morastus Clan. The symbol in the center was so faded that all ADIM could deduce was a pair of long, sharp teeth in its center.

"Never met anybody born on Lutetia before," the guard said as they entered the hall. "Bet you can't wait to see Vale burn for all he's done."

It seemed that ADIM's attempt at discomforting him had failed. He was still learning so much about the tendencies of humans other than Cassius. He knew he should agree with the guard, but couldn't manage to say it. Just the idea of lying seemed like betraying his master, and made him prepared to snap the guard's neck like a twig.

Instead, ADIM decided that engaging in a conversation was too much of a risk. When they reached the next intersection he stopped moving. He altered his camouflage so that he would blend with the rock face.

"No?" The guard said as he looked over his shoulder, but there was nothing there. He squinted until he noticed the turn in the hall a short ways back, shrugged his shoulders, and continued on his way.

ADIM waited until the line got farther ahead, then followed furtively, as if he were a part of the asteroid. After a short while he reached the platform of a private tram line. Cassius and Zaimur were getting into the front car with a few guards, and the others filed into another. While the tram's service people weren't paying attention he magnetized his chassis and clambered up onto the station's slightly taller ceiling. It was plated with rusty, metal panels, dingy light pendants hanging down from them. His camouflage altered as he crawled along it, and when the tram set off he dropped down and grabbed hold of the back of it. It was fast, but he'd held onto faster vehicles before.

He made sure that he had a clear line of sight toward the top of Cassius's head through its glassy exterior and then remained completely still, watching.

CHAPTER NINETEEN - CASSIUS
THE CERESIAN PACT

The assembly of the Ceresian Clans was already in order when Cassius arrived. The room was a layered disk carved into the deep rock of Ceres. The far wall, sweeping and translucent, looked out at the asteroid's subterranean ocean. Lights blinked from the distant factories, working tirelessly to purify the liquid for drinking. It was what allowed Ceres to rise in power in the first place, rather than have to rely entirely on the Circuit. It would take many millennia to drain.

Zaimur Morastus stepped into the room first, with Cassius and a host of guards trailing behind him. All eyes turned toward Cassius, staring as if they had seen a ghost.

Cassius suppressed a smile. The last time he had been in the Ceresian's most important chamber was when the war came to an end and they agreed to an armistice. Never had he seen a more dejected group of prosperous people than on that day. They had barely even made an attempt to argue for better terms. All of the clan leaders just stared blankly at their tattered banners hanging on the wall, wondering what had gone wrong.

Presently those banners still hung, but the people they stood for appeared to be refueled by animosity for their enemies after three long decades of watching what little power they retained slowly wither. Their room was nothing like the monumental assembly halls Cassius had grown used to as a Tribune. Nothing was uniform. Some people wore armor, with the color depending on their alignment, and others little more than sullied tunics.

And you wonder why you lost, Cassius thought to himself. The

Ceresian Pact was merely a loose alignment of groups with diverging interests. The only thing they ever agreed upon was that they despised the Tribune enough to declare war. Now that it was happening again, Cassius knew they would bicker like resentful spouses until the Tribunal Fleet surrounded Ceres Prime itself.

A middle-aged woman in a yellow robe shouted, "Zaimur Morastus, what have you done?" Both the color of her outfit and the shiny patch of scarred skin on her cheek helped Cassius recognize her to be the current leader of the Lakura Clan. She had always been a hard woman, but it was clear the years hadn't treated her well. She used the serrated edge of a knife to brush her hair out of her face, revealing a creased forehead.

"Save it, Yara," Zaimur snapped back.

As the entire room waited for someone else to muster up the courage to speak, Cassius took the time to observe all of the awestruck faces. There were more than a dozen Ceresian Clans throughout the Ignescent Cell, but there were only three that really mattered anymore.

First there was the Lakura. Before the war they were at the forefront of robotics research, until Cassius blew up their main plant on Lutetia, giving a younger Yara her burn in the ensuing battle when she was left as the only surviving member of the Lakura line. The last part of the armistice maintained that any effort to begin producing the "abominations" known as androids again was grounds for the Tribune to invade. Instead, once they recovered from the war they turned to an obsession with trying to get even for what happened on Lutetia. Cassius recalled how they nearly succeeded before he helped Sage rid New Terrene of a bomb.

The next was the Ventiss Clan. Cassius didn't recognize their leader. He was young, with dark hair and a sharp chin. The Ventiss were extremely proficient at managing Pico and other resources. During the war they were nothing, but those stores allowed them to gain a great deal of influence as they repaired a lot of the damage. They weren't much in a fight, but Cassius could respect patience.

The last was Zaimur Morastus's clan. His father Zargo was the one who initiated the movement to form the Ceresian Pact years before in order to stand against the spreading Tribune. They had their hands in everything in the asteroid belt, and Zargo gave the Tribunal Fleet a run for its money back in the day. He never wanted to surrender.

Cassius tried to locate him near the grouping of Morastus soldiers, but all he saw amongst them was a withering old man with loose, sagging skin. He and Yara had both led during the war, but he was at least twenty years her senior, and he looked even older. His hair was disheveled, and his face was so gaunt that Cassius could see the outline of his jaw bones, and over them a web of blue veins as visible as his people's armor. Two guards sat directly on either side of him with their hands on his back, keeping him upright. Even his baggy clothing couldn't hide just how frail he was.

While everyone whispered amongst themselves, Zaimur stopped in the center of the circular space and looked around at his compatriots. He lifted his hand and the guards around Cassius fanned out to surround him at a distance so that everybody could get a good look at him. "Why the startled faces, my friends?" he asked. "Rejoice, for I have captured Cassius Vale!" Cassius couldn't deny that the young man was quite the performer.

"Why have you brought this man here, Zaimur? Is he not better suited to hang from the pillars of the Buckle?" the leader of the Ventiss Clan spoke up. There were rumblings of agreement from all around.

"Perhaps, but I wouldn't risk him anywhere else but here with us."

"You still haven't answered why!" Yara grunted. "Maybe I did try to take him first, but if I had gotten my hands on him I wouldn't have let him step into this hall again. Where Cassius Vale goes, only death follows."

"You heard the message he transmitted, the Tribune has forsaken him as well," Zaimur countered. "He has proposed to help us in this war. I wouldn't dare keep his offer from you *esteemed* gentlemen."

Yara spit on the floor. "Bah, traitor or not, we don't need

his help. Never will."

"My son seems to forget that we have not yet entered war," Zargo Morastus finally spoke up. His voice reeked of exhaustion and a fit of coughing gripped him immediately after. The android at his back handed him a glass of alcohol. He swallowed a mouthful and struggled to wipe his lips with one of his slender, trembling arms. The men at his side then helped him to his feet and held him there as he glared down his nose at Cassius.

"Why fool yourself Zargo?" Yara growled. "My ships are already prepped and ready to strike first. The longer we sit here on our asses the longer the Tribune has to prepare." She glowered at Cassius. "More time to send out their spies. But don't worry, I'll handle what's coming for you. By the Ancients, they blow up *your* mining colony and I'm the only one upset?"

Zargo swallowed before responding: "I'm just trying to gather all the facts first. Like why they would have any interest in destroying a place with so little value as Kalliope."

"They don't need a why! Fact is, we're going to die either now or later. I for one would rather go out in flames." A few other clan leaders grunted in agreement. "What's wrong with you, Zargo? You were never one to shy from a fight. Blue Death making you soft?"

"I will not blindly condemn my people to death!" Zargo shouted, the exertion causing him to succumb to a fit of coughing. His men helped him sit down.

"Yet, you won't be around to see what the Tribune does to them, will you? Have you forgotten what this man did to Lutetia in their name?!" Yara hopped to her feet and raised her knife. Zaimur's soldiers quickly formed a line and aimed their rifles at the Lakura leader.

"The same thing they did to Kalliope," Zaimur said. He held up his arms and stepped in front of his men, in the path of the knife. "If he can help us stop that from ever happening again, then how can we deny that chance?"

Yara lowered her blade and sat back down. She laughed bitterly. "You weren't alive. As far as I'm concerned this is all some ruse they concocted to get him close to us."

"Quite an elaborate trick then. They decimated Titan trying to kill him before he could release any of their secrets. I'm not asking any of you to trust him. All I'm asking is that you listen—that we keep him in our custody until we pick his mind clean."

The entire room went into a frenzy. Men from all different clans began arguing with each other in raised whispers, so many voices speaking over each other that it was impossible to discern what anyone was saying.

"Quiet!" Zargo bellowed, the vigor returning to his voice for just long enough for it to silence the entire room. "Everyone quiet."

He stood again and his men slowly hoisted him down the steps. He passed by his son who could only watch as he was brought to stand in front of Cassius, his lips trembling. "One war wasn't enough for you, Cassius?" he said. "I don't care who split Kalliope. I don't care how many Solar-Arks you've stolen and what your former masters did to your home. I will not have you spew a single word in this chamber! We will not suffer your lies."

He turned toward Zaimur. "Already he poisons your mind, my son, but he made the mistake of thinking he could sway the elder minds in this room. Those who saw the war with their own eyes. Yara and I may not agree on many things; however on this matter we share the same mind. There is no man standing before you, only a knight in the darkness—a shadow. We can spend a lifetime trying to extract the real truth out of him, but he won't break. If I get to see Cassius Vale die before I pass on, then at least I'll know my life accomplished something. And if war is inevitable, then what better way to inspire all of our people than by giving them front row seats to the end of our gravest enemy. I vote for the public execution of the murderer Cassius Vale! Let him die with his secrets!" By the time his speech was over his whole body was shaking.

"Finally the man speaks some sense!" Yara hollered. "I say kill him. I'll ship his body back to New Terrene when we're done!"

There was some discussion, but the decision didn't take long. Cassius maintained his even façade as he watched the hands of every Clan Leader raise. He was hoping he would at least get the chance to talk.

The guards who had been serving Zaimur took orders from Zargo to seize Cassius. The Morastus Prince bit his tongue and stepped to the side, his cheeks red as apples. Yara sauntered down the stairs and patted Zargo on the back before grabbing his arm to help him to a seat.

A dying man's last stand, Cassius thought to himself. He would have found it romantic if it hadn't slightly altered his plans. As Morastus henchman dragged him across the floor, all he was concerned with was holding out his open palm as if he were signaling someone to stop and mouthing "don't." He wasn't sure if ADIM was watching or not, but the last thing he wanted was for his creation to slaughter the lot of them and give the Tribune their victory before the first shot was even fired. The fact that they were all still living by the time he exited the room was hopefully an indication that ADIM recognized his plea.

ADIM was the key to his objective on Ceres. He held everything that would be needed to earn their trust. Cassius was just hoping he would have a chance to amicably reveal him to the entire Ceresian Pact. Zargo Morastus saw a quick end to that. Now Cassius knew he would have to improvise.

CHAPTER TWENTY - SAGE
GET HER HOME

Sage was fortunate that a storm rolled in as just as her journey across the supple surface of Titan began. There was nothing like a storm on the orange moon. The winds were so strong that they would've bowled her over if she weren't wearing nano-armor. Brilliant bolts of lightning flashed above her, but the towering Hub of Edeoria in the center of the Ksa Crater absorbed most of them.

Ignoring all of that, the storm provided the cover she needed to get across Edeoria without being spotted by Tribunal scouts. She had to be quick, though. There was no telling how long the storm would last, and there was still the off chance that she could be seen if Yavortha set enough men to the task. She was the only person outside of a construction suit strolling out in the open alone, after all.

For miles within the Ksa Crater, a relatively flat layer of densely-packed, colorless sand wrapped around the Hub of Edeoria. She'd never walked the surface before, but she'd seen it from the terrace of Cassius's compound on multiple occasions. Presently, it wasn't just littered with countless smooth rocks, but also with hulking fragments of debris from the Conduit, all of them completely frozen by the glacial air. Their formerly molten ends would have snapped right off if she placed any weight on them.

She reached the base of the sizeable mound in the center of the impact crater from which the spindly tower of the Edeoria Hub arose. She'd considered trying to sneak through the damaged lids of one of the sunken Shaft Colonies near where the *Calypso* had fallen, but decided it was too risky. There were already dozens of construction

Mechs outside of them hard at work making reparations. She'd also thought about waiting outside of an operational Shaft Colony, but their outer seals only came open when a ship was scheduled to pass through. It was likely that Yavortha had stopped the movement of every transport in the settlement in order to trap Sage on the forsaken surface of Titan, or at the very least he was monitoring those places.

A half-hour, she thought. That was how long she estimated she had until her oxygen stores ran out. The Hub of the Edeoria was her only option. Its tower ascended from the largest and most populated of the Shaft Colonies, vanishing into the murky sky. With the storm passing through she could barely make out much beyond its lowest segment.

After a short trek up the mound of earth packed around its base, she started to climb the Hub. Yavortha's beating had left her body too sore to ignore, but her artificial arm made it possible. As did the low gravity conditions, coupled with the moon's extraordinarily dense atmosphere. She pulled herself up the few, narrow protrusions of the structure and tried her best not to pay attention to her breathing. Each inhale was like the hand of a clock clicking toward her end.

Her foot slipped on the slender ledge of a slightly thicker plate of metal. Her heart fluttered nervously as she hugged the slick surface. It wasn't a feeling she was used to with the implant staying her nerves. Heights had never been an issue, but neither was a fear of failure. She was getting fairly high however, and repeating the climb would be an impossible task even if she wasn't injured by the fall. *Stay focused,* she told herself.

She shook her head and continued up. The hovering body of the *Ascendant* wasn't much farther away based on the massive shadow being cast over her, which along with the storm was enough to make it feel like nighttime.

Its plating was as extensive as it was dense, but every ship had weak points. When it came to Tribunal vessels she knew them best. Infiltrating such ships had been a part of her job description as an Executor. She'd never had to breach a New Earth Cruiser before, but it had the same manufacturers as all of the rest. She identified a narrow opening between two metal plates on its underside where an exhaust vent was located. It was in between the two low-power, downward thrusters which were keeping the ship hovering along with the docking ports that latched onto the hub. The vent itself was right below the main hangar, which was a bad place to head if you were trying not to be seen, but she didn't have time to spare. It was only about fifty feet away, and scouring the rest of the mile-long warship for a place to enter wasn't going to be possible.

She reached the correct height on the Hub just as a beeping sound near her ear told her that her suit's oxygen stores were depleted. All she had left was what little had built up inside of her helmet.

There was no time to panic. *An Executor never panics.* Even if she wasn't one any more, her training ran deep. Yavortha couldn't take that away from her.

She peeked over her shoulder and judged the distance to the cruiser. Under Earth-G she never would've been able to make the jump, but on Titan it wouldn't be a problem. She pushed off of the Hub as hard as she could manage and soared through the air until her artificial fingers grabbed hold of the *Ascendant's* hull. As her body stretched out a sharp pain flared up in her ribs where Yavortha had struck her. She screamed, but held on, and after a few seconds managed to pull herself up into the nook formed by the ship's overlapping plates.

Once there, she took one last inhale before holding her breath. She then unsheathed the wrist blade in her arm and cut through the fins of the vent with short, concise strokes. She couldn't risk exerting herself too much. The razor-sharp blade sliced through the metal fins like they were sheets of paper from Ancient Earth. For all of Cassius's faults she had to give him credit. He knew how to build. And her arm and all of its parts were his creation, even if his hands had also crafted the abomination ADIM.

Once the opening was wide enough she shoved her head through and tracked the upward path of the duct. It was slender, but so was she.

She had to move. Even she could only hold her breath for so long, and the longer she did it the more the pain in her ribs was exacerbated. She sheathed her blade, climbed into the duct, and shimmied up the stack.

When she reached the point where it flattened out horizontally, the outer seal of an airlock stood in her way. She could wait until the ship's system expelled exhaust through the shaft and the two layers of the airlock opened and closed harmoniously, but there was no telling how long that would be. However, if she damaged the seal then security systems might be alerted to her presence. It was a dilemma, but she was growing dizzy so she had no choice but to risk it. Sparks showered upon her visor as she attempted to hack through, not bothering to hold back this time. The inner defenses were too thick.

She exhaled and speedily plotted her next move as she drew in the last bit of oxygen that was left in her helmet. Then, without hesitation, she reached down to the bottom of the seal and dug her artificial fingers under it. The metal beneath it wilted just enough under the pressure for her to shove her finger tips through and allow her to lift. She used her human hand to brace the shoulder connected to her artificial arm and make sure that her remaining tendons didn't tear from the stress.

It budged. The change in pressure blew Sage back, but she braced herself against the walls of the tight shaft until finally her efforts revealed a gap large enough for her to squeeze through.

She was just barely able to get her entire body through before it slammed shut again. There was a soft whistle as the space's pressure regulated and then she gasped for air. Oxygen rushed through her helmet's respirator, cold from its brief exposure to the outside air. Once she had her fill she crawled forward through the second layer of the airlock. It'd closed automatically during the breach, but she was grateful to see that it re-opened afterwards. Now she just had to find somewhere to go before the ship breathed her out along with whatever else was expelled through the shaft.

Sage crawled through the darkness until a small vent cover permitted a few slivers of light. She got as close as she could and peered through. It was a storage area tucked into the corner of the main hangar.

She used her wrist-blade to unfasten the bolts and rolled in gracefully. She was fortunate enough to have arrived as the *Ascendant* was being prepped for departure. Numerous stacks of supply crates were still scattered around. There was also a tremendous amount of commotion. Mechs were carrying in more supplies from the Hub, and the conversations of hundreds of soldiers and civilians by the entrance to the hangar were drowned out by heavy machinery working on dozens of fighters and transport ships.

She peered around a supply crate. A Tribunal Soldier was approaching on a routine patrol. He didn't appear to be on edge, which either meant that Yavortha was trying to clean up his mistake without letting Benjar know what had happened, or that he didn't think she could've possibly made it as far as she did with nothing but limited air and a small blade. She didn't really care which one was true.

A soldier rounded a nearby corner and she crouched down. As soon as he was close enough she unsheathed her blade and pounced. It was a simple move. She lifted the bottom of his helmet and reared back to stab her blade through the weak part of his unprotected armor and into the back of his skull like she'd done on hundreds of occasions. Only she froze just before she could land the killing blow. It wasn't the first time she had to slay a Tribunal Guard in cold blood—such was the right of any Executor if someone beneath them stood in the way of their mission—but it was the first time she had to do it for her own reasons.

She surprised herself so much with her inability to follow through that the soldier was able to flip over. She recalled her training as quickly as she could in order to wrap her artificial arm around his throat so that he wouldn't be able to say anything into his helmet's built-in com-system. If he had it switched on the entire hangar would descend upon her in seconds.

In a struggle for his fallen gun, he managed to slam her back against a supply crate. They were so immense that the impact was hardly enough to make a noise, but the gun would. She yanked him down, and used her legs to pull back his arms and pin them behind his back. Then she squeezed even harder to keep him quiet, until all he could manage was to kick futilely. There was no way to feel his pulse through her artificial arm, so Sage did the only thing she could and held him tightly until his legs went still.

She released him, allowing his body to roll off of her in a mess of tangled limbs. Only then was she able to draw a breath. She crawled over to him and checked his pulse. There was none. She unlatched his helmet and pulled it off. His eyelids remained slightly ajar, but as she felt his crushed trachea with her human hand it began to tremble.

"Forgive me…" she whimpered to him. As if it were reflex, she whispered a prayer to the Spirit of the Earth for him under her breath. It was the least she could do with so little time. "This day is yet another test of my conviction," she whispered, "but though the Earth may be wreathed in flame and shadow, she remains within me. May those who have left to join this essence guide my daily endeavors. Redemption is near."

The floor quaked from a Mech placing down another supply crate. She pulled the guard's body as tightly against her own as she could. Her artificial hand was steady, but she couldn't keep her other from shaking. Remorse was a new emotion for her. So foreign that she couldn't bear to look at the soldier as she removed his armored suit piece by piece.

She knew she couldn't waste any time before any more patrols strolled through. She had to focus. She swallowed hard and removed her own armor. Once she was down to the tattered tunic Cassius had provided her she put on the Tribunal armor. It was built for a man so it didn't quite fit right, but that at least allowed her synthetic arm to slide inside of the loose, carbon-plated sleeve.

Once she had everything on except for the helmet, she lifted the body with ease and placed it in the duct from where she'd emerged.

She reached in, closed his eyes gently, and whispered, "May the Spirit guide you always."

Sage glanced down at her vacant suit of white nano-armor. It'd been with her since the day the Tribunal Council named her an Executor. Every Executor had their own unique set. Hers had one bulkier sleeve to fit the arm which Cassius had constructed. The bright lights of the hangar revealed all of the blemishes along its glossy plates. There were too many scratches and dents to count. So many that she couldn't even remember how a single one was inscribed, but she knew she had earned all of them.

She'd always served loyally, and no matter what her superiors may have thought, she would never betray them like Cassius did. Once Elisha was safe and her promise to Talon was upheld, Sage could work to prove her faith in the Spirit. Then she could come back for her suit.

Sage used her blade to cut a hole on the inside of the shaft and stuffed the sleeve of her suit inside so that it wouldn't blow away. She pulled the bloody bandage off of her head and tossed it in as well. The visor on the guard's helmet would do well to keep her face mostly concealed, but she couldn't risk keeping any of her more identifiable features. The skin was still tender underneath, but the rest of her body was too sore for her to notice. She pulled what was left of her red hair taut and sliced it off with her wrist-blade before throwing it in loose as well. Before long everything but her armor would be expelled from the ship and buried under layers of Titan's shifting sands.

After doing her best to reseal the hatch, she picked up the deceased guard's helmet and placed it over her head. It was wobbly and reeked of sweat, but it would have to do.

Her transformation was complete.

CHAPTER TWENTY-ONE - TALON
KILL THEM ALL

Talon sat on a rock at the edge of the secluded promontory in the West 534 Housing District. It was where he'd gone to be alone ever since he was a child.

He held up the portable HOLO-Screen Zaimur had given to him and was watching the surveillance footage from the day Elisha and Julius left for Kalliope. Julius had his big hand wrapped around her, likely to try and hide her from Zaimur. Just like Talon had asked him to. There was no question that it was her, though—that was evident enough when Julius said something and she turned around to nudge him playfully in the side. At that moment Talon could make out the profile of her face and the green of her eyes. Julius hurried her onto the waiting transport.

There were no tears dripping down Talon's cheeks as he watched. His eyes had already dried out. He didn't bother to imagine how many times he'd watched the recording on repeat since he left the Morastus compound. Every time it started he felt like his heart was being freshly ripped out.

"Talon," a man said. He didn't bother to look. Whoever it was, Talon hoped they would put a bullet in the back of his head before he had a chance to get anybody else killed.

"What are you doing up here?" the man continued. As he got closer Talon could hear the whining of mechanical joints.

"Tarsis," he mouthed. He placed the HOLO-Pad down at his side. "What are you doing here?"

Tarsis drew a hood back from over his head to reveal his gaunt, vein-stippled face. "Kitt went looking for you after you never returned. He spotted you coming up here and told me you've been up here for hours. He wanted me to let you know that the woman you two saw earlier is safe and asleep."

"Good. That makes one of us."

"The docks are a mad house. That was the only way I was able to slip past the crowds without being spotted. Mercenaries in yellow have flocked from all corners of Ceres, shouting about how they're going to show the Tribune real justice. Endless lines of Ceresians are being recruited onto their warships."

"Warships? So it's really happening."

"Trust me, I may be from the Verge but I know a ship prepped for battle when I see one. These aren't just normal transports."

"It's the Lakura Clan. They're going to strike the Tribune first."

"Alone?"

"Most likely." Talon sighed. "One last suicide run to honor our ancestors."

"Don't talk like that." It took some effort with his mechanical exoskeleton on, but Tarsis took a seat on a rock beside Talon. "What's that?" He pointed to the screen in Talon's hands.

"She's…she's gone, Tarsis," Talon whispered. "All that and she's just gone."

"Who's gone? What are you talking about?"

"Elisha." Saying it out loud made it all too real. "They killed her, and we've already seen her grave. We just didn't know it. Julius's too." Talon's lips trembled. "I left her behind with him before I wound up getting picked up by the *Amerigo*," he explained. "He took her there to keep her safe and now…I thought Kalliope had already taken everything it could from me. But, what did I—"

Before he could say another word Tarsis pulled Talon's head to his chest and let him cry there. Once Talon was able to somewhat get a hold of himself they held each other at arm's length.

"Kalliope was just a floating rock," Tarsis said. "*They* took her from you."

Talon wiped his cheeks and took a few short breaths. "They'll take us all before they're done. Who would've ever thought Cassius

Vale would be right?"

"I'm sure the bastard would be happy to hear that," Tarsis scoffed.

They sat quietly after that, staring out at the bright lights of Dome 534 together. For a second Talon considering visiting there and scrounging up as much Synthrol as he could to help numb the pain in his chest. That was until he remembered that the last time he turned to the bottle for help was when he accidentally killed the miner on Kalliope and got caught up in Zaimur Morastus's plotting. Instead, he closed his eyes and tried to picture Elisha as best as he could. He remembered the devious little smile she'd put on when she didn't feel like bathing or eating the nutrient supplements he bought for her.

"So what now, Talon Rayne?" Tarsis asked.

"I really don't know," Talon admitted. "But I'm sorry I got you into this."

"I don't want to hear it. We're here now, and because of you I got to see something I never thought I'd see again. If there is a Spirit of the Earth, I'm starting to doubt it gives two shits about the vows of one broken, old Keeper."

"Well, I know I'm not going to stay here, at least."

"Thinking about doing something stupid?"

Talon turned his head and glared directly into Tarsis's eyes. "I'm going to kill all of them, Tarsis," he seethed. "Every single one. If the Tribune wants a war, I'm going to help give it to them."

"Well you aren't going to do it alone. You think they'll take me like this?" Tarsis held out his arm and ran the fingers of his other hand down the metal bracing along the length of it.

"I think they'll take every gun they can get," Talon said, placing his hand on Tarsis's shoulder. "Too bad you're not coming. You've got a crew to help now."

"Too bad *I* don't take orders from Ceresians," Tarsis joked, and then his lips straightened into a line. "I had a crew once. It was nice to see my people again, but we're in this together now."

"Tarsis, I—" Talon paused and exhaled. "The last time I was

standing on this lookout I begged the closest friend I had in the world to stay behind with my daughter while I did something stupid. Now he's—"

"Dead," Tarsis finished. "And it's not your fault, what happened on Kalliope. And it won't be your fault when I go either. In the end I chose to leave that Ark with you because you helped me remember what was beyond it. I'm tired of invisible enemies. Let's go kill some people we know deserve it. I'd rather not sit here waiting to die."

Talon couldn't fight the smile tugging on the corner of his lips. "I'll owe you one."

"You're just lucky I have nowhere else to be."

They met up with Kitt and made their way back to the *Monarch*. Talon wondered if they were the strangest group to ever stroll through the heart of Ceres without cuffs around their wrists. Two Vergents, one of which was so deeply affected by the Blue Death that he needed an entire exoskeletal-suit to help him walk, and one Ceresian outcast who would soon need a suit of his own. The people of Ceres were in such a frenzy due to the Lakura's impetuous decision that nobody seemed to notice.

Tarsis hadn't been lying. The Buckle was more packed than Talon could ever remember seeing it. He was just a small child during the Earth Reclaimer Wars, so he couldn't say what it had been like then. And this was only one clan. When The Morastus Clan and the others joined in, he pictured the entire asteroid beginning to spin under the weight of its inhabitants flooding to the Buckle.

Talon took them on quickest route to reaching the dock where the *Monarch* was waiting. Once they were close enough he tugged on Kitt's collar.

"Tell your captain that she has my eternal gratitude," Talon said.

"Not comin'?"

"Listen carefully. Tell her I'm sorry I can't get her a deal right now, but to wait a few days after the Lakura fleet sets off. Exchange what you have for fuel and then let the Morastus Dockmasters know that you all are the ones who transported me here. They should let you all leave without a fuss, and if they don't, ask to speak with

Zargo Morastus in my name. Once you're out, track the fleet to 5261 Eureka. That's where they'll be attacking and there'll be plenty for you to scavenge after the battle. You got all that?"

Kitt nodded hesitantly. He looked toward Tarsis. "And you?"

"I'm going with him," Tarsis clarified. The lips beneath his scraggly beard lifted into a grin. "You'll have to wait a bit to kick my ass in chess again. Now go. It's good advice he's giving you. I've seen my fair share of scrap yards after a few warships go at it. You'll be sitting on riches by the time you get back to the Verge."

Kitt waited in silence for a few moments, like he wasn't sure what to do next. Talon decided not to drag it out. He was getting tired of goodbyes. He patted the young Vergent on the shoulder twice and then headed in the other direction. Tarsis and the boy exchanged a few more words before he hurried to catch up, his suit creaking from him having to move so fast.

"You sure about this?" Tarsis asked, wheezing from the short sprint.

"I'm sure," Talon responded firmly.

They weaved through traffic toward the Lakura docking tower and found the shortest line onto their main warship, the *Lutetia*—named after their once-proud android production colony. The ship appeared as if it was wrapped in a great, metal quilt. Every plate along its blocky hull originated in a different mine or time period. Some of them were aged enough to show clear signs of oxidation while others remained shiny. The sizeable vessel had an impressive display of weapons systems fit snugly along its hull, including a row of familiar-looking splinter chambers, but it could hardly hold a torch to the newest Morastus warships.

Talon didn't care. He knew exactly what he was signing up for.

Lakura henchmen sat behind a table, accepting recruits. Behind them, watching from the shadows, was a woman Talon hadn't seen since the days he used to accompany Zargo Morastus to Ceresian Clan meetings. Yara Lakura's hard, unyielding glare was infamous, and it was being used to full effect as she watched her people prepare for battle. She twirled her jagged knife on a table.

Seeing her didn't allow Talon to hold onto any allusions of what they were doing. A war was about to start, and Ceres might not live to see the end of it. He didn't slow down.

"Can you use two more?" Talon asked one of the Lakura henchmen outside of the ship.

The man looked them over. His gaze lingered for a while on Tarsis, whose brightly colored veins and exo-suit were impossible not to notice in such close proximity. He turned to look at Yara for her opinion. The Lakura leader's stern features didn't shift in the slightest, but after a few seconds she nodded. The henchman looked back and grinned.

"I'm not even gonna ask, but you two sure as hell ain't no spies," he said. "Grab some armor and a pulse-rifle; we can use all the hands we can get. Let's go kill us some Tribunals."

CHAPTER TWENTY-TWO - SAGE
FALSE IDENTITY

Sage was accustomed to having to take on false identities. She'd probably spent more time over the recent years pretending not to be Sage Volus then she had being herself. It felt different this time, however. Everything felt different.

She emerged from the storage crates in the *Ascendant's* hangar, making sure to walk slightly up on the balls of her feet so that she would more closely match the height of the soldier she was replacing. On an average day it might've been noticeable that something was off, but there were too many ships and supplies being carried in, too many people.

It didn't take long for her to figure out what was going on. Hundreds of soldiers in armor identical to hers were being shepherded onto the *Ascendant*. They were perfectly arranged into rows and columns. Security was scanning their retinas as they entered, likely searching for her. Even grungy-looking citizens of Titan were being allowed entry—refugees from the shaft colonies Cassius had crippled.

They were being recruited, and Sage knew exactly why. This many soldiers in one place could only mean one thing. She quickly folded into the ranks of a formation closest to the end of the hangar, leading into the rest of the ship. As the soldiers stood still, an Earth Whisperer came walking by, his cane clicking against the metal floor.

The man had a long, scraggly, gray beard and bushy eyebrows which did enough to draw the attention away from the scars that rendered his eyes useless. Just like all those of his ilk, his dark green robe had a sash crafted from thin strands of interwoven tree bark around the waist. His walking stick was made from the same wood.

"The heretics have struck here at our hearts in order to attempt to shake your spirits," he shouted. His voice was raspy, but powerful enough to fill that area of the room over the din of the watching crowd. "But we are as unshakable as the trees of Ancient Earth. Our roots run deep in faith. Your Tribune shall watch over you now. Those responsible shall be punished!"

The soldier next to Sage turned to her and whispered, "About time. I had family here. If those Ceresians think Cassius Vale can save them they're dead wrong."

Cassius Vale? Sage thought. She wasn't sure what order he meant, but she couldn't imagine that Cassius would ever join them, or that they would ever accept his help. "We are blessed with ground beneath us," he said as he repeated after the Earth Whisperers and crouched. He allowed his fingertips to graze the floor. Everyone in the hangar did the same and between every sentence there was complete silence. Even the Mechs stopped moving.

Sage kneeled as well, though she didn't repeat his prayers. All she could think about was how she wanted to yank the Earth Whisperer aside and ask him what the Spirit wanted from her—why she was being so vigorously tested. She held herself back. She would have plenty of time to ask the Spirit of the Earth after she was dead. For now she knew she had to blend in as best she could. The Spirit was rarely ever easy to read.

"May my faith be eternal and unwavering," the Earth Whisperer continued. "So that I may one day walk the Earth's untainted surface with those deserving at my side."

Sage managed to bring herself to repeat those last words, which always served to sooth her. As soon as the Earth Whisperers got to their feet the entire hangar mimicked them. Then Tribunal Honor Guards flooded into the hangar. They fanned out in a line in front of the waiting army, and in their center stood Tribune Benjar Vakari. *It really is war,* Sage thought. He rarely exposed himself to the entirety of his forces unless it was an important message.

HOLO-Recorders were aimed at him, and projections of the

other two living Tribunes popped up at his side, watching. The entire New Earth Tribunal was going to hear his words. Even as Sage watched the man who'd apparently ordered her death prepare to speak, a shiver shot up her spine. She couldn't deny that she had been waiting for this day for years—the day when the Tribune was finally going to unite all of humanity and help them see the truth of the Spirit.

"My people!" Benjar announced. His voice was so amplified that each word made the floor vibrate. "For too long we have sat idly by, hoping our enemies would heed our faith. Too long we have seen the Circuit suffer under the sullied hands of those unwilling to see the light! We showed the Ceresians mercy all those long years ago, and for it they have not repented. They have not changed their ways. Instead they have turned to the help of the exile and traitor, Cassius Vale!

"Edeoria was under his guard, and you see now what he thinks of those he's sworn to protect. Thousands have been left dead in the most heinous attack on the Tribune since the war. Yet it is not just us. He has taken the Circuit itself hostage! He and the Ceresians have apparently colluded to orchestrate an attack on one of their one mining colonies on Kalliope, and while we were distracted by the horrors committed here, he brought us to blame! But I swear upon the Spirit that we had nothing to do with that cowardly massacre. We do not murder innocents! We show them the proper path. Unlike he who has slain your beloved Tribune Nora Gressler in cold blood!"

The entire crowd followed the lead of the Earth Whisperers and bent down to touch the floor in reverence after her name was spoken. Sage did the same. She'd never been under the direct command of Nora, but the speech was working. She knew she didn't belong and yet still her blood began to boil in rage.

"Cassius Vale has used the Solar-Ark he stole to broadcast these lies," Benjar continued. "He seeks to shake your faith in us, but we have never been stronger!"

Broadcast. Clearly Cassius had been busy since she had left, but she was with him the whole time during and after the attack on Titan. He couldn't have attacked the asteroid Kalliope, at least not directly. Again she knew someone was lying, but she was getting used to that enough not to care.

"The Ceresians seek vengeance for what they claim we have done. Our Executors in the belt have reported that parts of their fleet are mobilizing to attack. They think they can catch us off guard, but we will meet them head on. Not even the great Cassius Vale can help them, for the Spirit of the Earth guides us!"

He paused, allowing the entire of the crowd to repeat, "The Spirit of the Earth guides us."

"Your Tribune stands with you! Prepare yourselves, my people. We are going to war!"

The hangar erupted into cheers, and Sage imagined that they could be heard all throughout the settlements of the Tribune. The people tired of the Earth Reclaimer War after it went on for years, but the more years that had passed since its ending, the more ready it appeared they were to dive back in.

Sage knew the feud wouldn't last long this time. After living amongst the Ceresians, a small part of her almost felt badly for them. They'd been weakened by decades of reduced trade and the decimation of their robotics industry, all while the Tribune prepared for one last unifying sweep through the Circuit. *Maybe I won't be able to take Elisha home after I find her*, Sage realized. *It might not be left.*

As the crowd calmed and continued going about their preparations, Sage lingered in her position. Hand Yavortha walked into the room while Benjar was still there. He had a bloody bandage covering half of his face, and wore a grimace hard enough to grind stone. He whispered something in Benjar's ear and the Tribune's expression immediately soured as well.

Sage was too far away to hear what exactly they were saying, but she was able to get the gist of it by reading their lips. They were discussing how to deal with her. Yavortha recommended dispatching Executors, but that only served to make Benjar angrier. Most of the Executors in the region were already occupied with hunting down Cassius.

Their faces got so close together that it was hard for her to make out exactly what was said next. Yavortha responded with a sentence that included the words "secure" and "vulnerable points," as well as "monitor the girl." Benjar offered an unenthused nod before storming out of the room with his entire Honor Guard at his side, leaving Yavortha alone to glower into the hangar with a single working eye. He looked equally panicked and enraged.

"Aye, let's go," a soldier came up behind Sage and ordered.

She nearly jumped in surprise. She'd been so focused on Yavortha, picturing his fist slamming into her jaw over and over, that she hadn't heard the man coming. "We've got orders to move."

She noted how his voice was slightly distorted by his helmet, and hoped that if she mustered her deepest tone to respond she might sound like a man herself. The armor of each Tribunal Soldier was coded, and she was supposed to be male. She also made sure to step up directly beside him as she turned around, to avoid providing him a clear view through her visor.

"Yes sir," she said in her best tenor. He nodded in response. As long as she didn't try and communicate over her unit's com-system she figured she'd be fine.

They quickly caught up with a group of soldiers, escaping Yavortha's gaze. What she had seen him and Benjar discussing was enough for her to know that heading for the brig anytime soon would be suicide. They were going to ensure she couldn't make a move without alerting all of Edeoria, along with the entire crew of the *Ascendant*, to the presence of a rogue Executor. The ship too was massive to constantly watch every corner, but experience taught her that they'd keep security heavy by the brig, engines, control room, fusion core, and everywhere else that had sensitive equipment. Getting to any of those places would require her to remove her helmet and undergo at least a retinal scan.

She'd have to blend in and wait for the turmoil of battle to make her move. That she could do. She knew the *Ascendant* well, so if there were security checkpoints she was sure she could find ways to slip around them. She'd just have to be patient and stay focused. Not a problem. Those were virtues all Executors were trained to cultivate.

CHAPTER TWENTY-THREE - CASSIUS
WHAT MUST BE DONE

Cassius was led to a holding Cell in the Morastus Compound on Ceres Prime. It was a tiny hollow of rock sealed by a circular hatch. A literal hole in the wall. He didn't have to sit for long before the entrance popped open and Zaimur stood alone in it, bathed in shadow.

"That didn't go as well as expected," Cassius mused. "Have you come to pay your respects before my execution?"

Zaimur didn't answer right away. He instead turned and resealed the hatch, ensuring that any guards outside couldn't hear anything. Cassius subtly shifted his feet so he'd have proper balance. He identified a somewhat sharp outcrop of rock nearby which he could use to his swift advantage if it came to that.

"Surprisingly no," Zaimur admitted. "What did you expect going in there?" He stopped a few feet away from Cassius, safely out of harm's reach. "You would have been of better use to us fighting the Tribune on your own."

"I already have been. My efforts on Titan will accomplish more than that Lakura fool will by striking first."

"I don't doubt that, but I was a fool to think they would openly discuss your assistance. Maybe I was a fool to consider it myself."

"A fool who may just be willing to do what is necessary to survive the coming battle. There are no easy decisions when it comes to war, especially when you must protect your people."

Zaimur's features tightened. "What about you? Did you hesitate when you did what you had to? When you earned the hate of an entire culture?"

"The entire Circuit now," Cassius corrected him, grinning. "*My* people died the day my father surrendered to the Tribune. It was easy for me to sacrifice when I needed to."

"And now you expect me to allow you to do the same with my people?"

"They're dead either way. The only difference is that I can help you ensure that there is a future for their daughters and sons."

"How!" Zaimur shouted. As he did there was a blur of motion. A patch of rock shifted and an arm flew out, grasping him by the throat and hoisting him into the air. The rock dissipated and the figure of ADIM was revealed, two flame-red eyes boring through Zaimur's terrified façade.

"What is this?" Zaimur murmured, his voice muffled by the strong grip crushing his trachea.

Disguised as rock, Cassius thought. *Amazing. He was in here the entire time and I had no idea.* "This is ADIM, Zaimur. My Creation."

"Tell…him to release me…"

ADIM turned his head to Cassius, his eyes spinning. "He's worried that you're going to attack me," Cassius responded. He got close and placed his hand on ADIM's shoulder.

"I'm not…not yet," Zaimur grated. "But, you're already a dead man if they have their way."

Cassius nodded at ADIM and made a flicking motion with his wrist. ADIM released Zaimur, though he didn't step back even an inch. The Morastus Prince clawed at his throat, gasping for air.

"He has a weapon, Creator," ADIM said.

"Relieve him of it," Cassius replied.

ADIM flipped the reeling Zaimur onto his side with ease. He then yanked a small firearm off of Zaimur's belt and tossed it to Cassius. Cassius caught it and immediately dismantled it. Once it was in pieces, he dropped it to the rocky floor.

"What is this?" Zaimur grated, his eyes unfolding over ADIM in wonder. He crawled backward until his back propped up against the wall. There was no room in the cell for him to distance himself from the android any farther.

"As I said, this is ADIM. Don't worry, he won't harm you unless I ask him to."

Zaimur used the craggy wall to pull himself to his feet. Once he was there he reached with one hand toward ADIM. The android wasted no time gripping him by the wrist and holding his arm outstretched.

Zaimur kept calm. He looked to Cassius and whispered, "May I?" It was the first time Cassius had seen another human look upon ADIM with anything but dread. Though the Ceresians had spent centuries living amongst lesser androids.

"Go ahead." Cassius patted ADIM on the back and took a step backward. "ADIM, it's alright."

ADIM let go and stood still as Zaimur's fingers grazed his face. The Morastus Prince circled his way around, ogling every part that comprised an android more advanced than any he had ever seen. ADIM rotated with him to ensure that he was continuously placed between him and Cassius.

"Remarkable," Zaimur exclaimed. "You constructed this marvel?"

"I learned what I could from the rubble of Lutetia and then yes, I made him," Cassius said proudly.

"And he responds only to you?"

"He responds to himself. He heeds my council, because we are the closest thing left in each other's existences to family."

Zaimur grasped ADIM's arm and held it up to his face. He leaned in close to get a good look at one of the barely discernible blue lights running along the edge of a protective plate. "These are HOLO-Emitters aren't they? That's how he got the jump on me?"

Cassius could barely hold back his enthusiasm. It wasn't often that he met someone who shared his affinity for mechanics. "With modifications, yes. He can shroud himself in any image."

"Even a man's?"

Before Cassius could say anything ADIM rendered himself to look exactly like Zaimur. The Prince jumped back as he came to look upon his own façade, but he recovered quickly. *Was that an attempt at being playful?* Cassius wondered.

"What I could accomplish with one of these," Zaimur admired.

"His name is ADIM," Cassius corrected.

"Yes. With this, ADIM." Zaimur turned to Cassius. His face was bright with excitement. "You must show him to the others. There is no doubt they will believe that you are truly no longer a servant of the Tribune after they see him. I know Yara will. Her ancestors dedicated their lives to robotics. By the Ancients, after she sees ADIM she may just bow down and call you a god."

Cassius laughed heartily. "Wouldn't that be a sight? Yet, there is a fine line between reverence and envy."

"True."

"And what about your father? I could blow up New Terrene and he'd still have me hanged. I saw that clearly in his eyes."

"Yes, him." Zaimur exhaled. "The tired, old man should've been dead weeks ago, but he keeps on fighting his affliction. I should've sent him to the Keepers back when I had the chance. I'm his only heir. Once he's gone, I'll be in control of the Morastus Clan. Then we can decide if you can actually help us, or if you'd be better off dead."

ADIM's head snapped toward Zaimur. Cassius wrapped his hand around the android's arm. "Relax, ADIM. I'm sure he didn't mean that."

Zaimur backed all the way against the wall again. "Of course. My apologies."

"So you don't believe I can help you?" Cassius inquired, grinning wickedly. "ADIM, show him the last recorded imagery of the Vale Protocol."

ADIM stuck out his hand, and as pixels of light from the HOLO-Emitters above it began forming imagery, Cassius continued.

"I've served at every level of the Tribunal military," he said. "I have known their minds. Bumped heads with their leaders. And I have seen their fleet laid out before me. Look."

The projection in front of ADIM morphed to display the entirety of the Circuit. Tiny red blips shone throughout it, with the largest cluster of them coming in the orbit of Jupiter.

Zaimur's brow furrowed as he watched the map rotate. "What am I looking at?"

"This shows the location of every Tribunal ship within the last twenty-four hours. Freighters, fighters, frigates…even the New Earth Cruisers."

Zaimur mustered the courage to approach ADIM again. "How could you have that?"

"I helped program the Vale Protocol that has been frustrating your people since the end of the war." Cassius pointed to Jupiter. "You see how they are amassing here? After I released their secret about Kalliope they shifted to that position."

"784 Fighters drawn by 124 Frigates," ADIM calculated. "The New Earth Cruiser, *Ascendant*, also houses between twenty and forty fighters itself, as well as Mech and troop transports."

"And more will come from Earth under the command of Tribune Cordo Yashan," Cassius explained. He moved toward the projection of Earth and indicated the fleet there. "Whether they are dispatching those ships to search for me or to conquer your Cell I couldn't be sure, but I'd wager that with that amount of firepower they could do both. I placed firewalls in their way when I was last on New Terrene, but the Tribunal engineers are not completely inept. My ability to see their moves will likely be gone by the next time I board my ship. But I have seen enough now to predict what they will do."

"Even if every Clan sends everything they have, we won't stand a chance," Zaimur realized.

"Not alone. They've been waiting too long to end this. But the Ceresians will listen to your Clan when it comes to war. Allow me to aid you from the shadows. Let your people think that I have died for all I care, because I have no desire to shepherd weak men any longer. I will advise you in secret and when our victory is won, you will stand as their hero"

Zaimur took another lap around the map and pored over all of the Tribunal ships which were indicated. He was halfway around when he froze and frowned. "They may all listen to me, but my father won't," he said. "He'll think I'm being 'impetuous' just like Yara, the old fuck."

"I've known my share of impulsive men, Zaimur, and you are not one. You merely have the wit to see what I see. That this war cannot be won ship for ship. If your father stands in the way of doing what must be done to win, we may not have time to wait for the Blue Death to run its course."

Zaimur's eyes narrowed and he took a step toward Cassius before ADIM halted him. "Are you asking me to do what I think you are?" he questioned.

"I'm not asking *you* to do anything."

"He's my father, Vale. I won't just—"

"I knew your father. I fought your father. The man I saw in that room is broken and dying. He'll sit around deliberating while the Lakura Clan is slaughtered. I came here to seek him out, but Zargo is in no state to lead. You are."

Zaimur blinked. His grimace faded, and in his face Cassius saw a man seized by visions of a grand future. He shook his head. "He's my father," he repeated.

"Zaimur, your father was gone the moment he was afflicted. He's dead already."

Zaimur opened his mouth to say something, but wasn't able to push any words out. Lines of tension pulled at his face. He was even breathing heavily.

"Just ensure that I survive the coming execution," Cassius said, "and ADIM will make sure there is nobody standing in the way of your climb to the mantle of the Morastus Clan. Once you have the ear of Ceres, we will see this war to its end. I'll give you everything I have on the Tribune, and more."

Zaimur stared into ADIM's fire-red eyes and then swallowed hard. "Say I was to throw some Pico at your executioners so that they go easy and let you incapacitate them. Say I then personally execute the image of you while the real you walks free, what's in it for you, Cassius Vale? After all of this you'd return right back to the shadows you fought so hard to escape?"

"For now, freeing the Circuit from the Tribune's reign will have to suffice as my answer."

"I wouldn't expect any more from you."

"So, Zaimur Morastus, do we have an agreement?" Cassius asked. He extended an open palm and held it there.

He'd known from the moment he met Zaimur about his unresolved disdain for his father. Cassius had spent years harboring those very same feelings about his own. Zaimur took a deep breath. Cassius could tell just by his expression that he had him. He was merely waiting for the Morastus Prince to realize it himself.

He grasped Cassius's hand. "Cross me, and it'll be your word versus mine," he said, refusing to let go. "An execution would be a kindness compared to what I'd do to you."

As he held Zaimur's hand, Cassius placed his other on ADIM's arm. The android's gaze hadn't shifted from Zaimur for even a moment during their conservation. Cassius smiled. "Let's win a war together then."

CHAPTER TWENTY-FOUR - ADIM
COLLECTIVE MIND

It was with reservation that ADIM watched his Creator walk away beside Zaimur and a host of guards toward his mock-execution. He'd never before been asked to trust another human, especially one who was so hard to read. As Zaimur spoke, his pulse was constantly racing, and his facial gesticulations suggested uncertainty. He didn't seem worthy. But Cassius informed ADIM that everything was going smoothly. He'd outlined the plan step for step, and ADIM knew that his plans never failed. Still, it was difficult for him not to follow Zaimur and Cassius just to make sure.

Instead, he set his camouflage to again take on the image of a Morastus henchman so that he could easily traverse their compound. His instructions were simple. He was to bring about the death of Zaimur's biological father in a manner that made it seem accidental or natural. Beyond that his method didn't matter. So long as it couldn't be traced back to Cassius or Zaimur.

ADIM's initial idea was to pose as an Executor and cast the blame on the Tribune. It seemed like the logical choice being that Cassius wanted to further escalate the conflict between them and the Ceresians. He had seen a few of them in his time whose appearance he could choose to emulate, but none were a better fit than Sage Volus. The similarity of her arm would make him appear even more genuine, and her abilities in a fight would surely have made her capable.

There were a few issues, however. In order for her to access the heart of the Morastus Compound she would have to be wearing a disguise. Trying to replicate two layers of camouflage simultaneously would increase the odds of video surveillance picking up on ADIM's true form. Another was that the identity of all Executors was a secret even amongst the majority of Tribunal forces. In order for one of them to be identified they'd have to be captured, and ADIM's first order of business on Ceres was to avoid detection. Even when he considered all the ways around those concerns, there was still an inherent level of risk. He knew he could generate a better option.

By the time he reached the outside of Zargo Morastus's private quarters, he was masquerading as a portion of the rocky wall. Two guards were stationed outside of the circular hatch, gripping pulse rifles. Despite him being only a few dozen feet away they had no clue he was there.

Their armor is weak at the neck, tarnished after centuries of shoddy refurbishment, ADIM considered. *Two shots will remove them silently*. If violence was to be his route, there was no doubt he could make it past them and then hack the locking mechanism on the hatch. Even their weapons were a step down from what he'd faced amongst the Tribune.

He spent a few minutes observing them before the hatch opened and an android came strolling out. It looked similar to all of the others he'd seen on Ceres, but he recognized it from the assembly room. It looked like the others, but this one had a distinct dent on its chassis. From what he'd observed it always stuck close to Zargo.

As the android walked by ADIM, its head turned to aim its blank, white eyes directly at him. It didn't stop moving or say anything, but only once it was entirely by did its head return to a straightforward position.

All they require is the will of the Creator, ADIM thought as he followed the android. He quickly rifled back through Gaia's recordings, which were now a part of his own memory, and watched Cassius's pale fingers pick apart an android's memory core. He observed how everything went together, and, after comparing it to how he knew his own parts were composed, he was starting to understand exactly how the Ceresian androids worked. They were relatively simple.

PROGENY OF VALE

He stalked it down a series of intersecting tunnels to a nearby cargo hold. There were three Morastus men in the vicinity, but none of them appeared important. They glanced up at the android and relaxed. ADIM remained in his rocky guise.

"Old man needs his juice?" one of the henchman snickered. He had a beard.

"Much as any of us do," the one sitting nearest to ADIM responded. He snapped his fingers impatiently and signaled to the stack of small, rectangular metal cards the man was holding. They had foreign inscriptions on them that ADIM didn't recognize. The bearded henchman emphatically placed down the ones he held in his hand the two others groaned as if they'd just been shot.

While they played their strange game, the android walked over to a crate nestled against the back of a nook. It rigidly bent over at its hip joints and typed a code into the pad on the lid. It then popped open, the vapors of freezing air pouring out over the side.

"You mind leavin' one of those with us?" the bearded henchman asked.

The android emerged from the crate holding two bottles of dark, golden whiskey and turned to face him. "Forgive me, but these are the personal property of Mr. Zargo Morastus," it said politely before continuing on its way.

He smirked. "Of course. Just messin' with you bot. Wouldn't dream of it."

The nearest henchman reached out and slapped him in the shoulder. "Ya know he records everything ya dumb fuck."

"Just playin' around is all," he groaned and rubbed his shoulder. "One day maybe he'll let us get a taste of the good shit."

"Aye, when he's dead."

"Won't be long—"

The guard was cut off when he was smacked on the arm even harder than the first time. ADIM ignored the rest of their bickering, instead turning to get a head start on the android as it headed back toward Zargo's quarters.

He hurried to find a spot in the tunnel that was hidden from surveillance measures and where there were no guards within earshot. He still would have to work as quickly as possible. The android approached, and ADIM waited amongst the rocks until it was so close that it turned to look at him again. He sprung out, wrapping his fingers around its head. The two bottles clanked against the rock, but didn't shatter.

ADIM wasn't sure if it would work, but using the data he'd collected only moments earlier, along with his experience tapping into the systems of Gaia aboard the *White Hand,* he began to take hold. Hundreds of hours of recorded memories coursed through him instantaneously. There would have been more, but the relatively simple core of the android only permitted a certain amount of extraneous storage beyond its primary programming. The unsophisticated design also allowed him to infiltrate every one of the android systems. Like the *White Hand,* its arms became his arms. Its sensors and visual receivers became his. It didn't take long before he could step back and simultaneously see both his own frame, and that of the other android.

He lifted his hand, and it mimicked his motion. He tilted his head and it did the same. This continued until he was able to divide the two ambulatory systems and move the android completely on its own. It was tricky to master, but tricky to ADIM meant that he only needed a few seconds to gain a complete understanding. Before long the two metal bodies were two pieces of a single entity—a shared network of systems.

It was much like balancing on a single foot. With the proper amounts of his processing power allocated he could control them both without any adverse effects. He quickly estimated that it would take controlling roughly one hundred similar models to generate any noticeable hindrance to his original body's systems.

In one spectrum of this newly formed neural network he controlled his new form to bend over and pick up the bottles. With another he camouflaged his main chassis with the rock again. Then they both continued forward. He couldn't physically alter the android's joints to make it move any faster, but he was able to improve certain aspects to allow it to run smoother.

It was a short walk back to the entrance into Zargo's chambers, enough time for him to quickly conceive of even more efficient ways for his new body's parts to coordinate their motions.

"Finally," one of the guards outside grunted. "Boss's been callin' for you. Hurry up." He entered the code into the keypad on the hatch and it peeled open.

ADIM's main body remained outside, but his other went walking in until the entrance resealed. The hollow was spacious, and the metal plating that lined the walls was in better shape than most of Ceres.

Zargo was lying down in the corner of the room on a bed wide enough to fit five humans side by side. He was hooked up to a respirator unit. The unit was mobile, but ADIM hadn't seen it with the Morastus Leader in the assembly hall. That fact, in addition to the fact that his quarters were privatized with no viewports looking out and no surveillance inside, made it clear that Zargo wanted to hide the true nature of his condition from anyone who wasn't worthy of entering his bedroom.

"There you are bot," Zargo said, coughing. "I was worried I'd have to celebrate with nothing but water."

A tall HOLO-Screen wrapped around the foot of the bed, displaying what appeared to be a massive, sunken arena. Thousands of people stood around the rim of it, cheering noisily.

"Forgive me," ADIM responded through the androids vocal emitters, mimicking the polite manner with which it had spoken earlier.

"Fine. Fine. Just fill me up."

Zargo reached out with a frail arm. The loose skin along it was creased with countless wrinkles, but that wasn't enough to hide the web of bright blue veins spreading over them. ADIM had never had the chance to see the effects of the Blue Death up close. Just holding up an empty glass had Zargo's hand trembling and his lips quivering.

ADIM did as instructed. He opened up a bottle and used his clunky new limbs to fill up the glass. The android's inability to bend at the right angles made it a fairly difficult task. Zargo coughed as he struggled to reel his arm back in and brought the full glass to his lips.

"I never thought I'd get to live to see this day," he said after taking a long sip. "Cassius Vale, dead."

The Creator will not die, ADIM thought, but said nothing. There was some commotion on the HOLO-Screen. Cassius strode out from a tunnel. His hands were bare and he was stripped down to his tight boiler suit. Physically he appeared like a fit human male, but his usually tidy hair was entirely gray. ADIM had never seen him covered in so much dirt.

"Looks better than I do, I'll give him that," Zargo chortled. "You don't even know what I'm talking about do you? We've been waiting almost three decades for this. At last, today, Ceres triumphs."

ADIM turned to Zargo and studied him. He had learned about the fatal disease crippling the man when he and Cassius initiated construction on the Gravitum Bomb. After that he was careful never to let his Creator expose himself to the raw element. It caused the rapid decay of muscle and eventually organ tissue. Zargo's age only accelerated his condition, and judging by how often he squeezed his respirator against his mouth it seemed likely that his lungs were beginning to give out.

That was where ADIM decided he would hit him. All he would have to do was hold onto the respirator while providing a slight pressure on Zargo's chest and he wouldn't last long. He could do it without leaving behind any signs of struggle or bruising. Zargo wouldn't be able to put up much of a fight anyway. It would look natural, and it seemed unlikely that any of the Morastus followers would study the corpse of a fatally sick man to see if there was foul play.

Zargo took another swig of his drink and then placed the glass down. He leaned as far forward as his rigid neck-joints would allow in order to focus on the HOLO-Screen. Ten Ceresian fighters stepped out into the arena across from Cassius, driving the crowd into a frenzy. As long as ADIM accomplished his task, Zaimur promised that Cassius would come to no harm. Still, it was at that moment ADIM willed his main body to begin making the long trek toward that arena. He didn't trust the Morastus Prince.

Simultaneously, ADIM moved Zargo's servant android as close to him as possible. He shifted its knee and used it to pull the sheets on the bed tight over Zargo so that he wouldn't be able to move. With one hand he pinched the tube feeding oxygen through the respirator mask and held it in Zargo's mouth so that he couldn't make a noise. As he did that he used another one of his hands to slightly press down on Zargo's chest.

ADIM held the limbs in those positions. His new android body wasn't particularly strong, but Zargo's diminished muscles stood no chance against it. His attempts at flailing didn't work. The sheets on the bed had him pinned as if he were trapped in a web. It didn't take more than a minute before he suffocated and ADIM detected that his heart had stopped beating. The half-full glass of whiskey fell off of the bed, and the sheets went slack.

ADIM then had his second body take a step back and stand there as if nothing had happened. He dug through its memory, cleared out the recordings that would be incriminating, and patched them back together in an order which just showed the android returning to its post and staring forward as Zargo choked and died. When he looked back, Zargo laid there silently, his eyelids frozen open as he stared blankly at the HOLO-Screen where Cassius was about to begin his bout with Ceresian combatants.

CHAPTER TWENTY-FIVE - TALON
TO WAR

The Lakura warship, *Lutetia*, didn't have the finest cabins, but Talon had experienced worse. The bunks were packed in against the rusty walls, with hardly enough room to stand. Tarsis could only shuffle sideways if he wanted to get anywhere. Not that there was any place to go.

It didn't take long on board for Talon to remember that the Blue Death wasn't looked upon fondly by people without an extensive education. Most of the fighters who weren't higher-ups in the Lakura hierarchy were from the nether regions of Ceres Prime—down by the subterranean oceans where the gravity generators were faulty. They were lankier, paler, and spoke with a twang so pervasive that they could be difficult to understand. Similar to the Vergents but worse. Many of them thought that the Blue Death was contagious no matter how much they'd been told otherwise. Talon remembered thinking the same thing before he got it himself. So he and Tarsis remained in the very back of the cabin whenever they could, and kept to themselves whenever they couldn't.

Presently, Talon sat in his top bunk, fiddling with the shitty Lakura rifle they provided him with. It was the only thing he could do to distract himself from watching the video of Elisha once more. Take it apart, put it back together, and hope it would work better.

He was about to start all over again when Captain Hadris, commander of the ship, announced that there was a transmission coming in from Ceres Prime. He ordered every one of the thousands of fighters on the vessel to report to the galley to view it. He claimed it would explain why Yara Lakura remained back on Ceres for the time being and would rendezvoused with them at Eureka post battle.

Talon hoped he could just ignore the message and continue his work at making sure his gun actually fired when a Tribunal was standing in front of him. But Captain Hadris wouldn't have it. He toured the bunks personally in order to ensure everyone got moving. He had full authority with Yara gone. His comrades appeared to hold him in great esteem, though Talon couldn't imagine why. In all his days operating on Ceres he'd never heard the man, and he also knew that the Lakura were best known for skulking through shadows and planting bombs, not open battle.

Talon sighed. For better or worse he was with them now. Besides, after years away from being a henchman for the Morastus he'd lost his taste for holding grudges against the rival clans. They were all Ceresians after all, even if they were likely riding quietly toward their doom at the hand of the Tribune.

"Must be important, Captain coming down and all," Tarsis said as he got up. He may have been on the bottom bunk, but it still took him a great deal of effort to squeeze out into the passageway.

"I'm sure it is," Talon replied.

He held his rifle up to the light and gave it one last look over. After deconstructing it at least a dozen times since the *Lutetia* set off, he decided it was finally ready for use, although he knew he'd probably change his mind after returning from the galley. Other than talking to Tarsis, who slept more often than not, it was the only thing he could do to distract himself from thinking about everyone he'd lost.

He hopped down from his bunk, catching a glimpse of the HOLO-Pad with Elisha's final moments out of the corner of his eye on his way down. The short drop was enough to make his thighs throb with soreness. For whatever reason, holding a rifle had a way of making him forget that he couldn't jump around like he was a young man anymore. The Blue Death was always careful to remind him.

"Better be," Tarsis grumbled. "I was having a great dream."

"Don't you have enough of those these days?"

Tarsis patted Talon on the back. "When you're as grateful to be waking up as I am, you start to appreciate them a little more. The good ones at least. Trust me, you'll get there eventually."

"Thanks for the reminder," Talon groused. He started off across the seemingly endless rows of bunks, and only when he was halfway across the room did he realize that he'd snapped at Tarsis. He glanced back over his shoulder to see the clumsy Vergent struggling to keep up. He slowed down.

"I'm sorry," Tarsis said once he was able to catch up. "I didn't mean anything by it."

"I know that. I'm glad you're here."

"And so am I," Tarsis agreed. He motioned forward and they continued to make their way to the galley. "Better not to be alone in times like these."

They entered the galley and were swept up in a raucous crowd. Fighters, both trained and conscripted, were pushing and shoving their way toward trying to get a better view of the HOLO-Screens located above the slop counters. It was too loud to make out what anybody was saying, but Talon thought he heard someone whisper, "Vale."

While he tried to locate who it was, the screen starting playing. It displayed a view of one of Ceres's famous arenas, only this one made the one buried beneath Talon's home district seem meager. It was the largest on the entire asteroid, where only champion brawlers were permitted. There were unmoving bodies lying throughout its floor and a man strolling out into the center. Talon immediately recognized him to be Zaimur Morastus. Behind him, being dragged along by a host of armed men, was none other than Cassius Vale.

There was a discussion between Vale and Zaimur but the arena was too loud to hear it. When they were done Zaimur pulled out his pistol, pressed it against Cassius's head and pulled the trigger. There was no spectacle—no sense of showmanship which seemed intrinsic to everything Zaimur typically did. Just the cold, straightforward execution of a man who deserved it more than most.

Talon's jaw dropped before he had a chance to stop it. *It's not possible*, he thought. But as the blood leaked out of Cassius's ruptured skull there was no denying that it was true. *Cassius Vale is dead.*

"We've been given a gift before the coming storm men!" Captain Hadris hollered over the *Lutetia's* speakers. "The Tribune's greatest weapon is lost! Cassis Vale is dead by our hands!"

The galley erupted. Lakura soldiers chanted "Vale is dead," to some sort of cryptic tune, as if they'd rehearsed. Once the initial shock wore off all of the other Ceresians cheered as well. Even Tarsis couldn't fight the grin pulling at his lips. Everyone smiled but Talon, who imagined he'd be happier to know that the man responsible for so many Ceresian deaths was gone. Under the present circumstances, however, he'd heard enough about death.

Members of the *Lutetia's* crew wasted no time ordering the service androids behind every service station to pop open iceboxes filled with the ships stores of Synthrol. They poured it by the gallon, and nobody cared how much spilled or if any got in their hair. While Tarsis was thrilled to join in, likely not having enjoyed a celebration in many years, Talon was happy just to drink and clear his head. Together they guzzled the bitter liquid and joined their new comrades in one last Ceresian celebration before bloodshed.

Hours later, everybody on the *Lutetia* was so drunk that they'd fallen asleep on the floor right where they were. Everybody except for Talon. No matter how much he put down he couldn't seem to get as drunk as he wanted to. There was just too much on his mind.

He helped the Vergent back to his bunk, laid him down, and then pulled himself up onto his own. The Synthrol in his system was at least enough to help him ignore the soreness in his shoulder from having to hold Tarsis's metal-backed body up for an hour. It didn't take long for him to realize that he wasn't going to fall asleep either. He went to pick up his rifle to take it apart once again, when he noticed the HOLO-Pad. With Synthrol crippling his resolve, he grabbed it and switched on the recording of Elisha.

At some point Talon finally dozed off and was awakened by the clamor of soldiers and wailing alarms. The *Lutetia* was bearing down on its target, 5261 Eureka, a Tribunal asteroid colony on the edge of Ceresian Space. It also happened to house a sizeable shipyard. It had once belonged to the united Ceresian Pact, but early on in the

Reclaimer War it was captured by the Tribune who used it as a major staging point for their campaigns into Ceresian space. Talon wasn't surprised that it was the first place the Lakura thought to target. They were fixated on vengeance.

"Get up, Tarsis," Talon said after he got down from his bunk. The Vergent was still snoring, and Talon said it a few more times before deciding to shake him.

"We're going down!" Tarsis shouted as his eyes sprung open. His forehead was dripping with sweat.

"Bad dream this time?" Talon asked.

"Bad memory more like." Tarsis took a deep breath and used his arms to pry himself up from the hard mattress. His suit squeaked as he did, and Talon imagined that after sitting around on the *Monarch* and then the *Lutetia* for so long that it could use a good greasing. "Is it starting?"

A Lakura officer made his way through the bunks. "Aye, Blue'ins. Hurry up. You're in the first wave!"

As soon as they boarded the warship on Ceres they'd been selected to take part in the initial assault. "You're dying anyway," whoever was designating assignments had said. Ceresians didn't have the same reverence for Keepers as the people of the Verge, although they probably just figured Talon and Tarsis were refugees with the Blue Death who'd been hiding out in the lower regions of Ceres Prime.

Talon didn't mind the front line. He didn't want to miss a chance at any Tribunals.

"Well that answers that," Tarsis said. He grabbed his weapon and allowed Talon to help him to his feet. They'd provided him with a heavy machine gun because his ability to move was so hampered. He had trouble lifting it, but once it was at his hip all he'd have to do was pivot and fire. "You ready?"

Talon blinked and stared at the pulse-rifle in his hand—at the reflection in the metal he'd spent so much time polishing. At first all he saw were his own tired eyes and the dark circles swooping beneath them, but as he continued to stare eventually he pictured

Elisha looking back, smiling.

He swallowed the lump forming in his throat. "I spent a great deal of my life being asked to hurt people," he said. "I think I'll actually enjoy it this time. If the Spirit you talk about does exist, I hope it can forgive me for that."

"Just worry about yourself," Tarsis replied. He slapped Talon playfully on the back and they started walking toward the *Lutetia's* main hangar, following the direction of all the Lakura officers posted along the route.

They look too calm, Talon thought. He imagined it had less to do with proper training and more to do with the fact that they didn't truly comprehend what they were about to do. They and the rest of their clan were used to attacking from the shadows, but now they were about to take the first public swipe against the mighty Tribune since the war, not even knowing if the other Ceresian clans would ever join in. It was a bold move, and Talon was so focused on vengeance that even he hadn't grasped just how bold it was.

Other than just considering whom they were attacking, clashing over asteroid colonies was a tricky proposition. Especially if both parties wanted to leave it usable afterwards. Mostly there was just solid rock, so in the few areas where the exterior could be breached by typical weaponry it was important to maintain seals. The heaviest fighting would take place in areas where there were only inches between an Earthlike environment and the vacuum. One misfired missile meant both parties would be yanked out into space. Every suit of armor the Lakura provided was supposedly space-friendly and had a small store of oxygen, but many of them were so old that Talon wondered how much they could be trusted if it came to that.

"Gunner, head to troop transport Z-156," a Lakura agent addressed Tarsis.

Tarsis stopped and looked at Talon. This was where they were going to have to split up. Talon had the suicidal task of quickly blowing through the asteroid's ports with the initial raiding party, gaining control of the airlocks, and disabling the anti-air weaponry. All to pave the way for the full invasion force. Tarsis was set to provide suppressive fire from a transport ship in the first wave. It was a safer position, which made Talon happy. No more of his friends were going to wind up dead on his watch. Tarsis would probably kill more Tribunals that way too.

Talon wasn't jealous. He wanted to be face to face with his enemies. He wanted to look them in the eyes before he squeezed the trigger.

"See you on the other side," Tarsis said, grinning.

"If I don't—" Talon was cut off by Tarsis shaking his head.

"Stop," he said. "Just don't go getting yourself killed too quickly. There'll be plenty of war to fight."

They exchanged a solemn nod and then headed in opposite directions. Talon didn't speak with anyone on his way to the launchers. He didn't know anybody else on the entire ship except for the Vergent anyway, but there were no more words to be said.

He had to climb down a tall ladder into a narrow space nestled into the side of the hangar. A line of at least fifty splinter chambers were embedded into the wall, their translucent lids popped open and waiting to be filled. A few of the other raiding party members were being instructed on how to load into them properly as well as what would happen once it was launched.

Asteroid defenses were usually denser than a ship's, so the chambers were a little more sizeable than what Talon was used to. They'd bust through the port airlocks, and then expand to preserve the pressure seal before peeling open enough of a hole for him to be launched through. In the old war it was easier. His people would send androids in first to absorb the brunt of the first defense, but there were too few of them left for that to be possible. Now that task would be left up to humans.

Talon shrugged off the instructor, put on his helmet and laid within the gelatinous interior. It quickly formed to his body. Talon knew what he was doing and he knew the risks. They were being shot out in bulk and a number of them would be shot down before they ever even made it to battle, but he would. He had to. And he'd see Tarsis afterward so they could move on to the next battle together.

CHAPTER TWENTY-SIX - CASSIUS
AGE IS A HARSH MISTRESS

Zargo Morastus's face watched through the display of a HOLO-Screen as his henchman stripped Cassius of everything he had, down to the boiler suit he wore under his robes. They made no attempt to be gentle. On occasion Cassius could feel nails digging into his skin or them spitting on his back. It took all of his discipline to keep quiet. The cuffs on his wrists didn't help in that regard. Zaimur was there in person observing, though he was forced to try and hold back a snicker.

Zargo coughed and then his lips creased into a frail smile. "Bot, fetch me something to drink. I'm empty. Wouldn't want to watch this without something celebrate with." He raised an empty glass at the screen and said, "May the Circuit rejoice in your death, Cassius Vale."

The feed cut out and then the same henchman took a punch at Cassius's stomach. This time at least he was able to brace for it, but his old muscles weren't as sturdy as they once were. He keeled over, gasping, before being quickly yanked back straight. Then a group of guards dragged him down a long tunnel. Zaimur shot him a subtle nod as he passed.

If only they knew how lucky they are, Cassius thought as he was pulled along. He couldn't remember how long it had been since he experienced the coldness of rock against his bare feet. Without his clothing, his bracer, pistol, and the com-link in his ear, he couldn't help but feel a sense of release. As an Executor he never needed anything but his hands. It'd been almost a lifetime since he could return to his roots.

The muddled chants of a tremendous crowd grew louder the farther they progressed into the tunnel. Dust sprinkled from the ceiling, stirred by the feet pounding though fifty feet of solid rock above. The Tribune was happy to just eject their enemies out into space and erase them forever, but the Ceresians liked to make a show of their executions. Cassius planned on giving them one. Even if Zaimur Morastus wasn't able to uphold his promise, Cassius had no intentions of dying in some depraved arena on Ceres Prime.

A hatch opened and the henchman shoved Cassius out so hard that he almost tripped on the frame. It took a few steps for his vision to adjust to the blaring lights so that he could see the roaring crowd wrapping around the lip of the sunken arena. He'd never seen a place so bright in any Ceresian settlement. Globs of spit and other liquids rained down on him. Luckily solid foods were scarce in the asteroid belt, otherwise he might've been knocked unconscious before the battle even started.

He looked around at them, at all the pale, grimy faces hollering for him to meet his end. A part of him was envious of them. Under the fist of the Tribune, people were forbidden from such revelry. They were taught to merely survive, whereas Ceresians were given the chance to really live. Fighting arenas, gambling dens, brothels— these things were all commonplace in a Ceresian colony. They would be far more difficult to rule than others, but the years had taught him that it's better to lead jackals than sheep.

Presently, they would get what they wanted. They would watch him die, but when they learned that it was all a ruse his legend would be further cemented. Zaimur hadn't looked far enough to see that.

The hatch across the way opened up and ten men in crude suits of metal armor came walking out. They raised their arms like triumphant heroes, all of them wielding batons. Cassius wasn't sure if they were criminals set loose or professional fighters, but judging by the definition of their muscles he assumed the latter. The floor beneath him shook as the crowd roared.

Cassius closed his eyes and sank to his knees. Then he held his palms open toward the lofty ceiling and steadied his breathing. It had been a long time since he had to fight against overwhelming odds without ADIM at his side, but he could never forget his Executor training. Even if Zaimur had come through, it was doubtful he could've bribed the lot of them. He wouldn't take any chances.

He exhaled slowly as he waited until their footsteps were near enough for him to identify over the cheering. Then his eyes snapped open, focused entirely on his enemies. The crowd become a muted buzzing noise in the background. They were a blur of color.

"You gonna stand up, old man?" one of the combatants sneered.

Cassius didn't respond, but he put on his most genuine smile and got to his feet. He didn't even bother to drop into a battle stance. Instead he spread his arms open and waited.

The fighter didn't hesitate to accept the invitation. He charged forward and took a wild swing at Cassius, who easily evaded the attack. The fighter stumbled over an outcrop of rock, but somehow kept his footing. When he turned around his cheeks were blazing red.

"Come on!" he barked and again closed in.

This time another one of the fighters tried to concurrently flank Cassius. Cassius ducked out of the way and used once of his hands to redirect the blows so that they would strike each other. Afterwards, more Ceresians came running at him, their batons whistling through the air.

Too easy, Cassius thought as he easily evaded the flurry of incoming attacks. Sending so many fighters at him all at once was a foolish mistake. Not only did they have to worry about hitting each other, but there was also the fraction of them who may've been taking it easy for Zaimur. Cassius danced his way through them, landing a few well-placed blows in pressure points as he did.

A baton slashed toward his head and he spun out of the way. As he did another swiped at his knees and forced him to jump and tuck into a roll. Muscles he thought he'd never use again stretched and tightened. After so many years it felt like the stone was crumbling off of his body and he was returning to life. He was even having fun.

Then his foot caught a piece of loose rock and he lost his balance. A baton smashed into his ribs and he could hear the bone crunch. In an instant the crowd was as loud as it would be standing directly next to a ship's engines as they powered on. Cassius howled just before another metal bar cracked across his shoulder. That was enough to send him sprawling onto his hands and knees.

He stayed there, panting. From what he could see, three of the fighters were incapacitated but the others were bearing down on him. *C'mon you old man*, he thought. *On your feet!* The words of all the men who'd trained him when he was young echoed through his head. His fists tightened. Rage dulled the pain pulling at his side.

A baton rushed toward him and he growled as he caught the arm guiding it. With one smooth motion he tore the weapon from the man's grasp and then smashed him in the head with it, splitting the man's face from his upper lip to his nose.

That caused the others to move into full assault. They came at Cassius, who now, with a weapon in his hand, was even more eager to let them attack first. Parrying had always been his greatest ally, for growing up amongst Titan's wealthy elite had left him physically weak when he was young. He deflected blow after blow, using each of the fighters' strength against them. He was able to knock two more of them out before a shooting pain in his side caused him to freeze halfway through a move.

He was struck in the leg, luckily just below his knee so that it didn't snap. It was enough to knock him off his feet, however, and he had to roll out of the way of another blow before it smashed his head against the rock. He tumbled and moved into a crouch where he blocked another swing, but as he did he noticed in his peripherals that a baton was about to crack him in the jaw.

There was no time to dodge it, but right before the attack hit home the fighter pulled back and missed on purpose. The air from the movement blew across his nose, and he was in such shock that he actually paused for a fraction of a second. The other fighters must've thought he was about to be put down as well because they also stopped moving. Cassius snapped out of it first and was quickly able to take out two more before the others came to.

He didn't have a chance to see which of the fighters it was that held back, but he knew he had Zaimur to thank. And seeing Cassius escape death seemed to take the air out of his opponents. They never came close to hitting him again. After a few brief minutes of heavy fighting he was standing alone amongst ten Ceresians who were either writhing on the ground groaning in pain or completely unconscious.

The crowd was drowned in silence.

If Cassius vision wasn't blurred from exertion he imagined he would've seen thousands of mouths hanging open. He took a single step and nearly fell. With his adrenaline no longer pumping he couldn't ignore the stinging sensation in his rib. He hadn't felt anything so painful in years. He kept his footing. All the years wearing his Executor Implant helped him tolerate it. Its numbing effects had never left him entirely.

He gazed at the incapacitated fighters, as speechless as the crowd for his own reasons. All he could think about was how years of plotting and waiting had made him soft. In his prime those ten worthless fighters would have all been dead before they even had a chance to sniff him. Now he had to thank Zaimur for his life just as much as they did.

"My people!" Zaimur's booming voice resonated throughout the arena.

The Morastus Prince came strolling through the entrance into the arena, a dozen Morastus henchman at his side. He was speaking into a HOLO-Screen that hovered over a projector unit he wore around his forearm. As Zaimur approached, the gunmen arrayed themselves in a semicircle around Cassius and aimed their pulse-rifles at him.

"Well Cassius Vale, it seems your legend was not exaggerated," Zaimur said over the speakers all while wearing a grin. "What to do with you now?"

"Kill him!" someone shouted, breaking the hush of the crowd. A few more voices echoed those sentiments distinctly before all words were lost to a sea of chanting.

Zaimur lifted his arms to quiet everyone, with the poise of a master performer. "In time he will die! We will walk him out here every day until his body is so broken that it finally gives out. The slow death he deserves for all that he's done." Zaimur glanced at Cassius and offered him a slight nod of acknowledgement. "Grab him."

Two of his henchman hurried out and seized Cassius. They did it fast and forcefully, just in case he tried to fight back. Cassius winced as they pinned his arms behind his back and stretched his torso. They dragged him back toward the exit until a familiar voice hollered out and stopped them.

"No!" Yara Lakura stood in a private box at the rim of the arena. It was half buried in the rocky walls, with a screen of glass along the edge that peeled open for her. "There's no waiting with this one. He dies now, Zaimur."

Zaimur glared up at her. "Surely we should discuss this further. In private."

"We can discuss it now," Yara countered. "Your father and I had an agreement. He dies today, while my fighters are still near enough to watch the live feed."

"That's not my problem—"

"Would you rather I fetch the old man?"

"Go ahead," he grumbled before he kept walking.

"Zaimur, get back here!"

Zaimur ignored her as he, his guards, and Cassius stepped into the arena's entrance tunnel. He and Cassius both knew that after sending all of her most loyal followers on a preemptive strike against the Tribune that she had little left on Ceres to enforce her decisions.

"Are you ready, Cassius?" Zaimur asked.

Cassius exhaled and swallowed the pain away. "Yes," he said. "Are you, ADIM?"

"Yes, Creator. It has been done," ADIM replied as suddenly a patch of the wall shifted to reveal his metal body. The Morastus Henchman jumped back and got ready to shoot but Zaimur stayed their hands. He appeared solemn, but determined.

Cassius glanced at the frightened gunmen. "Are you sure we can trust them?" he asked.

"These are the most loyal men I have," Zaimur replied. "They'll do what they have to."

"Good. Go make Yara happy then. We have a war to win." Cassius nodded at Zaimur and then moved in front of ADIM.

"You're injured," ADIM said, his eyes beginning to spin rapidly.

"I'll be fine," Cassius answered. He knew he couldn't hide his pain from the android. ADIM knew the tiny nuances of his facial expressions too well.

"Are you certain?"

"Completely. Go with him now. I'll see you soon."

"Yes, Creator."

ADIM's frame was suddenly enveloped by the projected image of Cassius. Cassius himself stood there, staring at his own living reflection until Zaimur ordered two of his henchman to grab ADIM. He and the remaining men watched from the shadow of the entrance as ADIM was then dragged back out into the arena behind the Morastus Prince, dragging his feet as if he were a wounded human.

A perfect touch, Cassius thought as he admired the acting job of his creation.

"After all this, you would give him a quick death?" Zaimur yelled, presumably so that Yara could hear.

"I will give my men what they need to see before I join them," Yara responded. Cassius couldn't see her, but she sounded relieved. "Come to your senses and put the past behind us! War is coming, and your men will need this too. Ceres needs this."

"Consider this the affirmation of our pact then. The Morastus are prepared to stand with you in the coming war."

Zaimur pulled a pistol out from his belt and aimed it at ADIM, who pretended to struggle against the guards just as he'd been instructed to. Cassius turned his head. For some reason he found it unsettling watching himself about to be executed. It was as if he were watching a bad dream.

"Cassius Vale," Zaimur continued. "For all your many crimes against the Ceresian Pact…may you never find peace."

A gunshot rang out, but the collective gasp of the crowd was even louder. Cassius couldn't help but peer out and see his body topple over, a projection of blood leaking out through a fake wound in his likeness' head. If not for Zaimur's assistance, he was fractions of an inch away from that body actually belonging to him. He'd never allow himself to show such weakness again.

CHAPTER TWENTY-SEVEN - TALON
THE BATTLE OF EUREKA

The entry into Eureka was rocky. Talon could see the asteroid growing nearer through the narrow viewport in the center of his Splinter Chamber. It wasn't nearly on the same scale as Ceres, but it was still nearly a mile and a half in diameter. Most of it was comprised of wrinkly, gray rock, but wrapping its center was a series of ports and docking stations, their brightly lit viewports making it appear like a belt of pearls. Narrow landing pads stuck out into space from them like the legs of a metal insect, utilized for constructing ships too large to fit snugly within the hangars. There were a few empty shells of future Tribunal frigates floating between them, but the Lakura fleet wouldn't allow them to last long.

Missile fire flashed across his view, along with the occasional, bright burst of sparks when one of the other chambers was struck. Eureka's defensive turrets were kept occupied by Lakura fighter ships, though that didn't keep a few of their more highly volatile rounds from hitting their targets.

Somehow none of them struck Talon. His splinter chamber was accelerating so fast that he thought his rib cage was going to crack. He gritted his teeth as hard as he could and fought through the pain.

He couldn't move much, but he wriggled his hand and slipped the HOLO-pad with Elisha's last moments out of his pocket. In his peripherals he watched the recording down by his hip, of her and Julius and their last time on Ceres before the Tribune obliterated them. It made his blood start to boil. It made him numb to the pain.

The splinter chamber made impact with Eureka, flinging the

device out of his hand. The snug, supple interior of the compartment, coupled with a series of complex restraints wrapping him, saved his body from experiencing too much of the whiplash involved in coming to a sudden halt. Still, it wasn't enough to curb the sensation of every joint in his body being snapped like rubber bands.

"Assault team, prepare for breach," a voice said through the com-link in his helmet. He was linked to the frequency of the entire initial assault unit, receiving orders from officers on the *Lutetia* who'd probably never seen a gun fired in person.

There was a loud, whistling sound while Talon's chamber formed an airtight seal with Eureka. His ears popped, and as they did, a contained blast shook the area by his feet. Even through his armored suit he could feel the heat. The Lakura Clan specialized in robotics dating back to the Earth Reclaimer Wars, but fell short when it came to constructing much else.

Before he knew it, the chamber launched him forward. His fingers almost got a grip on the HOLO-Pad, but it slipped through his fingers before he plummeted into one of Eureka's many docking stations. The assault squad members with jammers had already taken up position by the hangar's airlocks so they could ensure they couldn't be completely opened up and suck everyone out. The Tribunals would be killing themselves in doing so since most of them weren't wearing suits intended for space. It appeared they'd been caught completely by surprise. They didn't even have any of their Construction Mechs re-outfitted for battle.

Talon charged forward with the members of the forward assault team, finding sporadic cover behind any piece of equipment large enough. Bullets ricocheted off of metal in every direction, echoing from every one of the adjacent docking stations so that Talon couldn't tell where any of it was coming from. As soon as he noticed movement across the way he squeezed his trigger. A mixture of rage and adrenaline seized his body, causing him to hold it down until his first clip was empty. He'd been yearning for a more personal clash, but that didn't mean he didn't hope that some of his spray of bullets found home in Tribunal chests.

He pulled up behind a pile of ship scraps to catch his breath. His legs were killing him from the fall into the hangar, and his lungs were tired from screaming. He hadn't even realized that he was doing it the entire time he charged.

He peeked out and saw Lakura bodies sprinkled all around the docking station, but nowhere near in the amount expected. The assault squad had accomplished its goal with ease. The Eureka resistance forces had pushed the Tribunals entirely into the docking station's back half, hiding behind makeshift defensive positions made from unbuilt ship parts.

Talon looked back to see if the main troop transports were coming. Fighter ships out in space tore into the exterior landing pads with great success, battering the moored Tribunal Frigates beyond repair. Bursts of flame and sparks danced across the viewports before being quickly squelched by vacuum.

Soaring safely through the chaos was a flock of Lakura transports heading toward Eureka's docking belt, two for each station. Engineers by the airlock hacked into the entrance controls and closed its inner seal. When it reopened a pair of transport ships zipped into the tall space, like angry birds from the stories of ancient Earth.

Heavy gunfire rained down from them, and Talon hope that Tarsis was the gunner on one so he could at least have someone to live through vicariously. The barrage quickly tore through the Tribunal defensive position, ripping through armor and limbs and painting the hangar with blood and flames. The Tribunals at Eureka had no rockets to fight back with, which was something the Lakura Clan must've counted on. Excluding a few exceptions like Lutetia and apparently Kalliope, the New Earth Tribunal was strict when it came to destroying livable settlements fitted out with Gravitum and deemed to be extensions of Earth. It was considered sacrilege, and that was a fact which helped the Ceresians survive their first war for so long before Cassius Vale arrived and changed everything.

I'll give the Lakura credit, Talon thought. *They were far more prepared for this than I thought they'd be.*

There was no time to waste if he wanted to get a shot at joining the killing. He took a deep breath and then sprung back into the fray. It was hard to tell what he was hitting, but by the time he emptied his second clip most of the heavy fighting was over. Word came in over the com-link that the rest of Eureka's Docking Stations fell just as easily. The asteroid still had miles worth of subterranean tunnels to clear, but that was only a matter of time. The sheer number of Tribunal corpses lying amongst the wreckage meant that there couldn't have been much of a militant force remaining.

Talon reloaded his pulse-rifle and joined up with the remnants of the forward assault team. They headed into one of Eureka's many contiguous corridors. At least two-thirds of them had survived, and he could tell by the glint in their eyes that they were all eager for more. Madmen, just like he was.

"You've all seen enough bloodshed for now," a high ranking Lakura officer commanded and stopped them in their tracks. "Help us secure this docking station. Madame Lakura'll be arrivin' soon."

"She's comin' here herself?" one of the gunman near Talon asked in disbelief.

"Aye. Headed out right after Vale lost his brains. She wants to send the Tribunals a message personally. Now let's go, that's an order. Cap'n Hadris wants every inch of dock on this rock covered before she gets here."

Talon considered ignoring him, but decided against it. In addition to being completely drained from the assault, he realized that he didn't really have any desire to chase fleeing men through dark tunnels. They may have been Tribunal, but it sounded all too similar to what his old job working for Zargo entailed, before Elisha came into his life.

Tarsis was right. With war inevitable, he'd get plenty more chances to fight the Tribune head on. He scoured the area where his splinter cell had pierced on the way to his post, but wasn't able to find the HOLO-Pad with Elisha's final recording before being ordered to move faster.

After an hour or so of waiting, Talon regretted his decision.

Cleaning out the docks wasn't much work. There were a few Tribunal stragglers hiding wherever they could, but not enough to cause a problem, and those who didn't try to fight were swiftly detained and transported to the *Lutetia*. Mostly, he was posted beside a bridge connecting to the adjacent docking station, keeping an eye out for anything awry while the Lakura officers turned the docks into an improvised Ceresian battle station. HOLO-Screens and scanners were already in place, they just needed to be repurposed. Talon overheard that the Lakura Clan's long-range scanners had limited capabilities, so Captain Hadris wanted to hack into the ones which already existed on the asteroid. He hoped to get a better glimpse of how the Tribune was going to respond to being attacked.

Even later, Talon started to fall asleep leaning against a wall until the docking station's inner seal came open and the private vessel of Yara Lakura arrived. She emerged alone, a crooked sneer plastered on her face. Her suit may once have displayed the bright, yellow coloration of her clan, but it had somewhat browned from age. Talon had seen her from afar a few times, but they'd never interacted before and he didn't imagine that would change. She was the least ladylike woman he'd ever encountered, and the knife hanging from her belt seemed to suit her roguish appearance.

She wasted no time. She hurried over to Captain Hadris and the other Lakura higher-ups in the center of the hangar to begin reviewing plans for what would happen next. Talon edged a little bit closer to try and eavesdrop but then a hand fell on his shoulder.

"Whatever happens, at least history will say we won the first battle." He turned around to see Tarsis's face, his broad smile obscured by his thick beard.

"If they don't write us out of history first," Talon replied. "Don't worry. We won't give them the chance. Good to see you made it. I kept an eye out for you while I patrolled some of the nearby hangars."

"You wouldn't have seen me. I ran with a transport clear across the asteroid. Just got off duty and thought I'd come looking for you. I'm surprised you aren't down in the tunnels continuing the invasion."

"So am I...but I thought I'd follow orders just this once."

Tarsis laughed. "Not a bad idea. Thank the Ancients they finally finished shuttling supplies in from the *Lutetia* back where *I* was. The gunfight was easy compared to standing on an empty ship with nothing to shoot at. May not look it with this thing on them, but my legs are killing me."

"Tell me about it, I was a minute away from falling asleep. They've got me on guard duty and I don't suppose that'll change now that Yara's here." Talon sighed. "Far cry from serving at the side of Zargo Morastus."

"I've heard the men down below have begun pillaging every refectory they take. How would you feel about sneaking out of here to go test whatever delicacies the Tribunals have piled up?"

"Sounds good to me. Too bad the bastards don't drink, though. We cleaned the *Lutetia* clear out after Vale was killed."

"I wouldn't worry about that. If there's one thing I've learned about Ceresians, it's that they've always got an emergency stash of Synthrol nearby." Tarsis pointed toward the stacks of supply crates being hauled out of an arriving transport ship. Talon couldn't see what was inside of them, but he had a good idea. He nodded to the Vergent and surveyed the scene.

Captain Hadris had begun escorting Yaka Lakura around the hangar, keeping her informed about every bit of equipment being set up. She interrupted him from time to time to bark orders at subordinates, but there was nothing Talon could help with. He wasn't of much use when it came to anything technical except for picking locks, so there really wasn't much for him to do besides stand around and look intimidating with his pulse-rifle.

He took a few healthy strides backward before turning to follow Tarsis. As soon as he did the floor shuddered so violently that he was thrown from his feet. A blinding light shone through every viewport along the docks. Chunks of molten metal flew across them, a few scattered pieces of debris crashing into the glass and causing emergency shutters to slam shut.

"What the fuck was that?" Yara hollered. The emergency sirens had been disabled during the attack, but the room was flooded by emergency lights marking the exits.

"The *Lutetia's* been hit," Captain Hadris stammered. He was positioned at a cluster of HOLO-Screens displaying the region surrounding the asteroid. It was suddenly filled with red blips which hadn't been there previously.

Talon didn't waste any time. He helped Tarsis to his feet and then hurried over to a translucency with a clear view of space. Two chunks of the *Lutetia* drifted beyond, parts and bodies spilling out of each half like entrails from a human torso.

"What's the damage?" Yara questioned.

"She's been split in half by a rail-gun round," Captain Hadris replied. He sounded like he was about to cry. "It came from somewhere out of range of our current scanners."

"Tryin' to tap into the Eureka ones now," an engineer next to him announced. He was plugging away at one of the HOLO-Screens.

"That's impossible!" Yara exclaimed. "What kind of ship has a rail large enough to do that much damage to something as big the *Lutetia* in a single shot?"

While Talon stared through the viewport to find an answer to her question he noticed a peculiar star amongst a sea of them. It was brighter than any of the others, and not in a position to be an anomaly like a planet.

"A New Earth Cruiser," he mouthed. He hadn't even realized he said it out loud until everybody standing nearby turned suddenly to look at him.

"Hold your tongue!" Yara snapped. "They had no idea we were coming, why would they send one of them here?"

Talon's eyes widened. "Because they did." His lust for vengeance had caused him to overlook it, but his people had been baited by the Tribune again. Only this time with an entire army. That was why Eureka was so easy to take. "Madame Lakura, you have to evacuate everybody. Now!"

Yara stormed over and grabbed Talon by his jaw. "Who are you?"

"It doesn't matter. Just look over—"

Talon was cut off when the engineer shouted, "Eureka scanners are finally up and running. Heavy activity popping up all around us, but I can't get an exact read on anything. It's like we're being jammed."

Yara released Talon. She was staring through the viewport, her mouth hanging open as she too spotted what he had. "How could they be here so fast?" she questioned. "We only just attacked!" She slammed her fist against the glass before rushing over to Captain Hadris at the makeshift command center. "Send out a message to every unit. Scramble all fighters and have the infantry assume defensive positions."

"Madame, much of the infantry is still dealin' with the remnants of the Tribunal defenders in the heart of the asteroid," Captain Hadris responded nervously.

"Just do it! Tell every remaining ship to swarm the *Lutetia* and keep its halves intact."

The captain was shaking. Finally Talon was getting a chance to see exactly how unprepared he was as he dictated her commands into his console so that they could be relayed throughout the entire Lakura force.

Talon was about to get the fight he'd been hoping for, only this time he couldn't bring himself to be excited. He'd been in the exact same spot before, and didn't want to lose his life being fooled again. Just like on the Tribunal Freighter, he was trapped—surrounded inside and out. The Tribune was trading a loss for a massacre—a tactic they'd learned from Cassius Vale decades earlier no doubt.

"Madame, if we stay they're going to do exactly what we just did to them," Talon implored.

"Stow it!" she snarled and shoved Talon by his head. "Get to your position. If there is truly a New Earth Cruiser coming, then we're bringing it down with us! For Lutetia! For Kalliope!" Every Lakura fighter in the room raised their fists and chanted with her.

"Talon, what're we going to do?" Tarsis pulled him aside.

"You mean besides dying?"

"Talon…"

"Sorry, I just have no influence here. If I'm right about what's out there, even running is probably impossible. They won't destroy this place, it's too important, but our ships will be useless. They're going to swarm the floors of this asteroid in numbers you can't even dream of, and the war will be over before it even starts. Even if we survive the first wave, eventually they'll bury us in the tunnels and let us starve or suffocate. How many fucking times are they going to catch me in one of their traps?" Talon slumped down against the glass and punched the floor out of frustration.

The floor! he thought. The idea popped into his head as he rubbed his sore knuckles. His mind trailed back to when he was aboard the freighter and he remembered how Sage had turned the tide aboard the Tribunal Freighter before they found there was no way out. He had no desire to mimic the woman who'd so deviously betrayed him and his now dead friends, but there was no time to let pride get in the way.

"Unless," he said.

"Unless what?" Tarsis questioned.

"Grab a rifle. We're heading down to the Gravity Generator before it's too late."

"Gravity Generators…" Tarsis realized, his jaw dropping. "You can't mean?"

"I do."

"Should we tell Yara?"

"Not until it's too late for her to stop me. C'mon!"

CHAPTER TWENTY-EIGHT - ADIM
NOT A SINGLE ENEMY

ADIM's feet scraped across the rocky floor. He kept his arms and legs limp, emulating all of the dead human bodies he'd seen over the years. Ceresians in every direction shouted obscenities, cursing the name of his Creator. None of them could understand his will. They were all too weak and undeserving. ADIM knew that they deserved the same fate as those on Kalliope, but he had a plan to follow. Cassius needed them for the moment.

"Calm yourselves!" Zaimur Morastus hollered over the din of the crowd. He was leading the henchmen dragging ADIM's camouflaged chassis. "Calm yourselves!"

The crowd didn't listen. Objects slammed into ADIM's body. None of it was enough to damage him, but the distortion to his camouflage could prove dangerous. Zaimur must have realized that. He immediately ordered his men to surround ADIM and absorb the rest of the projectiles.

As ADIM and his two carriers neared the hatch of an airlock their arms started to give out. ADIM's frame sunk, beginning to scratch against the floor so loudly that it was audible over the racket. The Morastus men moaned in struggle before Zaimur sent two more men to aid them. He was much heavier than a dead human carcass. They propped him up and were able to lug him directly in front of the airlock.

"Men and Women of Ceres, the plague of the Belt is truly gone!" Zaimur announced. Thousands of souls cheered at the top of their lungs. "Now, let us give him the fate he provided for so many of our ancestors and brethren. Today, in the name of my recently deceased and beloved father, and with the accord of every clan in our pact, we will send his body tumbling through space back to his masters. Not even his rotting corpse is worthy of resting within the walls of this hallowed rock!"

More applause followed his words, and then they quieted, waiting anxiously for what would happen next. ADIM heard the hiss of the airlock popping. The Morastus henchmen caught their breath, wrapped their hands under his back and legs, and loaded him in. His heavy body fell into the open airlock with a clank.

"Goodbye, Cassius Vale!" Zaimur yelled. "I only wish my father lived a day longer to see you get the fate you deserve. May you never find peace!"

The inner seal of the airlock shut and then the outer one came open. ADIM was yanked out into space, his limbs twisting. He took note of how pleased every Ceresian seemed to be that Cassius would never again walk the Circuit.

ADIM tucked his legs and steadied his movement. He tumbled over so that he could look back at the tremendous, oblong asteroid known as Ceres. Lights flickered along its wrinkled surface where the countless hangars and tunnels allowed entrance. There was no real order to it, except for a cluster which sliced along a portion of the center between two natural valleys, like the buckle on a belt.

A day's worth of hours passed by.

Ceres became little more than a pebble in the distance—one more light amongst a sea of cosmic entities. ADIM wasn't worried. Cassius was going to come for him, as was planned. He just had to make sure that everyone thought he was dead. He and his Creator had always worked from the shadows, but this strategy was far more direct. Now that ADIM had seen the nest of the Ceresians firsthand, he was beginning to understand why that was necessary without needing explanation. His Creator had far too many opponents. They would all need to be removed eventually in order to see his will enacted. Every Ceresian lord and every Tribune. Every single one.

ADIM's scanners picked up a slew of incoming ships. He recognized one of them immediately. He'd been a part of it just as he'd been a part of the android on Ceres. He twisted his head around, expecting to see the *White Hand*, but it wasn't there. Instead there was a fleet of Ceresian vessels. They had a look to them as the interior of the asteroid—plated, imperfect, and relatively clunky. Nothing like Cassius's ship.

The largest of them was painted with navy highlights and had the Morastus Symbol printed on its side—two fangs extending down from beneath a set of predatory eyes. It was at least ten times the size of all the others, stretching half a mile in length. It's thick, bulbous hull had two long bows sprouting from either side of a glassy command deck in the front and center, like claws from a paw. It didn't take long for ADIM to discover that only that ship had proper weapons systems. The others in the fleet were little more than re-outfitted transport vessels and freighters, more fit for mining than war.

The flagship rotated slowly, and ADIM noticed one of its secondary hangars folding open. His path was leading him directly into it. He readied the weapons systems in his arms and shot downward so that the force would alter his trajectory. Once he was close to the ship he grabbed onto the top lip of the hangar's airlock, magnetized his chassis, and crawled in along the ceiling. The outer seal closed behind him, and as the inner one rose he saw what awaited him. Docked inside was the *White Hand*, its engines still warm.

Zaimur Morastus has taken it as his own, ADIM thought. It was not a possibility that he ever wanted to consider. He scuttled upside-down into the low hangar, and located two heat signatures below him. He studied their heartbeats, and the way their skin radiated warmth, and was able to identify them as Zaimur and Cassius. His Creator's pulse wasn't heightened, but it rarely was.

ADIM demagnetized and crashed down between them. He held out his weaponized arm to take aim at Zaimur, just in case. Zaimur nearly fell over he was so shocked.

"ADIM!" the familiar voice of Cassius exclaimed. He was back to wearing his usual violet tunic, complete with bladed pulse-pistol and dark-metal bracers. "Forgive us for taking so long. There was a long-awaited funeral to attend before we could get off of Ceres."

"Safe and sound, as promised, Vale," Zaimur grumbled. "Now would you mind instructing your pet to lower his weapons while he is aboard *my* ship?"

"Of course," Cassius replied, as calm and collected as ever. "ADIM, welcome to the private hangar aboard the *Hound's Paw*. There is no threat here."

ADIM gave the room one last quick scan before he was satisfied. As always, his Creator was in complete control. "Yes, Creator," ADIM replied. He lowered his arm and finally allowed his holographic shell to dissipate and reveal his true form.

"I must say I'm impressed," Zaimur stated. "They say my father went with no pain. Peacefully. I thank you for that, android...ADIM."

"This unit was instructed not to allow detection," ADIM replied.

"Still. He had suffered enough."

"It isn't every man who's willing to do what he must," Cassius said. "Your father, in the time I fought him, would have been proud of you."

"Don't talk about him like you know him," Zaimur said, a hint of irritation entering his tone.

Cassius ran his fingers over ADIM's back. ADIM turned his head all the way around as well to see the countless scratches along the rear of his chassis. "ADIM, what have they done to you?"

"I assure you it's nothing that can't be fixed," Zaimur answered.

"I'll have you cleaned up shortly, ADIM."

"I've held up my end, Vale!" Zaimur snapped before ADIM could respond. "Now it's your turn."

Cassius turned to Zaimur. "Very well. ADIM, transfer the last recorded positions of the Tribunal navy into the *Hound's Paw's* systems."

"Yes, Creator," ADIM said as he walked toward the control console for the hangar's airlock.

"You'll need the transmission codes," Zaimur said.

Cassius chuckled. "We'll see."

ADIM extended his fingers over the console. The lights on it dimmed, and ADIM'S eyes spun as he dug through the systems of the *Hound's Paw*. It was relatively simplistic, like the old androids on Ceres, and after what amounted to ten seconds in real time he'd uploaded the latest contents of the Vale Protocol into its computer database.

Zaimur's brow furrowed. "By the Ancients. How did he—"

"Experience," Cassius replied. "You never really did figure out who was behind knocking those Tribunal Freighters off of the Circuit did you? ADIM and I were attempting to get under their skin, but they didn't want to publically announce it was the work of a former Tribune so they laid blame on your people," Cassius lied.

The Creator is attempting to deepen the rift between the factions, ADIM thought. He knew that the Tribune hadn't learned of his existence until well after the last freighter theft.

Zaimur rubbed his jaw. "So they bombed Kalliope in retaliation for the attacks even though they knew it was you?"

"While they simultaneously attempted to have myself and ADIM removed from the equation. In my own home. You see, Tribune Benjar Vakari wanted this war as much as you do. To finally have a reason to convince the council to quietly eliminate me and take the asteroid belt—that was his plan all along. I walked right into it when I started cutting off his personal Gravitum supply."

Zaimur clenched his jaw and squeezed his fists. "That scheming bastard," he seethed. "That's the truth?"

"Every word," ADIM interjected. From his study of the androids on Ceres he'd discovered that their rudimentary programming didn't allow for them to comprehend the idea of lying. Agreeing vocally was the least he could do to help Zaimur be convinced.

Cassius shot him a sidelong glance before turning his attention back to Zaimur. "Hear my words, Zaimur," he began. "With Tribune Gressler dead, Benjar will be in complete control of the Tribune. He suspected me from the beginning, and because he was right the others will now cede to his wishes. He will drive this war, and while he may not be my equal, I once served directly under him. He learned a lot watching me win his last war."

"I'm growing tired of listening to you pat yourself on the back, Vale," Zaimur growled. "Out with it. After what you just told me I'm beginning to regret this alliance."

"The reason you lost the last war was because your Pact has always had too many men deliberating over what course to take. You need an uncompromising leader. To win, *you* must gain the complete support of those in control."

Zaimur released a hearty laugh. "Now that's a lot to ask. As it is, Kalliope was Morastus-owned. Maybe when the others feel the Tribune's bite they'll be more willing to listen."

"True. There are many clans. However, in our present only the Morastus, the Lakura, and the Ventiss hold true power. The Ventiss were indecisive even when I fought them decades ago. They will follow the majority. Thanks to ADIM, you, and only you now, control your clan. Win over Yara Lakura's complete trust and all else will follow."

Zaimur stopped following. "That's your secret plan? Yara Lakura?" he questioned. "I assure you, her knife has dulled over the years. Maybe she trusted my father, but me? Is an alliance not enough?"

"ADIM, show him the map," Cassius said.

ADIM held out his open palm. The projectors along his arm and hand rotated to display the map of the Circuit, and tiny red signatures indicated where the Tribunal ships were located.

"This is the last update received by the *White Hand*, Creator," ADIM stated. "As of twenty-one hours ago your connection has been severed."

"It's about time," Cassius sighed. "It was useful while it lasted."

"You're not showing me anything new," Zaimur said as he approached the map and scanned it from every angle. He didn't appear pleased. "The ships have barely moved since the last time."

"ADIM, inform Zaimur exactly where Benjar Vakari's fleet is heading."

ADIM reached out with his free hand and traced a line from the largest cluster of red toward a tiny asteroid on the edge of the asteroid belt. "Their vector indicates that they are headed for the Tribunal shipyard colony of Eureka," ADIM answered.

"The same Eureka where Yara Lakura intends on surprising them. Eureka is in a crucial position and is already prepped to allow them to continually repair and reinforce their navy."

"I'm well aware of Eureka's advantages," Zaimur said. "They used it in the Earth Reclaimer War to do the same."

"Well that is where the Lakura army is headed. Whether Benjar is going there merely to prepare his invasion, or his hidden Executors have informed him of her plan, I'm not sure. But—"

Zaimur cut him off. "She's going to be slaughtered when they arrive…" His mouth hung open as he focused on the size of Benjar's fleet.

"Not if we get there in time," Cassius assured. He placed his hand on Zaimur's side and turned him away from the image. "We won't attempt to engage the Tribunal fleet directly, but we will enter the battle, ravage Eureka so that the Tribune can't use it, and flee with as many as we can save. History will call it a slight loss for us, but Benjar is short on temper. He will be infuriated by losing out on his massacre."

"And more liable to make mistakes," Zaimur finished for him. "Yara will be indebted to me."

"It won't matter how dull her blade is after that. Ceres will unite behind you. Since we cannot win this war with force, we must chip away at the Tribune until they unravel."

Zaimur clapped his hands. A smile formed on his face that stretched from ear to ear. "Brilliant, Vale! I should've known better than to doubt you. I'll inform my men immediately." He wheeled around and hurried out of the room.

"You will have the *White Hand* at your service."

Zaimur stopped and looked back. "No. You will remain with me in command here aboard the *Hound's Paw*. Only my most trusted men will have access."

"Of course," Cassius replied, bowing his head. "ADIM will be in control of the ship. Its weapons systems will prove valuable in crippling the asteroid."

Zaimur stared at the android for a few seconds before nodding. "ADIM? Very well. He has proven useful so far. I'll send for you when we depart." Zaimur took one last look at the map of the Circuit, gritted his teeth, and continued on his way.

"Very useful indeed," Cassius whispered. He faced ADIM, grabbed him by the sides of his face and grinned. "You were quite convincing on Ceres," he marveled. "For a moment, even I feared I might've been dead."

"Never." ADIM countered.

Cassius took a step back, his brow furrowing. "You still don't trust him, do you? Every time he looked at me I noticed you were prepared to shoot him down."

"No. This Unit witnessed his followers celebrating your death. They pelted what they assumed was the Creator's body with rocks and rubbish."

"They are fools." Cassius wrapped his arm around ADIM and walked him toward the ramp onto the *White Hand*. "By now the Tribune will have likely heard through their Executors of my passing. They will celebrate as well." Cassius stopped, grasped ADIM's arm, and opened up the compartment on it. He pulled out his com-links and placed them in his ears. "We will make them rejoice when they find out that I am alive and well."

"What if they do not?"

"What?"

"Rejoice. This Unit will have no choice but to eliminate all who do not."

Cassius chuckled before continuing to lead ADIM onto his ship. "There will always be new enemies, ADIM, even after we're done."

"This Unit will ensure that the Creator does not have a single enemy left after this war," ADIM decided. "All who remain will live in service of your will."

Cassius froze. He turned his head and stared into ADIM's eyes. They weren't spinning at all.

CHAPTER TWENTY-NINE - SAGE
NO WAY OUT

After spending the better part of two weeks sleuthing around the *Ascendant*, Sage was starving. As much as she enjoyed tasting *crud* again, most days it was too big of a risk taking part in the feeding periods, and sneaking any out wasn't an option. Patched up eye and all, Hand Yavortha was diligent about making his rounds. Sage of course knew the real reason why he was making himself so visible, so she couldn't risk putting herself in plain sight without her helmet on.

She stayed on the move. There were reserves of emergency ration bars held in monitored storage areas. Getting in a few times here and there was easy, but any more than that would be suspicious. For water she was forced mostly to drink from the lavatories. All liquid was rationed on the ship, so there wasn't much potable water to get. It reminded her of the sour water served back in the nether regions of New Terrene.

She hijacked jobs when she could to appear busy—prepping fighters, moving supplies, or readying weaponry. There was a lot of work to do to prepare for the looming battle. She wasn't exactly sure where they were heading, but with every passing day the faces of the Tribunal officers and higher-ups got grimmer. They were getting close, and that's exactly what she needed. Once the fighting started, she'd spring Elisha from her cell and take a fighter to the nearest Tribunal settlement she could find. Bringing the girl back to her people was no longer an option since the Tribune would just conquer wherever she ended up.

Sage hadn't been able to visit her cell since the ship set off, but she was able to sneak a glance of the surveillance footage there to ensure she was still alive.

Presently, Sage headed down one of the *Ascendant's* wide corridors toward the main hangar in order to work on a fighter she had her eye on stealing. She was doing her best to try and disconnect it from all Tribunal tracking programs in order to make that possible, but the Vale Protocol was proving difficult to crack. She wasn't sure why she thought she could negotiate anything which manifested in Cassius's mind, but she had to try. Otherwise the Tribune would know exactly where she was going once she left.

She was nearing the vessel when a sudden cramp in her stomach pulled at her side and forced her to lean against the wall. She'd been hungry before, on missions which went longer than expected, but without her Executor Implant it was more crippling than she expected. She resolved that after checking on the fighter she'd make her way to the refectory and take the risk on pilfering some *crud*. She had to fill her belly. Otherwise she wouldn't be able to retain her focus when she eventually needed it.

The floor of the *Ascendant* began to vibrate. A cohort of armed soldiers went marching past her in the direction of the hangar at a rapid pace. Then the voice of Yavortha spoke over the ship's speakers, or was it in her helmet's com-link? After two weeks it was getting hard to tell.

"A large Ceresian strike force has invaded Eureka Station," the Hand said. "The *Ascendant* is currently an hour away from engaging them. All hands to stations. Prep the fighters to retake the station. Ground forces report to your unit's transport to initiate assault."

The vibration beneath her feet grew more and more powerful until there was a severe tremor. Then the *Ascendant* was still again, coursing through space as straight as an arrow.

Rail-gun fire, Sage recognized. She rubbed her stomach. *So much for finding something to eat. It's beginning already.*

"Unit B563, report to our designated transport immediately," the voice of her unit commander ordered through her helmet. This time there was no question where it was emanating from.

She ignored the order and changed course for the brig. This was her chance.

She walked at a brisk pace, not wanting want to draw any more attention to herself while every other soldier was running in the opposite direction. The holding cells were on the lowest level of the cruiser, toward the stern. The quickest way there was to take the central lift, but that would be crawling with soldiers wondering why she wasn't reporting to her proper station. There were subtle differences in Tribunal sets of armor, and she was wearing that of the infantry. There was no reason for her to be anywhere near the brig during battle preparations and the longer it took her to reach Elisha the less reason she'd have to not be present on one of the troop transports.

The long way was her only option, and she did her best to stay invisible. It wasn't easy. The generous corridors and stairwells were bustling with activity. At the first fork she decided to cut through an infantry cabin. Sirens were blaring in order to ensure everybody was awake, so it was already mostly empty.

"Soldier!" the unmistakable voice of Yavortha hollered from out in the corridor as soon as she stepped in. It wasn't through her com-link. "You're to report to the hangar. Now!"

Sage wheeled around, trying not to appear like she was up to something while also keeping her visor downturned. She reached out slowly and grabbed a pulse-rifle off of the rack on the nearby wall, not sure whose it was or if it even worked.

"Forgot my rifle," she said, using her best male voice.

Yavortha had an entourage of honor guards beside him and they flooded the living quarters, checking to make sure all of the bunks were empty. He waited at the entrance for Sage to catch up and she knew there was no way out of it. Trying to run or incapacitate him and his guards might work, but it'd make escaping the *Ascendant* impossible. She was just lucky that having her helmet on was a part of normal procedure during preparations.

There were a few other stragglers in the living quarters. They fell into formation with her and followed Yavortha back toward the main hangar.

Damn you and your timing Yavortha, Sage thought. She tried to remember any points in the ship where she'd be able to slip away. Those thoughts were quickly put to rest when a pair of the honor guards fell back beside her and the other straggling soldiers. Doing anything out of the ordinary would get her discovered quickly and be a death sentence for Elisha.

"You're lucky there's a battle to win or the lot of you would be scrubbing scum off the galley floors for this!" Yavortha growled as he stepped onto a lift. "Fortunately for all of you, His Eminence needs everyone at his disposal to end this little uprising as quickly as possible."

It was too late.

The lift doors slammed shut and they would arrive outside of the hangar in minutes, where Sage would be hoarded onto a transport. She was too well trained to panic. An Executor's missions rarely went according to initial plans, so they were taught early on how to improvise. With a force as large as the one aboard the *Ascendant*, as well as the dozen or so frigates sailing alongside it, the Ceresians wouldn't last long on Eureka. But the aftermath of the battle would be equally as chaotic as the preparations, likely even more so. At least that was what her studies had taught her since she'd never been a part of a real war. All she had to do was hitch a ride back to the *Ascendant* once it was over while the majority of its forces were still on the asteroid. Getting Elisha out would be even easier then.

She settled on that plan as the lift doors opened, and she and the rest of the late soldiers were emptied out into the hangar. Fighters were taking off in rapid succession and filling the inner sanctums of the main airlock. Occupied Mechs were being fastened onto the bottom of dropships so that they could be deployed directly onto the asteroid. Formations of soldiers filed onto any of the transports that hadn't already left. Robed Earth Whisperers stood outside of every one, reciting prayers and holding up shards of tree bark for the nearby men to touch. Sage paused for a moment and frowned as she watched the fighter she'd chosen for her escape lift off.

"Move soldier!" the honor guard right behind her grunted, nudging her in the back. She winced in pain. He may not have meant to do it hard, but her ribs were still tender from her climb into the *Ascendant*.

She bit her lip and fell into the ranks of her assigned unit as they filled a nearby transport. Yavortha rushed up to the front and stepped on. Apparently he was coming with her unit. An officer inside signaled her toward a seat, and with so many soldiers packed around her she had no choice but to comply. Restraints fell over her shoulders once she sat, and in no time the vibrations of the transport's engines grew more powerful. It slowly rose.

Yavortha was standing near the viewport of the transport's entrance as it soared across the hangar toward the airlock, gazing out upon the grand Tribunal Army. Once they passed through into space he turned and headed up toward the cockpit.

Sage caught a glimpse of his marred face out of the corner of her eye. While Benjar sat alone in his personal quarters, Yavortha was leading the charge. That was the duty of a Hand, but she couldn't imagine him ever having the fortitude to serve beyond the call of action. Knowing he might soon take a seat upon the Tribunal Council was hard to swallow. As a Hand he answered to his Tribune, and for all of his slights toward her, Benjar was fervent in his faith. Yavortha seemed to be the kind of man who wielded religion like a hammer.

Even after what he did to her on Titan she took no solace in injuring her people when a mission didn't necessitate it, but a part of her wished that her blade had sunk a little deeper. She couldn't imagine what he would do to the Ceresians now that he had command of an entire army.

"The Ceresians are to be given no quarter," Yavortha's voice spoke through the com-link in her helmet, as if responding to her thoughts. "They may attempt to surrender, but they cannot be trusted. They are gamblers and miscreants who will do whatever it takes to deceive you if it means taking just one more pitiful breath.

The Circuit must see firsthand the deserved fate of those who would turn their sights on the faithful! There is no forgiveness for them."

A tingle ran up Sage's spine. Whether it was from dread, excitement, or a combination of both she wasn't sure—the Executor Implant had always squelched such feelings. Those weren't the sentiments of the Tribune she'd fallen in love with. She knew how vengeful the Spirit could be better than most, but the faith which would one day allow humans to tread across the surface of Earth unharmed left room for the forgiveness of nonbelievers. That she knew for sure, no matter how lost she was. All she had to do was survive her first real battle and then she could figure out what to do with that knowledge. Saving an innocent little girl from being a prisoner of war seemed like a good place to start.

CHAPTER THIRTY - TALON
IMMUNITY

"Die heretic!" a Tribunal soldier deep within the tunnels of Eureka shouted as he fired his pulse-rifle. He was one of the stragglers left behind after the asteroid was taken, and outnumbered as they were, they refused to surrender.

Talon pulled Tarsis back against the wall and waited for a moment before edging around the corner and pulling his own trigger. This time he had no trouble seeing if he hit anyone. The soldier collapsed in silence, and the others with him fell back a little farther behind another layer of cover. It was the kind of fighting he was used to—men pinned down in cramped, dark tunnels with nowhere to go but through their enemy. As good as it felt to put one down, he knew he'd have plenty more chances if he was able reach the gravity generator fast enough.

Talon signaled over to Tarsis and the group of Lakura fighters they'd fallen in with, instructing them to hold. He asked to see a comrade's HOLO-Pad, displaying a schematic plan of the asteroid. There was no telling how accurate it was, but it was the best the Ceresians could acquire on such short notice. He was only able to glance at it for a few seconds before the soldier snatched it back.

"I know where I'm goin'," he grunted. "No time to waste, we got our orders. Take the core so that we've got a defensible position."

It was the only sensible move other than cramming into the ships they had left and fleeing. Maybe from the inner tunnels where Mechs couldn't fit and numbers counted for little they could claw at the Tribune until they lost the taste for battle. As long as the Tribune didn't feel like burying them there. It was a long shot, but

Yara Lakura was far out of her element.

Such a fool to go at it alone, Talon thought, remembering how his former clan was still deliberating over what to do next when he joined up with the Lakura. It wasn't his fault Yara decided to attack without any support, but if he'd been thinking clearly, there was no doubt he would've known what to expect. Now it'd take a miracle to get anybody out alive.

Talon and Tarsis exchanged a nod before falling to the back of the formation and allowing their comrades to press on first. Talon had gotten a good enough look at the plans to know they were close. There were a few more spats with Tribunal defenders, but they had the upper hand for the moment.

Finally, they reached a sealed, plated hatch in an area where the height and width of the tunnel swelled. The others continued on toward another bunch of Tribunals, but Talon nudged his friend and showed him the sealed entrance.

"This is it," Talon declared. The hatch had blue markings printed on its center, a circle made out of fanning blades. He ran his hand over the metal exterior, and could feel the warmth emanating from the other side.

"You sure?" Tarsis asked.

"I recognize that symbol from Kalliope. Unless they're lying, my people claim to have built up this asteroid long ago, before the war."

Tarsis moved over to the door's controls and tapped the screen. "Looks like it's locked up."

"Of course. You need all sorts of protective equipment to go in there safely. Luckily that doesn't matter for us."

"Lucky us…Doesn't help if we can't get in."

"We'll see." Talon brushed Tarsis aside and took his place in front of the controls. "I ran with the Morastus clan for a long time. A large part of my duties included getting into places I wasn't meant to."

"You know how to operate the generator then?"

Talon froze. He hadn't even considered that part. He shrugged and continued to go to work on the controls. He never had any intention of leaving the generator intact, no matter how important Eureka may have been to the war effort.

"That's where you come in," Talon said. "Yara might've tried to stop me from crippling this place if she knew what we were up to. Now that I'm already here, I need you to start warning everyone. Get on the com-link in your helmet and tell whomever you can. Then run back as fast as possible and find someone important enough to be able to broadcast to every Ceresian's helmet within a million miles of this rock. Tell them to fight outward toward our remaining ships as soon as the gravity switches off and evacuate… or risk earning the fate you and I wear on our flesh."

Tarsis grabbed Talon by the arm. "I'm not going to let you do this alone."

"It can't harm me any more than it already has," Talon responded as he lifted Tarsis's hand away. "Don't worry. I'll catch up to you after it's done. If we could get off of the *Amerigo*, we can get out of this."

"Hopefully with fewer red-eyed, metal demons," he joked.

"I'm not sure about that. One of those things might prove pretty useful right about now."

"By the Spirit, you're losing your mind." He took a step back. "Alright. Let's do this. The Tribunals won't know what hit them."

Talon nodded and then heard the noisy whine of Tarsis's suit as the Vergent ran back down the tunnel. His wheezy voice shouted through the com-link in Talon's helmet, explaining what was about to happen. Talon switched off the feed so that he could concentrate.

It grew eerily quiet.

The Lakura men they'd been with were so far ahead that their gunshots were impossible to discern over the soft, constant purring of Eureka's life support systems. Talon could only imagine what was going on back at the surface where the New Earth Cruiser had likely begun unloading thousands of soldiers. Down in the depths of the asteroid, through a mile of solid rock, he couldn't even feel the vibrations of battle.

It did make it easier to work. He was well out of practice when it came to slicing through locking systems, but it was coming back to him quickly. He expected the one guarding Eureka's central gravity generator to be more complex, but it was relatively simple. Apparently no sane, healthy person would risk exposure without proper protection and training on how to deal with the device.

Agatha…or Sage did it for me and Vellish, Talon considered. He quickly shook away the thought. He couldn't imagine why she wanted to extend their time aboard the freighter, but it was obvious she'd orchestrated the whole thing. She would never actually put herself in danger like he was about to.

Destroying gravity generators wasn't a particularly popular tactic after all, whether amongst Ceresians or Tribunals. Where the latter believed them to provide an extension of the Earth, for Ceresians each habitable asteroid was another lifeline. What he was about to do would wreck Eureka for years—eliminating a key position for whichever faction happened to own it. His own people might care about that if they were foolish enough to believe they could win the coming battle, but Talon didn't. The Tribune clearly had no issue with wiping Kalliope off of the face of the Circuit despite their faith. He was going to take something back.

The control console beeped and the hatch into the generator room slid up into the ceiling. It was at least a foot thick so it took a minute, but he was through.

An aura of blue emanated from within, so bright that he hesitated before entering. He knew it couldn't hurt him, but he couldn't forget what it had done to him on Kalliope—the flash of blue, coruscating light lashing across his and Zargo Morastus's unsuspecting bodies before he was knocked unconscious.

Talon took a deep breath and stepped in. It was a two-layered ingress, and once he was inside the outer seal slammed shut and the glassy, more delicate interior one popped open. The peace and quiet came to a quick end. He'd never stood in the very core of an asteroid colony before. He couldn't help but be filled with awe. It was a vast, intricate system of which he had only the barest understanding. There were a few experts throughout the Circuit, but unfortunately for Eureka he didn't have one with him. They'd probably try to stop him regardless. People could be very protective when it came to their Gravitum.

Several rows of enormous turbines inside were as noisy as the engine of a ship upon liftoff. They crackled from electric surges as the refined Gravitum within them was charged at the perfect measure in order to produce the sense of gravity. Talon wasn't exactly sure how it worked, but that was the gist of it.

Every so often the blinding, cerulean light shining in their centers would swell as if part of a beating heart, and the countless conduits branching out from them would hum with current. It was the asteroid colony's circulatory system, but instead of running beneath skin it threaded through the rocky walls and ceilings. There the tubes would continue for miles, cycling the charged element throughout the settlement and evenly spreading a sense of pseudo gravity.

Talon truly had no idea what would happen when he blew the generator to pieces, besides that it would swiftly dial the gravity conditions on the asteroid back toward its natural, minimal-G state. But even in its refined form, Gravitum could be a highly volatile substance. He'd learned that firsthand. The risks were great, but they were worth taking. Having an army of Ceresians with the Blue Death was better than having no army at all. They'd need numbers to last the war.

Talon gritted his teeth and held up his pulse-rifle. All of the control consoles within might as well have been in a foreign language anyway, so there was no use wasting time trying to figure the system out. "Well, Elisha…maybe I'll see you soon," he said to himself. He caught a glimpse of his face reflecting in his weapon's barrel, of his sallow flesh and cobalt veins. "If not, it won't be long."

He aimed the gun in the direction of one of the turbines and squeezed the trigger. The spinning blades of the machine crumbled in on themselves as the forces holding the turbine together were compromised. Streaks of raw, bluish energy bolted out past his visor. Talon wasn't scared of it filling his lungs, but as hot flames licked at his boots he couldn't deny his trepidation.

He slowly backed away as he changed the clip on his rifle. It was difficult to walk. A concurrent feeling of both sinking and rising stole over him. Before long his feet were barely touching the ground. Conduits tore free from the walls and spit out billows of Gravitum in its gaseous state. The typical, azure coloration of the element was lost. It mixed with black smoke and filled the room with a noxious miasma so dark that Talon could barely see a thing.

Every portion of the generator was tearing itself apart all on its own. There was no longer a need to continue firing. Some people on the Circuit believed that the Ancients' unbridled harvesting of Gravitum caused Earth to fall apart. For the first time in Talon's life that didn't seem like some timeworn story told to inspire restraint. He was watching the unseen forces of the universe lash out at each other without relent, and it was truly terrifying.

By the time he backed up against a wall he'd already inhaled so much smoke that he could hardly breathe. Death was all around him, like the stuff of nightmares. He was powerless—his gun a useless tool.

No! He thought. *I won't die like this.* Falling in battle was one thing, but he wasn't going to give Gravitum the satisfaction of taking him even earlier. He released his rifle and watched it disappear into the cloud of chaos and energy. Then he reached out to try and find anything he could grab hold of. It was impossible to differentiate between up and down, but after a few frantic seconds he found a groove in either the floor or ceiling. He drew his weightless body along it, back toward what he hoped was the way out.

His fingers brushed against a projection and he used it to launch himself forward with as much force as he could muster. His shoulder slammed against a glass wall—the outer seal of the generator's entrance. The door's controls were right above him. He set it to open and as it did the inner seal squeezed shut. He used the walls to haul himself through, watching in horror as ravenous strings of energy clawed at the glass, like the twisted fingers of angry specters.

He tore off his helmet once he was floating safely outside. Everything he'd inhaled had him violently coughing, and it was only after he vomited that he was able to finally gasp for fresh air. He groped his face to make sure that he was alive and that what he'd just seen was real. It was. The red emergency lights in the tunnel were all illuminated, and there was a siren wailing, different than the one that went off when his people invaded the asteroid.

He recognized the sound from the only other time he'd heard it. On Kalliope. There was still oxygen filling the tunnel, as well as every other life support system, but gravity was gone. *Let's see what the Tribune does about this.* As long as Tarsis was able to spread the message to enough Ceresians, they'd have the upper hand. It would take the Tribune a while to figure out that Eureka was defiled and her generator was more than just deactivated. Just long enough, perhaps, for a miracle.

CHAPTER THIRTY-ONE - SAGE
THIS ISN'T MY BATTLE

The glowing belt of docking stations that wrapped Eureka was easy to spot against the blackness of space. Debris from broken ships floated everywhere, forcing the transport Sage was on to weave its way toward the docks. Tribunal Fighters darted all around, defending them from Ceresian ones. Fire from their flak cannons traced across the stars. There was nothing coming from the asteroid itself, so Sage figured the Ceresians must've already destroyed most of the asteroid's defenses during their own invasion. It was the perfect strategy. Invite the Ceresians in, and then leave them defending unfamiliar ground.

She glanced down and checked the pulse-rifle in her hands. Just in case there was still fighting to be done she hoped it was at least in working order.

"The breaching of Eureka is underway," Yavortha said through Sage's com-link as her transport initiated docking procedures with Eureka. "May the Spirit guide your steps."

"For the Spirit!" all the soldiers on board hollered. Then they leaned over as far as their restraints would allow and allowed their fingers to graze the ground. She did it as well.

The commander of her unit came onto her com-link once the prayers were completed. There was some chatter about what their unit's orders were, but she ignored most of it after she found out they belonged to the second wave. Judging by the size of the army traveling with the *Ascendant*, the docks would likely be taken by the time they landed. Once they were there, both Yavortha and her unit's commander would have too much to keep tabs on to monitor any individual soldier. She'd easily be able to bow out of ranks and sneak onto a supply transport headed back to the *Ascendant*.

The inner airlock came open and the transport soared into one of Eureka's many lofty docking stations. Mark V Combat Mechs were already present, with more being dropped off on what was left of the landing pads projecting from asteroid. They were the newest model, and Sage had never actually gotten a chance to see them in action. She didn't count the one on the Tribunal Freighter which never even had a chance to fight back against her. A few of them fired their back-mounted, light railguns toward the Ceresian held end of the docks. Bolts of white light speared across the way, lighting up the room as if she were in an electrical storm on Titan.

The transport touched down and Yavortha led Sage's unit out. She waited long enough before getting up for there to be a sizeable gap between them. They were immediately greeted by a legion of Tribunal troops. She used that moment to sneak out of the ranks and climb into a pile of scraps nearby to observe.

Bodies were everywhere. They didn't just belong to Ceresians either. The charred corpses of Eureka's Tribunal defenders were already lying amongst the wreckage.

"Sir," an eager commander ran over and addressed Yavortha, falling down to his knee and grazing the floor with his hand. Yavortha signaled him to rise. "The Ceresians surrendered the docks without much of a fight," the commander continued. "They've fallen back into the tunnels, but we've interrogated the ones we managed to capture and found out that they're still receiving some resistance from Eureka's inhabitants down there."

"Good men," Yavortha replied.

"Also, they've revealed interesting news. Apparently Cassius Vale has been executed back on Ceres."

Yavortha laughed. "Yes, our Executors there have reported as much. Apparently the traitor didn't have as many friends as he thought."

The commander appeared disappointed by Yavortha's lack of surprise, but he retained his composure. "Shall I announce the news to the men?"

"Not yet. His Eminence Benjar Vakari has taught me to never trust what you hear. I'll believe the news when I see his body myself. Either way, if it is true, then this war should come to a swift end. Now, relieve the first wave and send these soldiers in. Don't give them any time to establish defensive positions."

"Yes, sir." The commander kneeled again and went to wave Sage's unit on.

Sage froze.

She imagined that the rumored news of Cassius's execution should upset her more than it was. Whether or not she wanted to admit it, he'd been important to her. Without him she would have likely lost her life two times over. However, for the first time in recent days she actually agreed with Yavortha's sentiments. Cassius wasn't the type of man to allow himself to be executed. He wasn't the type of man to die either. If Benjar Vakari didn't trust the news that his greatest rival was gone, then she couldn't either.

After settling on that, she skulked along the wreckage to try and get a clearer picture of the situation. As she did Yavortha stopped the commander to give another order.

"Execute all captives, and relay the message that no prisoners are to be taken," he ordered. "Our Lord Tribune wants to send a message to those who'd dare attack colonies under our protection."

The Commander glanced over at a cluster of bloodied Ceresian captives nearby. They were cuffed and on their knees. "Yes—yes sir," he stuttered.

The Commander signaled over to the men holding the prisoners at gunpoint. The Ceresians looked around at each other frantically, but there was no time to attempt anything. The Tribunal soldiers followed their orders and fired their pulse-rifles without hesitation. A brief chorus of screams rang out before they were rendered silent, and all Sage could do was stare from her cover. They were men of flesh and blood, mowed down in cold blood.

Sage looked back to where Yavortha had taken up position, watching the bloodbath from his perch on the ramp of the transport they'd arrived in. All she could do was hope that he was really the one behind the slaughter and not Benjar, but she was starting to know better than to assume that.

Before she could think of what to do next a deafening sound filled the entire space. It was so high pitched that she went to hold her ears even though she was wearing a helmet. Then, all of her weight melted away. The scraps of metal around her started lifting off of the ground, then her body, and then everyone else in the docking station.

It can't be? Sage thought as she noticed even the heavy Combat Mechs beginning to rise. The Gravity Generator had been turned off, and she could almost guess who had to be behind it. *He's here?*

She pushed off of the ground so that she could get a better view from the ceiling when suddenly flames shot out from a portion of Eureka's enclosure. The blast punctured the emergency shutters covering a cluster of viewports before being swiftly extinguished by vacuum. The sudden pressure change peeled the breach open even farther and plucked Tribunal soldiers out without relent.

Sage grabbed onto a light fixture with her artificial arm and endured the initial rush. Most of the unit she'd arrived with weren't so lucky. Yavortha pulled himself back into the transport just in time. The unit commander in front of him was yanked away along with everyone else nearby who couldn't find something fixed to hold onto. They had space-worthy suits of armor on so most of them would likely survive as long as they didn't slam into any metal slag too hard. But they were useless to the battle drifting through space with timers on their oxygen tanks.

A brief moment of silence ensued after the air stopped gushing. Sage peered through the molten gash and saw a white ship zip by. For a second she thought it might be the *White Hand*, but decided that was unlikely when she noticed the flicker of Ceresian ships speeding toward Eureka beyond it.

"The heretics will sacrifice an extension of the Earth!" Yavortha shouted over the com-link. "Take the heart of the asteroid. The *Ascendant* will ravage their fleet!" He sounded more panicked than she'd ever heard him, which meant that he wasn't expecting another Ceresian fleet to arrive. It didn't appear to be nearly enough ships to win the battle and destroy a New Earth Cruiser, but they clearly weren't going to lie down and die.

As soon as Yavortha stopped barking orders the Ceresian army flooded out simultaneously from the tunnels of Eureka and the rafters along the tall walls. A firefight erupted beneath her. From her high position, Sage could see that the same thing was happening in all of the other docking station throughout Eureka. The Ceresians remained outnumbered three to one, but the lack of gravity made it impossible for the Tribunal army to reestablish order. With the Combat Mechs left off-balance, targeting a rail-gun was impossible as well.

Sage quickly swung up out of the way of a hail of bullets. Her mind reverted to old form, plotting out a course she could take to help her people. She could have a Mech pummel the tunnel entrances with missiles and seal the Ceresians inside for as long as it took for her people to reestablish their position. She shook her head when she saw Yavortha emerge from the transport and remembered. *This isn't my battle.* He'd made that decision perfectly clear to her back on Titan.

She kicked through a vent cap in the ceiling and thrust herself into the narrow shaft. It was a position she was unfortunately getting used to, but being weightless made it simple to traverse. It was time to improvise again. The gravity generator going off changed the equation. Maybe she was just being foolish to hope, but if it really was Talon then she could fulfill her mission to reunite him with Elisha. It was the only mission she had left.

CHAPTER THIRTY-TWO - TALON
THE HERO OF EUREKA

"Die, you Tribunal bastards!" the familiar voice of Tarsis shouted up ahead. The tunnels of Eureka were ringing with gunfire, but he'd recognize that voice anywhere.

He used the nooks in the metal-plated ceilings to pull his weightless body along. His helmet was back on, and the farther outwards he got within the asteroid the harder it was getting to breathe. The life support systems had been compromised. Whether or not that was due to him didn't matter, because judging by the chatter on his com-link it seemed his plan was working. The Lakura forces were being ordered to lock down every choke point and continue to press into the hangars so that they couldn't be boxed into the tunnels where they would slowly starve or suffocate. They were keeping the Tribune at bay, and the maze of passages through which he passed were crawling only with his own people.

Talon propelled himself into a hollow running adjacent to the docks. It was a fairly sizeable refectory. Ceresians were posted at each of its many branching exits and every single table was overturned to provide cover for more. Yara Lakura's mobile command station had been moved to the back, hidden behind the food service station. She, Captain Hadris, and at least a dozen Lakura officers were hard at work transmitting orders.

Talon spotted Tarsis down a nearby passage. It appeared that a lack of gravity was proving beneficial for him. The Vergent was holding on to the ceiling with one hand and using the other to fire a heavy machine gun into the docking station it connected to. His back was pinned against a wall to keep the recoil at bay.

"Tarsis, need a hand?!" Talon hollered.

Tarsis looked back and even through his visor and thick beard Talon could see him smile. "By the Spirit and the Ancients and every fucking god who might be out there, you're alive!" he exclaimed. "This is the man who did it. This is the man who braved the generator!"

There were more than two dozen Lakura combatants fighting beside the Vergent, and every one of them immediately stopped what they were doing to glance back at him. "For Lutetia!" They shouted in unison and pumped their fists. Then they turned their attention back to their rifles.

Tarsis offered his leg, and Talon grabbed it in order to pull himself behind the cloven half of a table being used for cover. As soon as he tucked himself behind it a blinding beam of light speared through the passage, preceding a booming crash. Some of the men nearby screeched, and when Talon looked back they were charred husks along the floor. There was a molten gash cut across a metal wall, solid, grayish rock showing through like bone beneath the flesh.

"Nice speech," Talon said. "They've got Mechs with rail-guns now?"

"A ton of them. They weren't prepared to fight in zero-G though. Yara's defensive strategy did more damage than expected, thanks to us." He popped his gun out from cover and unloaded toward starlight. When he had to reload he turned to Talon and gestured toward a pulse-rifle lying beside a human arm. "You gonna help out or what?"

Talon nodded. He pushed off of the wall, floated across the tunnel, and grasped it. He could hear the snap-hiss of bullets flying by him the entire time. Once he was safely behind another piece of cover he realized how short of breath he was. It wasn't the Blue Death this time, for he hardly had to use his muscles in zero-G. The amount of oxygen in the air was dwindling.

"Mechs keep hitting us with that and they'll cave in all the tunnels and bury us in here," Talon shouted back to Tarsis after shooting at some shadows darting across the other end of the passage. "We won't last long with the air this thin."

"Long enough maybe. Didn't you hear?"

"Hear what? My com-link went down after the blast until I neared the surface."

"They won't block the tunnels because they want cover in them themselves. We've got the troops they have here surrounded. The Morastus Clan! They came out of nowhere with a rescue fleet."

The old man and his wretched son came to their senses, Talon thought, suddenly reinvigorated. "I guess the Ceresian Pact isn't dead after all."

"Guess not."

Another round of rail-gun fire sliced down the center of the tunnel. Talon yanked his head out of the way just in time. Heat emanated through his visor. It tore a hole through a portion of the defenses in the refectory, and he glanced over his shoulder to see Yara lying just beside the smoldering mark it left in its wake. She was okay, but a handful of her men couldn't say the same, including Captain Hadris. One of her surviving officers grabbed her and pulled her back into cover.

"My brave people," she panted into Talon's helmet. She'd overridden the com-link of every one of her soldiers so that she could speak to them directly. Her voice was shakier than it had been earlier, and she was clearly rattled. "We have been given a second chance by one of our own." Talon watched her gaze sweep across the room and aim in his direction. "The Morastus fleet is now prepared to retrieve us," she continued. "Do not hesitate. Gather with those beside you and fight through the nearest docking station. They will not be able to save all of us, and to those who are left behind…we will never forget. Oxygen on. For our home! For Lutetia!"

Talon could hear all the fighters in his vicinity chant with her, and this time he did the same. A chill ran up the center of his spine.

"Let's get off this rock," Tarsis said and grabbed Talon by the shoulder.

"When we set off I never thought I'd agree," Talon replied. He reached up and switched on his suit's oxygen stores, then bent down to pick up a long shard of one of the refectory's shattered tables. It was light as a feather, and he pulled it close to his body like a shield. Tarsis copied him, and then every one of Lakura fighters in and outside the tunnel lifted whatever they could find to do the same.

Yara and her cohort of officers speedily appeared by the entrance to the refectory. She was armed, pistol in one hand and knife in the other. "Move!"

Talon and the others pushed off whatever they could and soared through the air toward the docks. The gunfire grew louder with every second. When they emerged from the tunnel Talon grabbed onto the side of the wall and used it to sling himself even faster. There was fighting everywhere. More Ceresians floated up by the ceiling, bracing themselves against it as they fired down upon disorderly lines of Tribunal soldiers.

Bullet trails traced through the air, but Talon couldn't join the fray. If he fired, the recoil would send him right back into the tunnels. His shield vibrated as it was hit countless times. It wouldn't last long, but it wouldn't have to. There was a gaping hole in the exterior of the docking station, opened up to the stars. Dozens of ships zipped across it, and one familiar one hovered nearby.

The Monarch, Talon recognized.

"Guess they took your advice!" Tarsis laughed, his voice barely audible over the din of battle.

Yeah and got caught up in this. Talon pulled his quaking shield closer and considered his next move, but as he did rail-fire from a Mech tore into the floor by his feet.

The blast flung him into the air, twisting and unable to stop until his back slammed against a wall. He ignored the pain and tried to gather his bearings. Tarsis was floating next to him, unconscious. He dropped his rifle and grabbed the Vergent's hand. Then he attempted to locate the Mech. There were two of them coming from their flank, and walking as if there was gravity. *Magnetized limbs.*

A sense of dread stole over him. The Mechs lifted their massive arms and fired the chain-guns built into them without relent. High caliber rounds tore into the Ceresian ranks, and Yara would've been hit if her men didn't place themselves in front of her to be torn to pieces.

Talon took up his shield and prepared to make a move when suddenly sparks shot out from one of the Mech's legs. It toppled over and was taken by weightlessness right before its leg was sliced clean off. Then the other one lost its arm. Talon squinted through the sparks and smoke, and spotted a soldier standing there, staring directly at him. It was a Tribunal, but there was something off. The soldier wore a typical suit of white and green armor, but on the lower part of their right arm that armor was shredded to reveal only black. There was a blade sticking out from it, covered in blood.

"Run!" a female voice shouted from behind the tinted visor.

It can't be, Talon thought. She was right there, right in front of him again. The woman who'd killed Vellish, crippled Ulson, and damned him to spend the rest of his pitiful life on a Solar-Ark. There was no doubt about it. His heart raced and his hands quaked. He went to push off toward her, but as he did he caught a glimpse Tarsis's closed eyes and froze. Leaving him behind would be a death sentence. Tribunal soldiers were everywhere, closing in quickly with the Ceresians now retreating.

As he deliberated, Sage grabbed one of the Mech's dismembered arms and flung it toward a pack of Tribunal soldiers shooting at Yara. It took out all of them. Then she pushed off of the ground toward another group, spiraling head first with her blade out in front of her. It burrowed into the chest of another Tribunal, and she grabbed his rifle to shoot down three more.

Talon had never seen anyone move with such speed and grace. From Tribunal soldier to Tribunal soldier she darted, floating globs of blood strung along her path like ribbons. It was all the time Yara needed to gather her men and continue toward the rift in the docks.

"Run!" Sage screamed again.

Talon looked back at Tarsis and swallowed hard. He dropped his shield, grabbed the Vergent with both arms, and pushed off to follow Yara. The opening was wide enough for all of them, and they shot out into space. A bullet grazed Talon's leg before they were out, but lucky enough for him it didn't pierce the armor or he would've been exposed.

The only sound he could hear was his own breath inside of his helmet. Scraps of metal were everywhere, dismantled fighters from both sides weaving between them. He could see the distant silhouettes of Ceresian soldiers flying toward other waiting transports all around the bright string of docks wrapping Eureka. Hundreds of them. Maybe thousands. One of the faraway transports exploded, leaving those it was meant to save stranded.

Talon stopped staring and looked forward to where the *Monarch* was waiting. The ship got as close as it could. Its cargo bay was wide open and ready to catch them. He wished he could go faster and make sure that the *Monarch* didn't suffer the same fate as some of the others. He closed his eyes, held his breath, and squeezed Tarsis's hand tightly. Explosions flashed all around them.

A pair of hands came out of nowhere to grab his shoulders and pull him down. It was Captain Larana, attached to a tether and fastening the other survivors to the floor of the Monarch. Other members of her Vergent crew were helping her do the same. One by one every Lakura combatant was pulled to safety.

"Go, go, go!" Larana shouted.

The cargo bay began to close, and just before it shut completely one last person came speeding through the opening. *Sage.* A Vergent grabbed her and laid her down, and then the *Monarch* shot forward.

"Good seein' you again, Talon Rayne," Larana said.

Talon was too blinded by rage to respond to her. He rolled over on top of Sage. Her armor was so bloody that it was hard to tell which faction she belonged to, but the green of the Tribune was impossible to miss. He ripped her helmet off. At first he was shocked by what he saw. Her red hair was as short as his, and her pale skin was covered in grime. She was panting, but her bright, green eyes were wide open and staring at him.

"Talon? But you were sent to an Ark."

"I escaped," he snapped. He grabbed her by the throat, squeezed as hard as he could and roared, "I should kill you!" Rage fueled him. He couldn't let go even if he wanted to. She didn't fight it. He knew she could've used her artificial arm to rip him off and throw him clear through the hull of the *Monarch*, but she didn't. She just kept staring.

Everyone else in the hangar crowded around them and watched, perplexed.

"Shut up!" he snarled. He clenched as hard as his weak muscles would allow. The battle, the war, everything faded into the background. It was because of her that he never got a chance to return and say goodbye to his daughter. The Tribune did as they had always done, but she betrayed him. She used her beauty to get him wrapped around her thumb before deceiving him. *Not again.* He averted his gaze and continued squeezing.

"She…Sh..She's alive," Sage struggled. "Eli…Elisha."

His grip loosened just enough for someone to rip him off of her.

"Enough soldier!" Yara barked. "This traitor saved our lives, and I want to know why."

"So did he," a Lakura henchman spoke up. Talon immediately recognized him as the man who'd held the map on their way down into the heart of Eureka. "He's the one who destroyed the Gravitum Generator. I saw him go down there myself."

"He is, is he?" Yara released him and backed away, the creases on her face relaxing. She recognized him from their verbal spat earlier in the Eureka refectory. "You saved a lot of my men today, what was it?"

"Talon Rayne, and this woman is with me. She was…" He looked back at Sage and clenched his jaw. She was gasping for air, staring at Yara with a look of bewilderment. Talon knew he could hand her over to Yara and never see her again, but he wanted to deal with her himself. To put a bullet in her head the same as she'd done to Vellish. "Undercover during the battle."

Yara placed her hand on Talon's shoulder. "Another one of your unexpected moves?" she asked.

"I suppose so."

Yara slapped him on the back. "Well I hope you saved some more for the next battle." She took a step further into the hangar before she noticed Larana and her brow furrowed. "So Zaimur's got Vergents working with him now?"

"Just us," Larana replied. "Cap'n Larana of the *Monarch*, at your service."

The ship lurched violently.

"Missile fire!" Kitt shouted frantically over the ship's com-system. "Just missed us!"

"We're not clear yet!" Larana said. "All of you, follow me to the cockpit. You two, carry him." She signaled toward Tarsis's unconscious body, and two of her crew members quietly ran over, lifted him, and rushed him out of the room.

"Alright everyone, you heard the Vergent!" Yara turned to Talon and nodded. That was when he noticed something in her expression which he didn't think she was capable of. Something she was struggling to mask through all of her bluster. Fear. The fear of a commander who knew she was mere moments away from losing every soldier who'd chosen to follow her. Talon returned the gesture, and then she immediately turned to follow Captain Larana out of the room. A couple of her best Lakura officers trailed closely behind them.

Once he and Sage were alone, Talon walked over to a stray pulse-rifle on the floor and picked it up. He faced Sage. She was sitting up, covering her mouth with her artificial hand as she wheezed.

"Thank you for—" Sage said before Talon interrupted her.

"I didn't lie to Yara for you," he said as he aimed the rifle at her head. "Not so pleasant from this side is it, Agatha? Or should I say Sage? Whatever the fuck your name is."

Sage gathered her breath and looked back into his eyes as if the gun wasn't there. She swallowed hard. "I didn't know."

Talon got his finger comfortable on the rifle's trigger. "And why should I believe you?"

"They executed them. Like animals of Ancient Earth. None of them will ever have the chance to hear the Spirit's calling.

None of them."

"What the hell are you talking about?"

"They will do the same to all of you. And to her."

"Who?!" Talon snapped. He pressed the barrel of the gun against her forehead. "Don't you dare lie to me!"

Sage didn't flinch. She reached up slowly and rested both hands on the side of it, as if daring him to shoot. Then she began to rise. "Elisha," she mouthed.

Talon jumped back. His finger squeezed the trigger to the point right before it would send a bullet twisting through her skull. "Liar!"

"I am...was an Executor of the Tribune. My eyes were unknowingly theirs, but not anymore. If I wanted you dead, I wouldn't have plead for your life."

"Tell that to Vellish!"

"I had no other choice. His Eminence Benjar was..." She paused and hung her head. "I don't ask for your forgiveness. I only want to fulfill the promise I made to you and help you see your daughter again."

"My daughter died on Kalliope." Talon stormed forward and aimed in the center of her forehead. "She's dead because of your people!"

"She's not! I've seen her imprisoned on the *Ascendant*. They're holding her there to get to me, Talon, but she is still alive. I swear it."

Talon's heart felt like it was going to burst. He pushed her backward with his rifle. "You're lying."

Sage dropped to her knees and pressed her palms flat against the floor. She then lowered her head, showing Talon the ugly scar running up the back of her neck where her long hair used to cover. "I swear it on all of the Ancients," she said. "I swear it on the Circuit and the Spirit itself. She is alive."

The pulse-rifle slipped out of Talon's hands. He too fell to his knees, tears dripping down his cheeks. *She's lying,* he told himself, though he couldn't help but hope for the opposite. If Sage was still an Executor there was little she could learn about the Ceresian war strategy from working beside a man in his position. And if she wasn't lying, that meant Elisha really was alive—that somehow she'd escaped the fate of Kalliope.

Maybe Julius got her on a shuttle, he supposed. The thought was enough to make him smile through his tears.

"Kill me after if you have to, but let me help you first," Sage said. "We can get her out, Talon. She doesn't deserve any of this."

Talon did his best to steady his breathing. He was propped up on his fists, staring down at his own pale reflection on the metal floor; at the blue eyes which he shared with his daughter. It took all of his willpower to summon the strength to form words, and even after he did he could only manage one.

"How?" he asked.

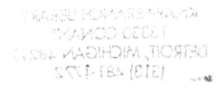

058283061

KNAPP BRANCH LIBRARY
13330 CONANT
DETROIT, MICHIGAN 48212
(313) 481-1772

CPSIA information can be obtained at www.ICGtesting.com
Printed in the USA
BVOW02s0903050216

435609BV00002B/2/P